D1491913

Fake Accounts

FAKE ACCOUNTS

A NOVEL

Lauren Oyler

4th ESTATE • London

4th Estate
An imprint of HarperCollins*Publishers*
1 London Bridge Street
London SE1 9GF

www.4thEstate.co.uk

HarperCollins*Publishers*
1st Floor, Watermarque Building, Ringsend Road
Dublin 4, Ireland

First published in Great Britain in 2021 by 4th Estate

1

Copyright © Lauren Oyler 2021

Lauren Oyler asserts the moral right to be identified
as the author of this work in accordance with the
Copyright, Designs and Patents Act 1988

Book design by Jordan Koluch

A catalogue record for this book is
available from the British Library

ISBN 978-0-00-836652-0 (hardback)
ISBN 978-0-00-836653-7 (trade paperback)

This novel is entirely a work of fiction. The names, characters
and incidents portrayed in it are the work of the author's imagination.
Any resemblance to actual persons, living or dead, events or
localities is entirely coincidental.

All rights reserved. No part of this publication may be
reproduced, stored in a retrieval system, or transmitted,
in any form or by any means, electronic, mechanical,
photocopying, recording or otherwise, without the
prior permission of the publishers.

This book is sold subject to the condition that it shall not, by
way of trade or otherwise, be lent, re-sold, hired out or otherwise
circulated without the publisher's prior consent in any form of
binding or cover other than that in which it is published and
without a similar condition including this condition being
imposed on the subsequent purchaser.

Set in Adobe Garamond Pro
Printed and bound in Great Britain by
CPI Group (UK) Ltd, Croydon

MIX
Paper from
responsible sources
FSC
www.fsc.org **FSC™ C007454**

This book is produced from independently certified FSC™ paper
to ensure responsible forest management.

For more information visit: www.harpercollins.co.uk/green

Fake Accounts

BEGINNING

CONSENSUS WAS THE WORLD WAS ENDING, OR WOULD BEGIN TO end soon, if not by exponential environmental catastrophe then by some combination of nuclear war, the American two-party system, patriarchy, white supremacy, gentrification, globalization, data breaches, and social media. People looked sad, on the subway, in the bars; decisions were questioned, opinions rearranged. The same grave epiphany was dragged around everywhere: we were transitioning from an only retrospectively easy past to an inarguably more difficult future; we were, it could no longer be denied, unstoppably bad. Although the death of any hope for humanity was surely decades in the making, the result of many intersecting systems described forbiddingly well, it was only that short period, between the election of a new president and his holding up a hand to swear to serve the people's interests, that made clear what had happened, that we were too late.

I didn't believe all this, necessarily, though as the news got worse and more bizarre I wavered. I've always been drawn to pragmatism, just not exactly a natural at it; as my brain says, "Calm down," my heart says, also weirdly calmly, "A paradoxical comfort can be found in drama." It was and still is my official position, if you were to ask me at a party or something, that the popular turn to fatalism could be attributed to self-aggrandizement and an ignorance of history, history being characterized by the population's quickness to declare apocalypse finally imminent despite its permanently delayed arrival. We don't want to die, but we also don't want to do anything challenging, such as what living requires, so the volubility with which certain doom was discussed made a tedious kind of sense: the end of the world would let us have our cake and eat it, too; we would have no choice but to die, our potential conveniently unrealizable due to our collapse. Until such time, the idea that everything was totally pointless now was seductive, particularly as a mantra you could take advantage of when it suited you and abandon when life actually started to feel alarming. I myself was soon using it to indulge some of my naughtier impulses, by which I mean that in the first hours of a morning in early January, when the sky was still dark and the government still inevitably hurtling, I decided to snoop through my boyfriend's phone while he was asleep.

I'd never really had the urge to go through another person's things before. After a few disappointing experiences with high school boyfriends' instant-message histories, I'd learned that poking around the by-products of other people's thoughts usually yielded the mundane, the predictable, and the unattractive. Even with men I respected intellectually, I never found myself caring enough to breach their trust; before Felix my boyfriends exuded the wholesome, loving, deep-down reliability of hot dads on television shows, despite being, as far as I knew, not hot, nor dads, nor on television. Another way of putting this is that before Felix I had good taste. (With the exception of a water-polo player I once showered with in college, a handful of celebrities, and anyone else I may find myself dazzled by in the future, I avoid obvious physical attractiveness because I believe it presages suffering.) But over the year and a half we'd been together, Felix had revealed himself to be completely unrevealing, insisting over and over as I baited and nagged and implored him to tell me his innermost hopes, fears, and childhood-formed biases either that there was nothing to tell or, conflict-ingly, that he'd told me everything already and it wasn't his fault if I didn't remember. It was humiliating and typical, and per the usual narrative I assumed he was hiding something, probably other women.

He almost always slept with his cell phone under his pillow. At first I'd thought this was just an arbitrary thing he did, or that it was related to some concern about emergencies transpiring in the night or a previous lack of side table, but after he started acting different—not strange, but different—I became certain he did it because he feared I would read his emails and text messages. That his bedtime cell phone habit predated his change in behavior from funny, somewhat reserved guy to slightly less funny, somewhat more reserved guy didn't matter: regardless of motive, it was weird to sleep with your phone under your pillow, and I'd failed to think about that until his subtle shift in comportment had me examining everything he did in a new light. There wasn't much to go on, but that didn't matter, either. Sometimes, lately, when we were texting each other, little ellipses would appear in the chat to indicate Felix was typing to me for an extended period of time, perhaps an entire minute, but then the message would never arrive: he'd have typed whatever it was and deleted it, and instead of sending something less delicate or elaborate in its place he would just stop texting me, as if we were fighting. This seems like a relatively small thing until it happens to you twelve or thirteen times.

His password, numerical, was long and, as far as I could tell, random, and I was only able to figure it out after weeks of surreptitiously watching him tap it out whenever I could, acquiring new numbers out of sequence one by one. He frequently bragged about not being addicted to his phone, so this took longer than it might have otherwise, especially because we didn't see each other as often as I understood other couples of our status to see each other. (About once a week, when it should have been at least twice.) I was resentful about this—my sense that I was being wronged was more power-ful than my growing ambivalence about the relationship, which was surely related to the distance between us he'd created but not entirely—so part of it, the snooping, was also about revenge. I briefly considered trying to place his thumb on the circular recessed fingerprint sensor (which is, as I write this, already becoming obsolete, replaced by facial recognition, which is of course even worse) while he was asleep, but I'm not a reckless person—my risks are calculated, and my dishonesty is dignified.

I'd had a few other opportunities to act before, when he went to the store to buy beer and forgot his phone on the table, when he was in the shower on one of the rare occasions he stayed long enough to want to bathe at my apartment. His phone was always pulling at me, like my own phone did but in a more sinister way. He was private but never thorough, a manner that I guess might have convinced me he wasn't hiding anything if I hadn't been so sure he was; instead I considered these lapses either evidence of his incompetence or, more likely, a misdirection strategy. But until that night I'd been hesitant to pick up the phone and confirm my suspicions. Part of it was that I tried to avoid, as much out of elementary-school habit as out of genuine belief in the importance of collective reciprocity, doing things to others that I wouldn't want done to me. A bigger part of it was that I dreaded getting caught, a tense confrontation in which I'd have to pretend to feel remorse and ask for forgiveness I didn't really have any use for—the relationship being in my mind already basically over—which is almost certainly what I'd do. I'm not given to screaming fights, especially those that require me to dig in and defend my own questionable honor; I can never come up with any memorable insults, and I tend to come out looking like a shamed child instead of a passionate and self-possessed woman. The righteousness Felix could wield over me if it turned out he wasn't sleeping with other women—the vindication I'd need for my sneaky actions—was also discouraging. It would hasten the inevitable breakup, which would be a relief, but I would seem totally pathetic.

Serendipity arrived on the wings of the Grey Goose. Felix and I had gotten moderately drunk at a bar down the street from my apartment, and he came over afterward. "I'm tired, I'm tired, I'm very, very tired," he sang on the way home. "I'm not even going to brush my teeth!" Such goofiness was uncharacteristic; it put me on edge. When I'd nod my head along with the music in a café or put on some minor performance of impromptu joy, he'd often look distraught or even ask me, glancing around, as if truly uncomfortable, to stop. He did brush his teeth, in the end, and then proceeded to my bedroom, humming the "I'm tired" song and doing a cute, contained dance. Where was this coming from? I felt I was being manipulated, but I couldn't say how. On my way to the bathroom, I saw he'd left his phone on the bookshelf, where it sat all-knowingly next to his keys, wallet, and stray stick of gum. I got a little nervous jolt, like it had just asked me on a date. In the bathroom mirror my face was flushed.

My skincare regimen is more extensive than I'm proud of. I'd recently learned it was important to let each product "fully" absorb before applying the next, and while I did not spend forty-five minutes each night sitting in the bathroom awaiting transcendence, the layering approach I couldn't unlearn did give me plenty of time to consider my options. After a swipe of special water supposedly popular in France, I thought, I won't do it. After I cleansed a second time, with cleanser, per the recommendation of Korea, I was pretty sure I wouldn't. After I used a dropper designed to look scientific to apply serum to my nose to decrease redness and "purify," I thought, Great social revolutions are impossible without feminine ferment. After a pat of stinging, very expensive foam, the effects of which I was not convinced, I thought, Ha, that's funny. By the stroke of moisturizer I was dewy and resolved: I had nothing to lose but my chains.

Immediately I began to worry that my chance would slip away, that, though Felix was not on social media through which he could mindlessly scroll in the dark before bed, imperiling his eyesight and disrupting his sleep cycle, he might be overcome with an urge to check tomorrow's weather or his email or to look up the definition of a word (I don't know what people without social media use their phones for) and retrieve the phone from the

shelf. No. Still there. When I went to the bedroom, quietly past my roommate's door, he was breathing evenly, his blocky elbow jutting onto my side
of the bed. I took off my glasses, got under the blanket, and lay on my back
with my arms uncomfortably close to my body to avoid his painful joint.
Felix shifted. I stared into the darkness and began to wait, the possessed
radiator occasionally scaring me with a shaming clang.

I dozed and woke suddenly, dozed and woke suddenly, until the familiar font said it was 03:12 and I was tapping out his passcode as if in a
trance. Bedroom door: I closed it slowly to avoid creaking and did not let
it click. Hunched forward on the couch, elbows on knees, the glow of it
around me, I noted that it had opened to the home screen, so I should make
sure to return to the home screen before going back to bed. At first there
was too much information to take anything in; I felt frantic, like I had just
entered a Walmart with the whimsical idea that I might get some socks,
maybe a magazine, maybe a new kind of frozen burrito, and instead was
confronted by the overwhelming vagueness of my desires. I looked to my
bedroom door and trusted I would hear the bed creak if he left it. I was so
nervous that, though I do not believe there is such a thing as bad people,
with the exception of the water-polo player I once showered with in college
and a handful of celebrities, I felt a strain, the sense that I must be a bad
person, to be willing to feel so awful in order to commit the pretty minor
offense I was committing. I suppose my definition of "bad person" might be
more self-centered than others', though, really, worrying about being a bad
person is entirely self-centered regardless. Good people do not think in such
categorical terms.

It was a normal iPhone, with the pleasant rounded corners that had
recently been at the center of a (punted) Supreme Court ruling. Lined up
according to his inscrutable personal preferences were the little square icons
with more pleasant rounded corners, each featuring a nice image someone
was paid a lot of money to develop into something recognizable, if not memorable; all were different colors yet somehow of equal brightness, creating

an effect that never allowed the eye to focus but didn't exactly exhaust it, either, making you feel as if you were seeing too much and nothing at all. The manual camera, the color wheel, the maps, the better version of maps, the clock that displayed a real ticking digital timepiece, two ways to call a taxi, the weather partly cloudy yet always bright blue, the notepad. The apps that came with the phone and couldn't be deleted: the app store, the upsetting health monitor that tracked how many steps you took per day and how much damage your headphones did to your hearing, the wallet that meant you could skip printing your boarding pass, the internet browser that was a compass but also a safari. His battery was half charged; he was automatically connected to the internet in my apartment. I tapped the messages tab and saw it was open to his conversation with me, trying to arrange a time and place to meet. Since we both had iPhones, like everyone else, to send texts we used the app that comes with the phone, iMessage, in which the phone owner's text bubbles are bright blue and the correspondent's are light gray. Seeing our conversation in reverse, the one in which I remembered participating hours before, was jarring. The flair I'd thought I'd infused into my punctuation choices was gone; I was only identifiable because I knew the facts of the exchange, that I too had suggested to Felix that we meet at eight thirty at the dark bar with the fireplace so I would have time to get a slice of pizza beforehand. My name at the top of the message history did not seem like my name; it was as if I were only one of hundreds of people that another person might virtually engage with at any given time, and whatever I'd said or not said was no different from what anyone else would have.

The rest of the messages were unremarkable; over the last few days, Felix had texted his mother, a coworker, a friend I hated, his building superintendent, and a pair of artists he had an ongoing group conversation with. There were girls, but I knew at least broadly who they were, and their exchanges were just wilted attempts at flirting, random instances of either Felix or the girl being reminded of the other by something; they consisted mainly of inert *haha*s and *cool*s. I tapped back over to our conversation so that when he opened his messages it would show up first, as before, and returned, less nervous and less excited, to the home screen, where I went to his email and did the same thing, searching his ex-girlfriend's name and looking through the Sent folder and Trash. I was about to abandon the project, disappointed at how boring he was and now very tired, when I saw the single icon containing images of tinier icons, situated in the bottom right-hand corner of his screen, labeled *no*.

Tapping it expanded the little box into a bigger box containing two messaging apps I'd never heard of and a social media app on which I'd been led to believe Felix maintained no account. He'd deleted them soon after we got together, he'd said, in a display of resolve that impressed me even though he'd never been particularly obsessive about the internet in the first place; I didn't know why he was bothering. I immediately thought of the obvious: expressions of yearning, photos cut off at the neck or the belly button, meetups arranged in areas of the city I'd never known him to visit. I could imagine him fucking stupid women, young women, women he could easily wriggle out of, and assumed this would be what he was pursuing here, maybe even with a pseudonym. I smiled ridiculously in the glow of the phone, though I was also disturbed by the instant onset of joy.

I tapped one of the icons, Instagram, and a familiar layout expanded to fit the screen. A row of circular user photos along the top indicated accounts that had posted Stories, photos that would disappear within twenty-four hours, images I thought, out of an abundance of caution, I shouldn't view; if I looked, they would later show up at the end of the row without an ombré ring around them, suggesting that someone else had watched them. A new-message tab said 68. Beneath these was the start of his feed, populated by people he followed. Because reading was not what this app was for, it had always been my instinct to skip over words—captions, usernames, tallies of likes and comments—but as I scrolled down, careful not to tap twice and add Felix's heart to someone's post, I found that all the accounts he followed posted images that were dark, fuzzy, and uncultivated, or else they were crude cartoons, their meaning unclear and the user's purpose in posting them even more so. When I quickly reached a notice from the app—"You're all caught up! You've seen all new posts from the last two days"—I didn't experience the shame that usually followed when I got the same message while scrolling through my own feed. Instead, it was surprise: Felix must have been looking at Instagram all the time. At the bottom of the screen was a row of understated line drawings, a house, a magnifying glass, an addition symbol, a heart. The rudimentary silhouette of a figure took me to his profile, where I saw I would need to consult the text.

The topics ranged from science to politics to business to national security and were illustrated by images heavy-handed and amateur: crisp blue skies crisscrossed with lines of puffy white; doctored gatherings of Barack Obama with George W. Bush, Bill Clinton, and Jacob Rothschild, one of their arms stuck out at an unnatural angle to point a gun at the viewer; frowning women next to cell phones emitting harmful energies; the blurry Twin Towers in the moments before and after they were struck; all inscribed with warnings in big, artless fonts. The government at fault somehow. The Jews at fault somehow. Incredible, unbelievable facts. I noted the username, tapped out of the app, swiped the app out of the phone's open queue, locked the phone using the button on its side—thankfully the sound was off—and placed the device back on the bookshelf at precisely the nonchalant angle at which I'd found it. I was overtaken by a sense of purpose unlike anything I could recreate in a workplace environment. My boyfriend was a conspiracy theorist. I could have laughed, but I would have woken him up.

Searching @THIS_ACCOUNT_IS_BUGGED_ from my own phone, I got a sense for how popular he was: tens of thousands of followers, hundreds of comments on each post, immense gratitude for his being one of the rare few to not only admit the truth but also strive to expose it for the benefit of others. Instead of outrage or hurt feelings I felt suddenly, magically free. I wanted the relationship to end. I didn't want things with Felix to be significantly different, as in better, than they had been for some time, or for the uneasy not-niceness of our relationship to transform through no effort on my part into copacetic peace; I wanted riddance and finality, a cessation of concern. I may have gruesomely hoped he had been cheating on me, but this was more conclusive: operating a popular Instagram account that promoted (and maybe devised) conspiracy theories meant he was no mere betrayer of trust or casual manipulator, but rather a person of impossible complexity whose motivations I was now liberated from trying to untangle. He might make sense, by some twisted logic, but I would not be the one to determine how. Because Felix wasn't a wayward soul down on his luck, uneducated and left behind, who had turned to conspiracy as a way to explain his pain; he did not believe the government sprayed trails of chemicals from high-flying aircraft for unknown but surely nefarious reasons, causing in the innocent and unsuspecting population below cancer and Alzheimer's and flu-like symptoms and malaise. He did not believe the world was governed by a small group of highly influential Zionist conspirators or that ambient Wi-Fi eroded miscellaneous but important "cells" that impact sleep and cognitive functioning and immune response. He did not believe that the terrorist attacks on September 11, 2001, were carried out through internal U.S. government missions aimed at justifying the invasion of Iraq and Afghanistan. I knew these things about Felix as much as I knew anything about Felix, which in retrospect I suppose was not that much. Nevertheless, I'm pretty sure he was Jewish, so it would have been strange for him to be authentically propagating anti-Semitic conspiracies—possible, but strange. He was annoyingly logical, always asking for sources and proof even when shooting the shit after many drinks in the early hours of the morning. He was resistant to health trends aimed at eliminating harmful substances like *toxins*, which he thought were fabricated to sell things, the only science they appealed to being, he said, the one used to dress up petty feeling. We once got into an argument about organic milk. (I'm in favor.) *BUGGED* was also not a word true internet conspiracy theorists used—it was a knowing appropriation of the past, a wink, a clue. One of his photos, posted nineteen weeks earlier, was a triptych zooming in on a fuzzy form apparently latched on to the side of an ashy World Trade Center building that, in each image, became progressively hazier; in the last photo the indistinct thing was circled and exposed as a DEMOLITION SQUID. An inside joke masquerading as a relatable typo. He usually slept with his cell phone, as you know, under his pillow.

As I sat on my couch gleeful and frenetic, many options appealed. I could stomp into the bedroom and throw him out, with or without explanation. I could get back on his phone and cause mischief, through the account itself or through his email, text messages, etc. I could do nothing except begin to insert provocative phrasing into our conversations, suggesting but never confirming I knew something he didn't want me to know. Or I could procrastinate: put off leaving him until I could approach the endeavor with the calm dignity befitting the partner of a person who *needs help*. I don't think I would have cared if he got help, really; this was the final straw in a relationship that had always been porous and insecure, and the weightless feeling of righteousness this gave me was something I wanted to enjoy, a secret of my own, and one far more original than your typical "When I say 'I love you' I no longer mean it." I imagined the satisfaction of saying, falsely curious, "I went through your phone and discovered you were operating a popular conspiracy-theory account on Instagram, and I just wanted to know . . . why?" But I wasn't sure that was the absolute best way to play my hand, and I wanted to play my hand in the absolute best way. My last boyfriend I had dumped cruelly, clumsily, and nakedly (literally), blurting out that I had something to tell him as he used his underwear to wipe semen off my stomach, a postcoital ritual I now view as sweet. I wanted there to be no question this time of any mishandling or callousness on my part; this was my chance to be purely and entirely the good one. I checked my Twitter account for notifications and decided to wait.

Maybe it seems to you damning that I would go back to bed with someone who could do such a thing, that I would not be repulsed enough to immediately throw him out of my house and life. If he were spreading misinformation in a more usual, deceitfully earnest way, in an editorial published online, say, he would be condemned, and anyone who didn't condemn him would be questioned, if not condemned themselves. The more ethical alternative—engaging the to-be-condemned person in a frank conversation about what he is doing and why—was also unappealing to me, particularly at the time, when I was feeling nihilistic and base. That said, I understand the reasoning I provided above isn't quite good enough. I don't know why I put down the phone, opened the door slowly so as not to wake him, laid myself on my side of the bed, and pretended to unread everything I'd seen. I didn't have trouble falling asleep. The next day I woke up calm. Now sometimes I fantasize about what might have happened if I'd raged into the bedroom and shaken him awake—he hated being startled during sleep, always acting as if he were personally offended by sudden noises made when he wasn't conscious—and demanded he tell me what the fuck was going on. In the fantasies, whatever he has to say for himself, half-asleep, worried, mad, doesn't suffice, and holding his phone in my hand like a love letter from a secret girlfriend I kick him out into the night. Sometimes in the fantasies I throw the phone down the stairs after him; other times I just keep it. I believe the latter would be a more empowering outcome.

Or maybe I'm being misleading. Maybe there were lingering feelings of tenderness toward Felix I'd like in retrospect to obscure, given what my association with him must say about me, and I'd rather say I was strategizing than admit I was conflicted about what to do. I'm sure that's true, though it doesn't feel true. And I'm sure some of you might say strategy is immoral. Regardless, a few days later, we went on what would become our last date, to a restaurant on the Lower East Side, a new venture by the owners of another place popular among people in the art world, and the serenity of my upper hand turned me into a gracious conversation partner. Everyone *was* going to Japan right now, I agreed, looking over the menu and citing the Instagram accounts of a colleague and a friend of my brother. It was too bad, I added, because it meant that now you couldn't go there without looking like a trend-following dabbler, and I also wanted to go. Felix had been and thought it was exciting but preferred South America, which to him was "grittier." Mmm, I said, in agreement, though I hated grit and objected to the appropriation of it. He had a thick beard, trimmed neatly, that he pulled at with one of his meaty hands as he made this pronouncement. The music was ambient, the plants were bountiful, the menu was a mix of Spanish, Italian, and French influences, and though the cocktails were egregious the wine was reasonably priced.

I still recommend this restaurant to people; I harbor no complicated feelings about this restaurant. Soon after we sat down, Felix told the waiter, a smooth and beautiful gay man, that we were there to celebrate my acceptance to a PhD program; the waiter, when he heard where I would be studying, raised his eyebrows and said congratulations. Felix smiled across the flickering table at me. This is another reason I knew Felix was not at his core a paranoid misspeller known on the internet as @THIS_ACCOUNT_ IS_BUGGED_: I had not been accepted to any PhD program, much less one at Harvard, but Felix liked to tell strangers little, inconsequential lies and build slightly alternate realities out of them, a game with no objective except to delight himself and fluster me. We had once been in on it together, or at least I'd thought we had, and it had felt good-natured and fun, but now it just seemed like a way to assert intellectual authority over un- and never-to-be-witting strangers. Would I have even found out about a PhD acceptance by early January? The timeline seemed ill-considered, though I had no idea. I practiced being alone by flirting with the waiter, whose name I'd learned was Dean, about burrata, such a great cheese, before Felix one-upped me by saying we would have champagne, "to celebrate the genius." When Dean whisked back I downed the bubbly dramatically as soon as he poured my glass, the kind of social display I knew Felix hated, and smiled a smile I imagined imbued with smug superiority. Dean, shaking his head as if we were old friends and I were simply always adorably like this, declared me "an inspiration!" He refilled my glass as I wiped some liquid from the sides of my mouth. Later he brought us dessert on the house and Felix did not eat any of it.

BACKSTORY

THE STORY OF HOW WE MET IS FUNNY, ENOUGH THAT IT MAY help answer one of the questions you probably have so far: Why was I with him? Keep in mind that right now, at the outset of this paragraph, I don't completely know the answer—that this writing is as much an effort to better understand my*self*, the person I can't help but feel is the most important figure in this narrative (if not, apologies, the most intriguing), as it is an effort to enchant an audience, promote certain principles I feel are lacking in contemporary literature, interpret events both world-historical and interpersonal (perhaps at the same time), etc. Keep in mind, too, that once you get with someone it's easier to stay with them than to leave them, and that once you dedicate a certain amount of time and effort to a relationship or hobby or whatever, it feels as if that time will have been wasted if you stop. One of the best lessons I ever learned comes from the single lecture of ECON 101 I attended, in which the concept of sunk cost was explained, but this is another thing I'm better at advising other people to take advantage of than utilizing for myself.

Anyway, June 2015: I was on vacation in Berlin, where I'd been followed by a couple of Brazilians I'd met at a hostel in Vienna. They were so happy, repetitively thrilled, to learn that I was not only heading to where they were heading, I was going to be staying down the street. They insisted on taking my phone number and synchronizing our sightseeing plans. Since I hadn't made any sightseeing plans, the synchronization was pretty easy. I nodded along and expressed interest in their suggestions, most of which had the word *underground* in their marketing. At first I found the two of them sweet, their accents charming and their enthusiasm fresh; on that trip I'd been trying to open my mind to the beauty of new people and experiences. Is this not what travel is all about? I asked myself, eating a schnitzel. That Berlin is not an uncommon city to be heading to from Vienna only made cuter their excitement at what they considered our fated acquaintance; maybe Prague-to-Berlin is a more common trajectory, but the Brazilians and I had both narrowed down our itineraries to German-speaking countries only, though none of us spoke German. "Prague . . . it is like Disney," they said, rolling their eyes. They resented their parents for sending them to an American international school instead of a German one; any asshole can pick up English—everyone speaks it!—but now because of their stupid parents any German they managed to learn would be deficient. Were they trying to learn German? I asked. No—there was no point now. Once we'd all arrived in Berlin, them on an overnight train and me on a plane (the ticket prices were more or less the same—we agreed this was incredible and that they should have researched transport options as thoroughly as they had investigated all the activities that can be partaken in former bunkers), I instantly regretted my friendliness, in this context seeming detrimentally American, and wondered if I would be coerced into clubbing (not the cool kind). I should have let their messages float unanswered. I could have pretended to be a flaky person, someone who just doesn't check her phone very often—there's a certain nobility in that—and if I'd run into them in the street I could have made something up to counteract any spur-of-the-moment invitations: meeting an old friend, tickets to a play for which I was about to be late. Don't usually see plays, but I thought, When in Europe!

Instead they dragged me on a pub crawl sponsored by a tour company, first by disabusing me of my belief that we "don't really do pub crawls in the U.S." and then by seeking to frame me as a sleepy Puritan, even going so far as to ask if I was afraid I'd miss my "boat home, the *Mayflower*." "It's only eight ay-or-ohs," they said, sexily, "and you get all the beer for one hour!" An hour of beer for eight euros sounded like a good deal to me, someone who had never before been to Berlin and so didn't know how much beer could not cost there. I also felt guilty about the one-sidedness of our mutual cultural awareness—I have no idea what the Brazilian equivalent of the *Mayflower* is, much less the kind of familiarity with the country's history that would allow me to use it in a joke at a native's expense. Finally, my journalistic curiosity—I was a journalist, sort of—pushed me over the edge. I told them all right, I'll go. I wouldn't have understood most of the plays on anyway.

The group convened in Mitte and was wrangled by a young but enforcing Polish woman with a clipboard and a tall guy of ambivalent affect who kept putting his hands on his hips and then crossing them and then putting them back on his hips again. He had thick brown hair cut into a normal male shape, a little rectangular with some movement at the top, and was wearing, like his coworker, a red polo shirt embroidered with the tour company's name, the sleeves hitting him too low on the arm. The sun had only just begun its slow summer descent and reflected orangely on the nearby tram tracks. As other tourists approached the pair to fork over their eight euros, he flirted with each man and woman in turn, responding in a game-yet-contained way to their jokes and questions, like a middle-school teacher with a naughty inner life: when he's on the clock it's just a subversive source of confidence to him. They asked about where the Reichstag was in relation to where we were, about the route our tour would take that evening, about which bar was his favorite, about whether he would go to the bars we were going to even if he didn't work for the pub crawl, about whether where we were standing was in the former East or former West. When it was my turn I looked him in the blurry eyes over the top of my glasses—I am tall but not as tall—and offered a closemouthed smile that I hoped conveyed my skepticism about the experience we were about to undertake together, wagering that he probably hated his job and if he didn't then it wouldn't matter if I had expressed skepticism because I would abandon my interest in him and move on to someone who also believed organized pub crawls were but one of innumerable humiliating excesses of desperate post-globalized economies. He gave a closemouthed smile back, not perfunctory but not innuendo either, and because I returned just then to an upsetting experience from college in which I used my twenty seconds at the front of a line to try to banter with a renowned author while he signed my copy of his novel, I retreated without attempting any little comments. When it came time for him to give an introductory spiel, he hopped to the top of some stairs, introduced himself, and outlined the terms of the evening with practiced gestures: four bars on foot, then eastward by S-Bahn to a club, do not bother the Germans, they do not like you. Kasia introduced herself as such and tried to smile. Most of the non-native-English-speaking participants did not seem to really understand his sarcastic comments, which gave him a certain creative freedom that surprised and attracted me, and as we trooped down the street and across a green space I thought miraculously large and empty considering we were in the center of a major city where drinking outside is legal, I found myself, Brazilians at my heels, trying to get closer, not walking exactly next to him but in proximity. He was talking nicely with a couple from Slovakia who, I would later learn, were on their honeymoon, and although that was very depressing it seemed a good sign that he could manage a chat without insulting them. We arrived at a row of empty, hut-like establishments along the river, the Spree; a few casual drinkers, seeing the chattering horde of accents approach, dispersed from their idyllic spots in the grass, forfeiting direct views of the river and the grandly European-looking Museum Island.

A keg, flanked by stacks of plastic cups, was set up outside one of the squat, dark bars, and we were instructed to enjoy all the beer for one hour as an unspeaking presumed German watched from the doorway, unmoved.

I took a seat on the ground with the Brazilians and confessed my interest in our guide. It was a strategy I often used with my mother: offer some tidbit of what most people would consider intimate information but which you do not care about sharing with others—anything romantic is what I choose—and the person thinks they are close with you, that they know some essential thing about your character, and you can get whatever you want from them, including to be rid of them at your leisure. The Brazilians cooed and shrieked and said I had to talk to him. I replied, in my gossip-girl voice, I know, but what about? I was not in the habit of hitting on men, I admitted—they usually came on to me, ha ha—but something about him was compelling. They said to ask him what I should do in Berlin. This was a terrible suggestion, I thought, so I told them, Good idea. Though I had no international data plan and so could have received no updates, I looked at my phone out of compulsion, took a sip of beer, and stood up.

If I thought of Kasia as competition it only helped me. She and Felix were talking to three American study-abroad students who were in town from Spain and looked like they must be cheerleaders, an initially daunting but easily surmountable task. As I approached the group I shifted into what my friends in college called "conquest mode," making my face warm and a little smug, collecting my hair against one shoulder to expose my neck and delicate earring; the latter I assumed he would not notice but the women would. Instead of grandly entering the conversation I integrated myself into the circle, with one person, Kasia, separating me and my target, so I could look at him but not directly, and began nodding along to one of the girls' descriptions of her host mother, who only allowed showers between 6 and 8 p.m. and inventoried the trash can every day to query any inappropriate disposals. I did not look over to see if he was laughing or seeming bored, hoping to establish that I was a social and fun person who had come

over merely to mingle equally with men and women alike, though I don't
know if I have ever intentionally mingled with women in my life. He asked
if they had been to Seville, where he had spent a month before moving to
Berlin. Etc. Just as another of the Spain girls was beginning to cite her (to
me, surprising) enjoyment of *Leaving the Atocha Station*, Kasia, to my right,
smoking a hand-rolled cigarette, turned to Felix and asked, "So what did
you think of the exhibition?"

You had to hand it to her. You really did. I was shut out of the conversation, both physically and in that I had no idea what exhibition she was
talking about. Having by that point only nodded along to tedious study-
abroad stories, I looked like a hanger-on. The back three-quarters of her
head had the same uniformly beige quality as her face, plus a tattoo of a
treble clef behind her ear, pierced several times, but impressed by her savvy
I reassessed the blandness as confident, unconcerned, maybe even elevated,
indicative of something like the humility of an excellent classical pianist trying to make ends meet in the gig economy, and myself as perhaps a little Po-
lonophobic. I took a moment to reflect on my biases and then, though Felix
had already begun to speak, put one of my long elegant hands out in a sort
of questioning gesture over Kasia's shoulder and asked, "What exhibition?"

An angling of eye told me he received this as obnoxious, even portentous of a dreadfully long night ahead, so I recalibrated my thinking,
always better at working with something than nothing: I could prove
wrong the idea that I was about to become a pesky drag, and I would ultimately seem even less annoying than I might have if I'd seemed totally not-
annoying at the start. In fact, I reasoned, I had made myself an underdog,
the best kind of dog a person can be. I could now come back from behind
and emerge victorious. As he began to explain the exhibition—something
something video something, sounded awful—I moved to refill my beer and
in doing so maneuvered to the other side of Kasia, excluding the study-
abroad girls, who were now gamely talking to a lone Romanian about in-
ternships and didn't need us, and looked at Felix for the first time from

a distance that allows true facial description. His nose was crooked, not with a bump but like the sculptor stuck it on at a slightly off angle, maybe initially as an accident but finding it was actually better this way, and his dark stubble, maybe a day's worth, covered evenly to his cheekbones, with sharp divots at the tops of his laugh lines. Lips of normal plumpness that seemed, like the rest of the visage, not bloodless but faded, which made him look weary despite the sense that his features might spring into action at any moment. I think it was the eyes, which had a look about them that straddled the line between flirtation and mischief, that suggested independent thought, a challenge for the sort of circuitous ego that makes a woman wonder if it wouldn't be good for her to have to pursue a man for once. As he was winding down discussion of the work as a cheap imitation of Martha Rosler by someone who had never heard of her—maybe this was what it was, actually, the combination of feminist art knowledge with unapologetic contempt for ahistorical hacks—I began to nod a little more purposefully than I had with the señoritas and asked, flatteringly, in a low, teasing voice, "Are you an artist?"

Kasia departed without fanfare. Here is the information I gathered:

—Yes, painter. Well, self-consciously, "multimedia," whatever

—Moved to Berlin in 2009

—Lives in [some neighborhood I'd never heard of, indecipherable to virgin ears, I shouldn't have wasted a question on this]

—Born in Montreal, to American college professors

—Lived in New Haven for some period of time, noncollege

—Italian nanny, unplanned by parents but good because now fluent, lover of Fellini

—Majored in art history (did not ask at what university because I did not want to emphasize that I am American, Americans being the only people who care about that and Americans abroad being the second-worst audience for other Americans abroad, after French people)

—Dropped out, on an exact date he will never forget because "it was the day the first iPhone came out"
—Likes chess
—Vegetarian, including no fish, particularly put out by the ravaging of cod

At this point two men of unannounced national origin had begun to hover as if to ask some questions of their own, and I left to refill my beer. Do these kinds of getting-to-know-you details even matter? I didn't think to wonder at the time. The *creative* New Yorker scoffs at them, his performance against the cocktail-party question "So what do you do?" lasting at least three times as long as a normal response would. *Don't ask me what I do; ask me who I am!* the New Yorker cries, hoping to make it big as soon as possible so that he can forget about such arbitrary distinctions. I always want to know these things. I say it's because I like to establish a context, though it may be that I like to talk about myself while imagining the person nodding along is curious enough to want to establish a context for me, and a certain amount of reciprocity is necessary in order to speak freely about oneself without looking like an asshole. *He didn't ask me a single question!*—worse than asking the wrong one. I do recognize that biographical information, likes and dislikes, the sort of stuff one puts in an online profile, can also be a red herring. People conform to type but also resist it. Where you're from and what you do for a job can mean a lot or nothing at all; the measure of any particular tidbit's significance usually falls somewhere in the middle, depending on how much of the story the person who came up with it has told you. Unfortunately, because of my own biographical information, I tended to be overawed by the kind of glamorous, intellectual upbringing Felix described, as well as impressed by the rejection of institutions implied by the dropping out, the living in Berlin, the working of a terrible job in order to (I assumed) pursue art-making. I didn't think to question his account, which was just interesting, not unbelievable. I might have been insulted by the flippancy with which he'd discarded a life that a younger me had wished she'd lived, but by that point the majority of people I knew were totally oblivious upper-middle-class types, "I mean we weren't *rich*," so I no longer cared. Besides, he expressed mild shame about it, and not through some falsely penitent acknowledgment of his *privilege* or "luck" but by seeming genuinely unsure how to present the concomitant summers in the family's villa, shaking his head at his younger self when he got to the part about dropping out, saying audibly and to himself, "Stupid." All this was good to know, or would have been if it were true.

There was still a lilac tie-dye look to the sky when we reached the second bar, which was indoors and literally underground, with exposed pipes running along the ceiling and some cavernous aspects; its most obtrusive decor was a silver, possibly papier-mâché sculpture of a human head with a comet's tail hanging from the ceiling that I assumed was meant to evoke the bug of the bar's name, Silberfisch, but I couldn't be sure. The people inside didn't seem to mind the sudden presence of an international crowd; upon closer inspection they were resoundingly Australian, in soccer jerseys. On the way I'd asked Felix where we were going, and he said, in English, Silverfish, and I said, "Oh, I think I've heard of that—isn't it supposed to be really cool?" and he produced mild noises in response. I was thinking of Silverfuture, a queer bar across town that had appeared on one of the Brazilians' underground lists, and when I realized my mistake while googling the next day I felt a vibration of embarrassment, thinking he might think I read the kind of publication or spoke to the kind of person who would recommend the kind of place Silver*fish* turned out to be. The Brazilians handed me a shot and an idiotic dawn rose in my mind: Jägermeister is German.

Eager not to seem eager I tried to talk to other people, keeping an eye on my target as I prowled around the room. I asked the Slovakians what they had seen in Berlin so far, I asked the study-abroad students about preparations of octopus they'd eaten, I asked the Brazilians if they were going to see one of the more famous underground attractions, an abandoned Cold

War listening station in the forest. (They said no, because it used to be that you had to sneak in through a hole in the fence and now all the holes in the fence were patched and a tour group charged a fee for entry, so it was no longer special. How they knew this I didn't ask; they seemed to know everything.) I made no new friends; I was barely paying attention. Kasia was squeezing behind Felix, her arms held wide like goalposts above the crowd, a bottle in one hand and an unlit cigarette in the other, as he looked over his shoulder and made nodding eye contact with her. A friendly see-you-later? Just checking in before we move to the next place? Acknowledgment of untold passions awaiting them after work, when they could finally hang up the just-coworkers routine? During this analysis the Brazilians had some-how disappeared from my side and were now literally if casually samba-ing toward me from the other direction, their heads impossibly level as they cycled their hips and laughed, saying, Watch out! Your boyfriend is flirting! You have to go get him!

But there was no path; he was deep in an impenetrable throng of Anti-podeans, apparently regaling. He made a swinging motion like he was telling a baseball story. I decided I could embark on a fact-finding mission until the final inning and hit my head on the overhang above the steps on my way out the door. I emerged embarrassed—Why is hitting your head on unaccom-modating structures always embarrassing? Surely an architect somewhere is the one who should be embarrassed—and annoyed. Hi, I said. Can't you smoke inside here? Kasia said yes "but not quietly." I laughed and then real-ized I'd gotten myself into a textbook-awkward situation by not coming out with a conversational game plan. She had smoking to focus on; I was just standing there. I could have asked her for a cigarette but since she rolled her own the request was more burdensome than whether could I merely deplete her supply; there was no hope of me rolling one myself. I regretted leaving the Brazilians behind. I dug through my purse for something to do. Lip gloss, technically "butter," which one has to apply with one's fingers and so must subsequently wipe off on available (ideally dark-colored) fabric. I took out my phone and tapped around, pretending it worked, reading old promotional emails as if they were important updates from everyone I knew. Kasia was looking diagonally away from me and exhaling as if coming to terms with a huge problem in her life. Suddenly, or maybe it just seemed sudden because I was in a fabricated trance about my cell phone, she was looking at me and asking where I was from.

We chatted for a few minutes, about Greenpoint, where she seemed to know more people than I knew in all of New York City, and as I was beginning to fixate on not having a cigarette Felix came out of the doorway, ducking. My two favorite people, he said, can I roll you a cigarette? A knight in shining armor, looking at me. He would go on to prove himself almost scarily anticipatory of others' wants, constantly hosting a party, but here it didn't seem extraordinary—he was just offering a cigarette to a woman outside a bar. Nevertheless because I had pressurized the situation I experienced total relief. To be put in a category with Kasia was additionally flattering and galvanizing; I no longer felt I had to compete with her, I had already won. (She herself had surely taken months to rise to joke-favorite-person status, which I had managed so quickly.) We agreed that the best course was to smoke the cigarettes and move on.

OK, get to the point, my ex-boyfriends are saying from the audience, not unkindly but not kindly either. They will listen to me talk about other men, but you can tell they don't really like it; they use any excuse to cheapen the experience. *You take so long to tell stories.* It's hard to say what it is they saw in me if they didn't appreciate this crucial aspect of my charm.

Felix rounded up the crawl by yelling down the stairs into the bar that since everyone had already paid him he didn't care if they stayed here but he was leaving in two minutes, that's zwei minutes. One by one pink and exuberant faces emerged, hitting their heads on the overhang. The route led along a cobblestoned street behind the redbrick S-Bahn tracks, the TV tower hugely and brightly there in the background. I decided to walk with Kasia at the rear of the group, saying it looked like something from *The*

Jetsons, do you know that show? It's a cartoon? She did not. Another pause threatened but soon she seemed like she had something serious to discuss.

"You know, Felix... he is a really weird guy," she said. My initial horror at being read too well was rendered irrelevant by more pressing concerns. "What do you mean?" I said, modulating my voice, trying both to seem cooler than I had apparently seemed before and, evilly, to make her feel as if I thought she was confiding in me her disappointment in Felix rather than warning me. "Like bad weird?" But she was much shorter than I was, so I had to lean forward, emphasizing my obvious curiosity about any bad weirdness I was hoping to make out with later. "No no, he is so charming," she said, "but there is something about him." "Yes . . ." I said, hoping to lead her to more, "he seems interesting . . ." Quickly she agreed that yes he was interesting. I was trying to mean "interesting" in a neutral way; she saw through the euphemistic veil of the word and could see that what I was really trying to say was that I wanted to sleep with him and, if that went well, that I would be open to the possibility of sleeping with him again. A standstill. Whether this was supposed to constitute a coded message I could not say; I didn't want it to so I didn't let it, though now I wonder what she knew, if she just had a feeling or if there was anything incontrovertible she had in mind.

Regardless, after about five drinks—the unlimited beer having been German and low in alcohol content—I finally became my true self. Felix and I talked, and talked, with the Brazilians occasionally giving me supportive glances across the subsequent crawl locations, which were as unimportant as the previous two described, though one was decorated entirely in a kitschy bright orange, the walls polka-dotted and the seating self-consciously lounge, and being also completely empty except for an apparitional ponytailed bartender it looked like the haunted set of an Austin Powers movie. There were stories from childhood and discussions of the news of the day. Finally, closing in on midnight, when we were en route to the S-Bahn to the crawl's final destination, an all-ages club called Matrix that played shrieking house remixes of Top 40 songs, he asked me if I would like to ditch the crawl and go to a "real bar" after he dropped off the rest of the group. I said yes. Actually, I said I had been looking forward to the club and wanted to "check it out" and watched happily as the horror on his face transformed into understanding of my joke.

As our train approached our point of disembarkation, a seriousness overcame him, and he began to brief the group chatting and scattered throughout the car: They all had their wristbands, so if they got separated from him and Kasia on the platform, which would be VERY CROWDED, they should go up the stairs, turn left, walk past the U-Bahn station down the hill, and the line for the club would be located through an underpass on their left. Also, just a reminder that if you had a good night we do accept tips. Winning smile. A fretful question appeared: I didn't need to tip him, right? I would buy him a drink. Or would this mark me as a callous enemy of the worker? He beckoned to me as the train came to a stop and put his hand up to my ear: In fact the pub crawl tour guides were not supposed to accept tips. I was getting excited and the adrenaline made jostling through the dense mass of people on the platform almost unbearably frustrating, just absolutely fucking infuriating. To look at one's phone while walking up the stairs is a hazard and a menace. To have been plucked special from one group only to be reincorporated into another more debased one is an insult to pride. I maneuvered irritated past bright stands selling unfamiliar pastries and sodas, left, past the U-Bahn station down the hill, keeping Felix ahead of me but not too far ahead. Bass advertised throughout the underpass as eyelinered girls finished off bottles of beer. Felix filed the rest of the crawl behind them in line, shared a look of camaraderie with the bouncer, and motioned that we would go back up the way we came. Three single-minded cyclists sped past the wrong way down the bike path, dinging cute bells at an errant reveler who had strayed into their way; when the bells did not jolt the offending pedestrian apologetically to the side, the leader shouted and set off a chain of maneuvers. At the top of the hill outside the glass-windowed U-Bahn station, its interior glowing with bakery and convenience-store signage, a barefoot performer's toothy smile dared passersby to ignore his ukulele.

Back at the bridge over the train tracks the crowd, speaking many languages, flowing out of the S-Bahn station and onto the narrow sidewalk, became tighter, encouraging us off the sidewalk and into the bike lane, and for several yards (meters) we walked in single file and I was leading him, though I had no idea where we were going. Past an opening where a group of crust punks and their dogs harassed one another, the line outside a couple of retro photo booths blended with the line outside a sausage stand. A tram rambled to a stop on the left, its garish yellow expressing the city's casual liveliness and nodding at its history (when the trams were also yellow). Felix returned to my side near the intersection, across which another barefoot hippie in billowing pants awaited the walk signal. This area sucks on the weekends, he explained as we turned right, into a group of leather jackets, and most of the bars around here, except the ones I'm taking you to, are terrible. I wouldn't live here if I had much of a choice, but finding an apartment is a nightmare. A large complex of squat warehouse-looking buildings enclosed by a high brick wall plastered with concert and exhibition posters to our right comprised what I was told was an OK Sunday flea market and beyond that several not-worth-it concert/exhibition/club venues. I said, You can take the guy out of the tour but you can't take the tour out of the guide. He said grammatically he didn't know if that was fully right, but fair. As we crossed the street and turned left he pointed and said he lived two buildings down.

The bar was packed and smoky, with a greenish light and rude bartenders. He bought me a beer and explained that it was called a Berliner Kindl. I said yes, I could read, is it special? He said yes, it's cheap. Ha ha, ha ha, jokes about my worth as a date.

Until we left the bar, the focus was on me; I had never, even with the sweetest, most generous of men, been asked so many questions about myself, my desires, my fears, my history. Despite Kasia's attempt at sisterhood it wasn't until then that I began to get truly suspicious—achieving the audience I'd staked out all evening was scarier, less satisfying, than I'd thought it would be. Was he buttering me up for some kind of obstacle I'd have to slip through? A sexual fetish? Though I often tried to imply libertinism, the truth is that anything beyond feet would have stirred in me serious soul-searching, and even that would have been a leap. Might this night become a sad blog post? Or worse? I checked my bag when I went to the bathroom to make sure he hadn't stolen my wallet. I reminded myself that I had pursued him; if he now had any criminal ideas, they were unpremeditated. Unless getting me to pursue him was part of the plan, and the pub crawl a handy way for a sociopathic charmer to find new victims, the kind who neither knew the city nor possessed the wherewithal to organize their own nights out in the global capital of nights out, the kind who generally think they are supposed to meet new people while traveling and so would always come to him? And what if this was not actually a real bar but a lair of some kind? I came out of the bathroom and noticed he was still wearing the tour-company polo shirt. I said I'd like to get my hands on one of those shirts. He said, Whoa whoa, we just met. Ha ha, ha ha. Would I prefer he go home to change? No. We decided to move on and bought beers at a Späti, he taught me the word *Späti*, and we took the beers to a little park a few blocks away. As the conversation turned away from me I accepted that I was not being kidnapped or somehow duped but rather having a fun night with an unusually attentive person who was interested in me, and that it was additionally cool this was happening in Berlin, where you can drink outside and the weather was, at the time, really great. I resented my mother and online feminism for making me so paranoid.

What we talked about is mostly lost to me now; I had accessed by then much more of my true self and sent the neurotic minute-taker of my thoughts to bed. I remember a lot of twentieth-century poetry—no recitations, thank God, just discussions, though I later learned he had it in him. But surely we didn't talk about John Ashbery for hours. I remember being impressed that a painter could discourse so confidently on poetry but then thinking that this was how college dropouts always were, especially those whose parents were, e.g., professors: smarter. I think I told him some stories about working at the mall as a teenager; he talked about what Berlin was like (good but not at all good), how he felt like a fraud for living there but also how he felt there was simply nowhere else to live, and how it was foolish to believe that cities in the past were better than they are now but nevertheless David Bowie, Nick Cave, Nan Goldin, etc. Even the GDR, he said, though the regime was . . . was something he wished he could have . . . how to put this . . . he didn't want to be insensitive but he wished he could have seen it. I didn't know anything about Berlin at the time, so I didn't think to question why his protonostalgic fantasies revolved around fleeting expats and not German punk or techno; instead, his brief monologue had the effect of making me feel like I didn't know anything about anything at all, putting me, I suppose, in a somewhat vulnerable position. I remember asking what his paintings were like and him evading by saying that he was, ha ha, taking a leaf out of David Lynch's book and refusing to explain his work to other people. I said I wasn't asking for an explanation, just information. Like: Are they oil or acrylic? Large or small? Abstract or figurative? Bad or good? At the last he laughed and said, They're OK. This I appreciated, a lot, because he didn't say it in a falsely modest way, or in a powerfully bemused way, the way a celebrated artist who knows you haven't heard of him and thinks that's precious might say his paintings are OK; he said it as if it were sadly true. Why would I want to fall in love with an admittedly OK painter? Well, I spent a lot of time with unadmittedly OK writers, and around them self-awareness seemed like the only personality trait that could not be learned, no matter how much it could be mimicked.

At around five in the morning, after I had pretended, outside a McDonald's at a train station where we'd used the bathroom (former East), to be only a little bit wowed that the sky began to get light at three thirty, we went to his apartment. I was on my period, information I provided as a courtesy, and he said, breathily, that he didn't care, as if that would make him seem especially sensually in thrall about the female body and not like every man I'd ever slept with before. That I could see through things like this, things that many men, mostly unbeknownst to each other, do, made me think I might understand him, that I might have the upper hand. And since he'd performed so well over the course of the night, withholding at some moments to suggest he might not be as interested as I suspected he was, showing off at some moments to demonstrate that he possessed all the good qualities (smarts, worldliness, humor, etc.), I caught myself tallying the score, wondering which of us was going to come away the more eager and therefore less attractive, forgetting I suppose that we lived in different countries and that truly smart, worldly, funny people have one-night stands in foreign cities without imagining who would "win" in their hypothetical relationship. He had a full, deep laugh, head occasionally thrown back, that I wanted to capture and keep as a pet. The sex was typical drunk first-time, a little too fast, too inevitable, the kind of open-and-shut case that clouds in memory whether genitalia made contact at all. We slept, but he had no curtains, apparently a local custom, so too-few hours later he got up to use the bathroom and came back with a considerately minty mouth, and that time I made myself come the way I usually do, on principle. I know it's tempting to read a lot into sex, but pace yourself, you still have a lot left to read; all that really matters in the beginning is can he kiss, does he make an effort, and is his sexism overt or merely residual.

After the sex it was 9 a.m., and I had to wait for Felix's roommate to get out of the shower so I could ask her to borrow a tampon. When she found me sitting in her kitchen legs crossed in front of the stale-smelling ashtray he and I had used a few hours before she looked surprised but just said sure, they were under the counter. He took me to a café owned by, he claimed, one of the members of The Knife; on the menu among its traditional German basket breakfasts was a "park bench": coffee, cigarette, shot of vodka. Neither of us ordered it, but I appreciated the gift of a good Berlin anecdote. We got along easily, which is not nothing, looking at each other and smiling at how well it was going, how surprisingly and nicely well, and though I can't remember the conversation I remember the fluidity of it, the lack of uncomfortable pauses. Uncomfortable pauses don't necessarily mean anything—sometimes things get uncomfortable because you are happy, for example, and unused to the feeling—but that's another piece of wisdom I find hard to use. Like most people I much prefer an easy conversation to a hard one.

Knowing what happens next (you're about to find out), and how he ended up performing as a boyfriend (you know some of this and will learn more), and what happens after that (this would be the conspiracy-theory thing, which you also know), and what happens after that (truly unbelievable, though in some ways not; you do not know this yet, unless you're one of the people I've discussed it with), I would like to deny that I liked him very much by this point. To my credit I can't identify with the past self who liked him very much by this point. That person seems like someone else, like one of my friends who is constantly getting into romantic scrapes, whose decision-making processes I just do not understand. One of these friends dated a mean clown—professional, not figurative—whom she met at a Balkan Beats concert. Unfortunately, my having liked him very much by this point is part of the historical record; I sent many pitiful messages to my confidantes about it.

Pushing through the crowd back the way I'd pushed the night before, smiling dumbly at the wide stretch of unused train tracks and dirt underneath the bridge, I didn't notice how strange it was that this open space in the middle of a city was not only huge but also harshly ugly, its steel and concrete expanding unapologetically to the east and west in seemingly random formations; when I came back to Berlin the sight of it was so shocking it was as if I'd never been there before. (Some of the pleasingly hideous construction would soon become an alienatingly hideous mall.) I crafted an email in my head as I threaded through the bridge's daytime crowd and reflected on the clear signals of attraction Felix had projected, clear signals of attraction being some of the most appealing things to reflect on. Every instance of possibly prolonged eye contact counted as evidence, but I don't know why I was focusing on these when I had in front of me the clearest signal of all, that when I dropped him off at his apartment on the way to the train he said, "Well, I guess we'll never see each other again," in a wistful kind of voice that suggested he might have been sad or he might have been joking, and then he gave me his email address. Already I was heading in the direction of fixation. When I met someone I liked I wanted him in my orbit, virtually or physically or mentally, at all times; I would want to know what he was thinking and doing and saying when I was not around; I would want to account for him. I'm aware this is considered unhealthy. I also suspect it's normal, that it's the aloof, pointedly independent people who should be checked on and deemed dysfunctional. The train came and I almost missed it because I wasn't paying attention.

Sleepy and useless back at the hostel I placed my valuables in my locker and took a shower. As rills of shampoo flowed down my body I looked down in horror: I'd forgotten to wear the rubber flip-flops I'd bought in Vienna. (*You did not look down in* horror, the ex-boyfriends are saying, shaking their heads. *You were not* horrified. *And even if you did get a fungus or whatever, you would be fine.*) With wet hair I took my computer to the lobby and sank into the internet. Because it was a little after 6 a.m. on a Friday in the U.S., nothing worthwhile was happening on social media; I scrolled through my feeds distractedly, opening and closing the same site multiple times in quick succession. I was a lab rat assigned to a random trial with the lowest frequency of reward. I knew that, and more importantly I knew it was an unoriginal observation, yet I couldn't stop myself from making it. I clicked on some news to try to add a useful element to my rotation but the article might as well have been in German because I couldn't read it. I was tired and jittery. I wanted time to move faster until my brain recovered and a suitable interval had passed so I could send Felix the message I couldn't stop thinking about sending, that I was definitely going to send, it was just a matter of when. I opened my email and wrote a bad sentence that I deleted. I wrote a summary of the night to a friend that incorporated a delirious number of ellipses and exclamation points. Across the room people speaking Spanish played Ping-Pong and at the opposite end of my table a good-looking man, my guess Greek, frowned into his own laptop, the tendons in his forearm flickering as his fingers hunted anachronistically around the keyboard. I became conscious of my staring, and as I turned back to face the unattended bar where cornflakes and muesli had probably been served that morning as part of the complimentary breakfast, inspiration struck: though I didn't know Felix's last name, I could search his email address. I had typed it into my phone but didn't need to look because I had already memorized it.

If you're wondering why I would search for Felix online when I already had a method of contacting him, I appreciate your purity. For one thing, I needed some outlet for my Felix-oriented energy that didn't involve immediately revealing it to him. More to the point, the chance of discovering some uncontained fragment of Felix's self that he'd left lying around on the internet was too exciting to sacrifice for some notion of respecting boundaries or Golden Ruling. Would I be mortified at the thought of a lover perusing my contributions to the college newspaper and Facebook photo albums of my time studying abroad? Yes. Of course. I'd swaddled my accounts in layers of gauzy privacy that offered an enticing amount of information to the idle googler but limited any meaningful access to people I knew. Beyond these measures, though, there was, lurking on the third or fourth page of my search results, the unfortunate evidence that I had once been less judicious. My impulse to look Felix up was both greedy and calculating: I wanted to know everything about him, and I thought I might be able to glean from his internet presence an effective way to approach him for a second date. I was also curious to see photos of his art.

On Google nothing came up. Someone with an email address that began with the same five letters as his was to be contacted by those interested in signing up for a knitting workshop at OSU in 2010. Facebook returned a profile for "Felix Biberkopf" next to a thumbnail image of an overexposed white poodle with its legs primly crossed. I didn't know the reference at the time so I assumed that could be his name. Even if I had recognized the allusion I don't know that I would have been immediately concerned; many people, particularly Europeans, use cheeky pseudonyms on social networks—they're more protective of privacy and less outraged by the idea of not getting credit for their idle musings. Anyway, at that point I believed Felix had lived in Europe for six years, so if I'd known that Biberkopf was taken from *Berlin Alexanderplatz* (and a mountain in the Alps on the border between Germany and Austria) and almost certainly not his actual last name, I might have assumed he'd adopted some of the continent's social media customs and was innocently using them to showcase his taste in literature/film. If the not-I who had gotten this reference were to stop and think about it for a few seconds, she might have been a little alarmed that the literary character with whom her imaginary new boyfriend chose to publicly identify was a drunk murderer who struggles to resist the cruel pressures of a careening society and the draw of fatalism as he makes shambling attempts to turn his life around; however, if we're being realistic here I'm going to say I doubt she'd have stopped to think about it for a few seconds, overcome as she would be by her yen for the scoop. Regardless, I was in the dark about the potential meaning of Biberkopf, so I skipped ahead to the About section, where I was soon noticing that the list of schools Felix had attended did not align at all with what he'd told me the night before. What's more, this said he was from Los Angeles.

I couldn't access the rest of the profile. I saved the poodle photo on my computer and searched the image—one of my favorite diabolical tips to share with less-savvy internet users is the fact that you can put an image into Google and search it—and found his Instagram account, which was not particularly active but did present further evidence that he had not lived in Berlin for six years, but probably about two. A caption revealed the poodle belonged to a friend in Boston whom Felix visited in 2013. A girlfriend-type figure took a series of photos of him the year before that, in the town where I now knew his impressive art school was located; her profile was private. The photos in which he was tagged demonstrated a casual hesitance to be photographed—he often, but not always, blocked his face, distorted it, or otherwise betrayed obvious discomfort—and it seemed he had a brother who got married in Italy, though the brother had no account.

After twenty minutes of this, I remembered my deteriorating posture and began to feel like a creep, and the fact that Felix had lied to me was only partially vindicating. I felt my high-level search-engine excavation skills were knavish and petty; they marked me as a member of a generation that grew up watching reality TV, without respect for fundamental principles of functional society and the human soul. What I was doing seemed to resemble, though I couldn't say how, a kind of violation or even theft. Felix's reluctant photos were evidence of pressure, from the dominant mode of contemporary life that required too much will to opt out of. If I'd been hacking, whatever that is, or even just digging journalistically, for some higher purpose, that would have been OK, but all I did online was assess the seemingly complex dynamics between people I didn't know, skim headlines, and occasionally read archived *New Yorker* articles with a friend's password; stalking was one of the most focused activities I participated in. I tried constructing hopeful analogs to the past to account for the time I wasted online, to convince myself that my drive to collect useless knowledge about strangers and acquaintances was not a new condition but merely a contemporary manifestation of a timeless problem, but any pre-internet activities I could come up with were in some way valuable: listening to the radio, tending a garden, anything classifiable as a hobby. Maybe before television and the internet people spent more time staring at the walls or ceiling, sort of depressed but really just absent. Reading? I certainly should be reading more.

But the problem was not attention span or gluttony; the problem was that I didn't actually believe the knowledge I acquired online was useless. I sought it out purposefully, defensively, as if it would one day become vitally important, provide the clue to some threatening mystery of my social or professional life. I closed the windows and opened my email again, glad at least that I no longer cared about pinpointing the most advantageous time and tone for my email to Felix.

"Hi. I had a great time last night/this morning. So overtaken was I by the greatness of the time that I mischievously put your email address into Facebook, which was . . . interesting . . . Sorry to invade your privacy (?). I was going to ask if you wanted to meet again before I fly back on Monday night. I would still ask that if your explanation is good enough."

I hate it when people sign emails with their first initial because it seems pointlessly literary, but I also wanted to convey a curt yet ultimately unbothered seriousness, so I didn't sign it.

The temptation to sit with my computer and wait for a response was great, but I remembered I had paid money to travel to Berlin to see sights and experience culture and that having a hangover and being tired and yearning pathetically for a particular email from a relative stranger were not excuses not to do this. I shut the computer. I had gotten three WhatsApp messages from the Brazilians over the course of the morning, asking me how it was???? and if I wanted to eat 1) lunch or later 2) dinner with them. Because the messages popped up in preview on the home screen of my phone I was able to avoid opening them, and therefore avoid making the little gray checkmarks that signified to the sender that his messages had been delivered turn into little blue checkmarks that signified to the sender that his messages had been read, and therefore avoid the Brazilians. They will not be back. I opened my computer again and searched for an important sight to see and decided to walk to the Berlin Wall Memorial nearby. Looking at it didn't take as long as I'd hoped, and afterward, thinking I should "just explore," I walked up a hill into the first café that looked sufficiently bourgeois, ordered a coffee, and asked with the forced nonchalance of an unskilled grifter for the Wi-Fi password. Because I didn't understand the way the barista was saying the letter *R*, I had to ask for it three times. I was logged in before I sat down and tried to be calm as I waited for my email to load.

Under promotions for several clothing stores and a response to my news from one of the female confidantes there was the desired Re:. He was so sorry. He felt really terrible, truly. He had had such a good time, but the thing was that on the pub crawl he usually had an awful time, so predictably bad a time that in fact he had never anticipated ever having anything close to even an OK time, and he certainly had never anticipated having a good time due to the presence of someone who had paid 8 EUR to PARTICIPATE in the pub crawl, the pub crawl which was so bad, the pub crawl put on by a company which owed him actually over 2,000 EUR; he did not envision that the Venn diagram of "people with whom he might have a really nice time" and "people who would come to Berlin and decide that the best way to partake of the city's bars would be to pay 8 EUR to have a guy in a polo shirt lead them around Mitte shitholes, some of which only opened for business when they could trick striving companies into paying them to do so" would involve any overlap. Anyway because he worked this job as he'd mentioned three times a week and because it can get boring introducing yourself and what you do and where you're from to the same boring types multiple times a night three times a week, he and the other guides tended to do this thing where they made up different lives for themselves each time, playing characters, usually not straying too far from the believable but messing around with it a little bit, coming up with stories more interesting to develop than "I'm from L.A. and went to art school," though sometimes they did swap personal histories to amuse one another, and anyway the point was just to manufacture some variety out of their *Groundhog Day* nights. Because of his incorrect assumption that he would never be interested in having a legitimate conversation with a pub crawl participant that continued after the Matrix, he initiated this game with me pro forma, and by the time he realized he was interested in having a legitimate conversation with me that continued after the Matrix it was too late, he had already said all that sentimental bullshit about Italian nannies and dropping out of college, and he felt that if he told me he had made it all up I would think he was a psychopath. Given that I was a tourist and presumably going home soon he had decided at the time that not telling me would be the best course of action, because it would allow us to have our purely nice night together and remember it fondly, but after I left him at the front door of his apartment building he realized that giving me his email address had been stupid because if I were as internet savvy as I seemed (not in a bad way), the email address would probably eventually become the negation of our nice night and therefore render in vain all his increasingly acrobatic lying about his background. He became so upset that he told his roommate, who being British tried to console him by making him a cup of tea. He knew this all sounded ridiculous and that I had no reason to believe him but it was the truth and if I thought it was a good enough explanation I could meet him at the bar Transit on Schlesische Strasse the next day at six. If I did decide to do that I shouldn't confuse this bar with the two Thai/Indonesian restaurants of the same name that were located on other streets in different parts of Berlin. Sorry again. —Felix.

People often say my generation values authenticity. Reluctantly I will admit to being a member of my generation. If we value authenticity it's because we've been bombarded since our impressionable preteen years with fakery but at the same time are uniquely able to recognize, because of the unspoiled period that stretched from our birth to the moment our parents had the screeching dial-up installed, the ways in which we casually commit fakery ourselves. We are also uniquely unwilling to let this self-awareness stop us. I had thought, then, before *accountability* became a word everyone used, that explaining oneself and one's motives was an appropriate addendum to an apology, that an explanation was almost better than an apology, because an explanation gave you something to do beyond accept or reject; it allowed you to understand. I found Felix's story compelling, too particular to make up and too hastily written to counterfeit, and today I still believe he was being genuine, that what I've described above is really what happened when we met. That it might have been both honest and a cloud on the horizon, a little cartoon cloud with a face drawn on that doesn't know it's about to join a storm but is waving a little red flag just in case, is probably the best explanation for its significance in this story, but that's also a bad analogy because clouds have no agency, they are created and moved by external forces, part of a system, and that's not something I want to suggest about Felix, at least not entirely, as it's since then become clear that I do not know much about what external forces were or were not acting on him. All I mean is that I know what it's like to have your past experiences and well-established tendencies converge into a new behavior or idea, and it isn't something you or any divine creativity planned from the start. I assume I'm dwelling on this because as in most relationships the beginning was for us the best part. I'm told I don't have to try to justify love, which contains at least a small percentage of unsolvable mystery, but I just can't stand the thought of seeming irrationally carried away by emotion and unable to freestyle my way back to the calm waters of reason. I believe it hurts the feminist cause. And, worse, makes me personally look bad.

In Berlin, we saw each other twice more before I went back to New York. One thing led to another. Neither of us liked sports or believed in God. If I had to locate it precisely, I would say that I began to have the usual feelings, beyond charmed fixation, when we were at a Vietnamese restaurant. The too-soon possibility of being in love sat down across from me and waited for me to object. It was as if before meeting this person I had been living in a bubble, or a hole, or under a repressive religion, like my life was just beginning now that I had met him, like up until I had decided on a whim to join a trashy pub crawl in Berlin my personal history was hazy from total lack of consequence. I considered changing my flight to a later date, taking two more days off work, but ultimately decided against it on the grounds of frivolous cost and unwillingness to make a grand statement. Back in New York, I quickly dumped the boyfriend I had at the time, citing a mysterious change in feeling that was really tearing me up inside; he briefly cried, and when I finally extricated myself from the traditional despaired rehashing of the problems of our relationship four hours later, I had a string of short funny emails from Felix in my phone and a spring in my step. We talked about the breakup during our next call and discussed our retrospectively disturbing shared love of the fresh sense of liberation that came after kicking someone to the curb.

The hilarious unlikelihood of our meet-cute sustained me for several months of distanced longing; I couldn't help but feel, though I knew it was wrong, that we had been destined for each other, or at least that I had stumbled upon great material for life or art. Emailing him frequently, thinking of little but what might impress him, I looked around and realized everyone around me was boring, more boring than even the most boring person I could make up, so boring that it might have made them interesting if I could have stopped thinking about the world's one interesting person who had rendered all the details and motivations of my life immediately clear. That this was how I felt every time I found a new boyfriend was something I recognized but did not care about. Women forget the pain of childbirth so that horrific memories don't stop them from going through with it again; my brain dismissed all those previous experiences of falling out of love soon after I'd fallen in it, and I thought: OK, yes, this is singular. (In the end, I wasn't wrong!) Let's do it, I said, when he asked, "it" being something along the lines of "everything, all the time, together."

There were tweaks of doubt, sure. His nihilistic opinions seemed to burst forth from nowhere, which made his usual placidity seem less the result of an easygoing personality and more the result of a cynicism so heavy that it calmed him like a weighted blanket. But was he *angry*? No. Nor was he rude, offensive, passive-aggressive, or spiteful. He kept to himself, even when he was describing himself and his problems, and although it could be frustrating, his refusal to allow anyone else to bear the burden of his presumably bad feelings seemed a kind of corrective to the tendency in our milieu to boast about being in therapy. Was it wrong to presume he had bad feelings? I'd thought it was the sensitive thing to do. There was a period, a day and a half, when we'd been communicating intensely on a couple of different platforms, flowing from instant messaging to video call to texting to instant messaging again to another call; we spent thirty-six hours together in a way, and then after that, I did not hear from him for four days. I assumed he just needed a break, because spending all day updating another person like that is tiring, the high of a new message, the anxiety of waiting in between them, the sick, gorged feeling of overindulgence, the guilt of neglecting everything else; I reckoned, too, that four days was not very long, especially because I spent them proudly waiting for him to text me when I could have just as easily texted him myself. Yet I couldn't deny that I felt abandoned, that I thought he'd met someone else. Because we didn't see each other very often—three visits during this period, him to New York twice and me back to Berlin once—these concerns were easily dismissed as the by-product of progress, getting closer, and I pretended, of course, to have barely noticed the pause. An advice columnist would say that the relationship's inherent strangeness allowed me to play down other things that were off about it, and I would say in reply isn't everything in life a little bit off? Isn't that why it's so hard? Our visits were cram sessions; we mostly stayed in bed. That, too, is a little off, but no one would say it isn't great.

Six months after we met, around Christmas, Felix moved back to the United States, on the grounds that he would be able to earn money without having to scrounge for gigs on a foreign, worse version of Craigslist, and for a while it was novel to be able to see him anytime I wanted. We would leave each other sweet notes in surprising places, buy each other thoughtful gifts, share knowing looks across the room at bad parties that I was proud to bring him to because I liked to prove he actually existed to acquaintances who'd heard tell but never met him. I imagined that many other men—ex-boyfriends, editors at work, people I knew from social media and had never met in person—sought my affection, but as in the early stages of other relationships previously mentioned I thought only of Felix. We spent many hungover mornings in my bed, doing nothing but good-natured complaining, getting too hot, throwing off the covers, getting too cold, pulling them back. There was some intimating, too, of course; when I said I'd thought he was too cool for me at first, he said he'd thought my confrontation of him, about the lying, was the coolest thing that had ever been done to him, including "weird sex stuff." Ha ha, ha ha. When I asked, wondering if I was insufficiently sexually strange, "What weird sex stuff . . ." he said he was just kidding, and that he had known as soon as he got the email that his aim should be to make sure I did not stop speaking to him, even if it was only platonic and across the Atlantic.

But then something changed. When he moved back to the U.S. he was broke, having been stiffed those euros by the pub crawl company in addition to some other factors that seemed related to the flakiness of expat employers in Berlin, and because he refused my offers to lend him a couple thousand dollars and got downright mean when I suggested he ask his parents, who were as far as I'd heard well-off in Long Island (dad) and Los Angeles (mom), he got an overpaid job at a startup, through some connection or other, doing social media strategy and *audience development*, and the forced cheerfulness of the environment, plus the insipid teamwork robot vocabulary, made him hate himself. He didn't want to admit that he hated himself, but he also didn't want to admit that he wasn't suited to the kinds of mealy shared apartments he'd been living in in Berlin, that he liked having money, and he expressed this internal tension as ranting directed vaguely at "capitalism" or the government but also often snapping at me. I think he convinced himself to blame his only secondarily manipulative girlfriend who never outright said, "Move back to your country of birth so we can be together!" but who was nevertheless not shy about saying things like, "Ugh, I miss you!" or "I had a *great* burrito for lunch . . . you know, the kind of thing you can't get in Berlin." He had wanted to renounce the U.S. and never come back, be transformed into a good artist by lifestyle politics and abnormal sleep schedules and elective struggle, but instead he came to believe that he had been forced, by the weather system of his strong and confusing feelings and therefore by me, to wait out our relationship in the comfort of a large paycheck, which he used to buy me dinner and decorate his apartment with intellectual posters. He talked about moving back to Berlin someday, with some of this New York Money, and though he would say this in a way that suggested I should or would come, it started to sound more like a threat, or at least an acknowledgment that we would one day break up and he would again be free. Donald Trump winning the presidential election gave him even firmer grounds for his belief, which we shared, that huge parts of the United States had nothing to do with him, but whereas I thought that even huger parts of Germany had nothing to do with me, he waved this off as "different." He said, "America is the sound of someone stepping on a plastic crate and cracking it, and it never stops," and while this sounded to me suspiciously familiar it was also sort of brilliant. You can opt out in Berlin, he'd say; you don't have to worry about constructing a public persona. I found this obnoxious, the first part especially, and would often reply, Because you don't speak the language? But I also hated my job, and was dependent on social media for a humiliatingly large percentage of my self-esteem, social life, and reading material, so even if I found his embittered watering of the other side's grass irritating, I also knew exactly what he meant.

MIDDLE

(Something Happens)

ON THE MORNING AFTER OUR LAST DATE I WOKE UP WITH AN overpowering desire to make Felix pancakes. He didn't really like pancakes, but that didn't matter. The knowledge that he had been lying to me and, in a slightly different way, to the rest of the good innocent people of the internet continued to be a source of cruel pleasure; I kept it locked up in a little cage in my mind, feeding it sad meals on a tray in the mornings and evenings. Curiosity about his motives occasionally threatened, but I was able to fend it off by arguing that his motives were fundamentally inscrutable. There was nothing to be curious about. He was beyond the pale. Conveniently his being beyond the pale did explain why he was in the end so frustrating as a boyfriend, and why I was totally justified in giving up trying to understand him. Though I did look at his Instagram account often, wanting to know what he came up with, seeking hints about his inner life in his misspellings and capitalizations. He posted every day, sometimes multiple times a day, and because I was so vigilant I usually saw a new image within ten minutes of its appearance. Sometimes I even checked the account while he was in the same room; once I checked while he was in the bathroom and the timestamp under his most recent picture (which warned of radio-frequency devices planted in the flora of every country on earth . . . except North Korea) said it had been posted forty-eight seconds before. I wondered if he scheduled posts in advance, as he often had to do for his job, or if he had gone into the bathroom to do it and we had been hunched over our phones looking at Instagram in different rooms at the same time, like a split screen in a very sad romantic comedy. His caption urged me to google "Silent weapons for Quiet Wars," but he came out wiping his hands on his jeans, a telltale rectangle outlined in his front pocket, before I could. "Kara's in Australia," I said, as if my colleague's kangaroo photos were what I'd been looking at while passing the fleeting seconds of his peeing. He did the only normal thing a person could do when presented with such information and said, "Huh. Cool."

On weekend mornings before Felix moved to New York I would get up early to read and type or exercise; with Felix, I stayed in bed awake, doing nothing and worrying about it, as he slept on. Lying on my back with one of my feet against the inside of my opposite thigh in a figure four, I would hold my phone above my head and look at the websites of all the stores I liked and think about buying things. Or I would read articles: a commentary on the new president's pick for whatever Cabinet position was being discussed at the time; an old profile of Andrea Dworkin; how to prevent going gray in your twenties. Going gray in your twenties was cool now, so what I really needed was an article about how to best make use of the gray hairs I already had, to make sure I either developed a fetching Sontag streak or went totally silver before I turned forty.

The only place I could get fancy-enough ingredients for the pancakes I envisioned was a grocery store fifteen minutes away, and although a fifteen-minute walk did not seem the best way to optimize my shrinking window of Sunday morning, nothing mattered anyway, least of all time passing, and I had been trying to make decisions and stick with them, lying around worrying being if nothing else a terrible default. I looked up a recipe, got out of bed, and went downstairs. Turning the corner from Bedford onto Lafayette I passed the homemade flier that read "The Star Of David / LOOK AT IT" and thought, as I did every time I passed it, about how having attainable goals leads to more success. About a block later I was texting a friend who'd slept with her ex-boyfriend the night before and nearly ran into a pubescent Hasidic boy. He looked startled, though it was unclear whether that was because of the pubescence or the near-collision or the fact that he was lost. "Miss," he asked, standing too close, "do you know where Bedford Avenue is?"

He didn't seem to understand what I was saying, but he nodded several times and then set off in the direction I pointed him in. Felix was always marveling reproachfully at how distrustful I am of strangers—the odd angle at which my body attempts to avoid people who just need directions and straphangers who, like me, are traveling at busy hours. Did I think this ultra-orthodox teen was going to rob me? I always replied to the teasing by either 1) saying, "You mean strangers like pub crawl tour guides?" or 2) tracing the tendency back to my first trip to New York, in preparation for which I had studied a guidebook that warned, several times, in the Before You Go, Transportation, Shopping, and Entertainment & Nightlife chapters, of the city's stealthy and ubiquitous pickpockets, and since then any urban environment took on a sense of lurking danger. Felix always replied that the latter thing was racist and ignored the former.

At the grocery store I bought ricotta, blackberries, eight-dollar grapefruit juice, maple syrup at a price I will not disclose, and two lemons, thinking that in addition to putting lemon in the pancakes I could start drinking hot water with lemon in the mornings, a *wellness* tactic dumb celebrities recommended that also made some kind of sense. While looking at the cost of lemons, written on a little chalkboard above the lemon bin, I realized that going to this grocery store had not really been necessary and considered that my new snap-decision policy was going to be a financial liability, prioritizing as it did my first choices, which always tended ignobly toward luxury. I also had to buy the things for pancakes one should already have—flour, baking powder, eggs—because I did not have them, and these too cost much more than they needed to. I have a friend who refuses to cook for men, even though she can cook pretty well and enjoys it, because she believes the gesture will never overcome its sexist connotations. I always feigned indifference when she went on about this because although I hate chopping onions and don't usually cook for myself, I like to cosplay hospitality. The fact that Felix was my boyfriend made me want to give him things, like pancakes he didn't want.

Outside my apartment building I saw the Hasidic boy again; he had not made it far in the half hour or so since we'd last met, and in fact I didn't live on Bedford Avenue, so he'd really made negative progress. I nodded at him, and as I was walking up the steps he lisped, "Excuse me, miss?" and came up to the top of the stairs to meet me. Again I became awkward and avoidant. He was sorry to bother me again, but he needed to know where Myrtle Avenue was now. After I pointed him north, a look of relief lightened his features. He tipped his hat and said thank you; I smiled and said he was welcome. I went into the first door of my building and, standing in the vestibule, began groping around in my bag for the key to the second door. With my back turned I heard the front door open; I turned; it was the boy, still looking terrified. He reached for my hand, which I allowed him, stunned; said, "Thank you, miss"; and kissed it. Then he banged out the front door and skittered away in the wrong direction.

Felix did not look like a painter, but he sometimes acted like one, erratic and moved by inspiration. I will admit that he has drawn me several times, in various states of dress, and that I was blushingly flattered every time the request was made, even if the ultimate representation was not something I would, say, post on Instagram. When I walked in the door he was at my kitchen table, which was in the living room, wooden paintbrush in hand and sketchbook open, his workspace surrounded by little stacks of thin white takeout napkins that remained untidied-up from the week's dinners.

Months before, without asking, he'd cleared out a corner in my closet and assembled a little altar of his art supplies and underwear, calling it "practical sculpture," and every time he wanted a pair of boxers he had to remove several colored pencils from their positions blocking the shelf where his boxers were and then put them back. I didn't have a lot of clothes or, crucially, shoes, so I didn't mind from that perspective, but I thought it was rude he had never asked if he could build a practical sculpture in my closet, just as I thought it was rude when he got up during a lull in conversation and went to the bathroom without acknowledging that he was getting up to go to the bathroom. I always took it as a slight. (*Because you're too sensitive.*) It was as if he was both invading my life and abandoning me.

"I'm sketching the man we saw last night," he said without looking up, understanding that artistic melodrama was usually tiresome but believing himself to be an exception. On our way home from the bar we'd passed on the sidewalk a tall man dressed in stylish and very white tennis shoes carrying a newborn baby wrapped in an equally white blanket. The man was very calm and unselfconscious, bouncing, and Felix was perplexed by the image, unencumbered as he was by background knowledge of the type of scene we were likely watching: the new father was trying to get the baby, who had been crying, to go to sleep without waking the mother, who was indoors and probably very tired. I lived next to a tall silver building with private parking and locked gates; one side was a column of living rooms whose floor-to-ceiling windows revealed which residents read books and which watched TV, and at the top there was a duplex that occasionally flashed purple and blue lights. The man and his baby had probably come from there, like the poodle crossbreeds that had proliferated in the neighborhood in the last year or so. I didn't explain any of this to Felix because I didn't want to seem maternal.

"I bought stuff to make pancakes," I said. He didn't respond, so as I removed the ingredients from my bag I added, "Guess what happened to me."

"What?" he said, rinsing off some purple in a *Harper's* promotional mug that had FUCK THE INTERNET printed on it.

"A boy kissed me in the street."

He looked up. He had padding around his edges, like a former athlete, and the teeth of a prom queen. The food in the U.S. made you fatter, he said. He could have snapped the paintbrush in two if he'd wanted.

I told him the story, adding the detail that the Hasidic boy had had red hair, making him seem even more ingenuous. Felix laughed and said I had probably changed his life.

"I change all men's lives," I replied, and I asked if he'd seen what Trump had tweeted about a senator. I kissed him on the forehead so that he wouldn't suspect anything was about to change but ended up enjoying the ripple of good feeling giving affection produced. We ate the pancakes as we read *The New York Times* on our phones, pausing frequently to wipe our fingers on the takeout napkins so the screens would not get sticky.

. . .

I DECIDED TO PUT OFF DUMPING FELIX UNTIL AFTER THE LARGE women's protest taking place on the day after Trump's inauguration. There were iterations of the event scheduled everywhere, but the big one was in D.C. I hadn't planned to go—not because I was ideologically opposed to the idea necessarily but because it seemed there would be a lot of pink, which in a feminist context signaled to me a lack of rigor. I also thought the traffic would be horrible. Besides those two considerations, I had avoided considering it, even as conversations at parties increasingly focused on how people were getting there, where they were staying, the unbelievability of the whole situation in general, and if we really cared shouldn't we have been at the protests against police brutality. Then, a week before the march, I went to a yoga class, and immediately following the nice but antsy conclusive period of lying on your back with your eyes closed, during which you're supposed to clear your mind of all thoughts and take a reflective break, the instructor—too peppy, I felt, for this job—announced that the following week's class was canceled because she would be traveling to D.C. for the protest. One by one the women rolling up their mats and putting their bodies back in order whooped, or raised a celebratory fist, or shouted, "Me too!"

I was overcome with the sense that I needed to go, and it did not feel good. The people at my yoga studio, which was on the more bourgeois side of my neighborhood, were primarily white women living in Brooklyn, and although I too was a white woman living in Brooklyn, I of course did not identify as such, since the description usually signified someone selfish, lazy, and in possession of superficial understandings of complex topics such as racism and literature. Besides working in the media (also a bad thing), the weekly seventy-five-minute session of possibly culturally appropriative contortion was the most white-woman-in-Brooklyn thing I did. It is OK to do yoga, I told myself, but I never really believed it, and each time I joined the perky line of spandexed women heel-toeing down the sidewalk on the way to the studio before class, stressed about getting there before all the good spots were taken, wondering if it was an anti-yoga impulse to indulge my impatient and competitive nature by passing the slow walkers, I hated my yoga mat, the purple of a pediatric dentist's office, and was ashamed.

I had assumed most of my cohort would, like me, not care to spend time and money traveling to lifeless Washington, D.C., in order to protest an administration that would not affect them particularly sweepingly, but after the election, being a white woman living in Brooklyn began to feel, very briefly, less repugnant; the white women living in Brooklyn, in the end, were ultimately just annoying, point-missing, and distracting, not the biggest problem. For a few months the political catastrophe seemed so dire that one's music and movie preferences were no longer considered the ultimate markers of one's moral fitness to fight *fascism*, which became, incredibly, a buzzword; though we could always *do more* or *do better*, there was a sense that our embarrassment of privileges could be set aside to focus on the task at hand, though what that task was I wasn't really sure. The emphasis was on *resistance*, a helpfully broad term the force of which was derived from social media, where you could not look away from the spectacle of previously apolitical coworkers and high school classmates and one-night stands rallying around paragraphs of drastic recommendations, often copied and pasted from users of *n* degrees of separation who would later emerge demanding credit for having started whatever *action* was scrambling into being. Watching debates about logistics coagulate in real time was tedious. Yet if you were out there protesting you were only a single person protesting; if you were out there posting photos of yourself protesting you could become, theoretically, multiplied, into the number of people you encouraged through genuine inspiration or quiet guilt to follow your example. Whether the righteous overuse of social media platforms fed directly into the fountain of power on which Donald Trump was a lewdly spouting statue was not worth thinking about. You worked with what you had, and you had to admit it was useful to be able to reach an audience like that, an audience that might as well have been everyone in the world for all your brain could comprehend. At the march itself I realized after seeing several signs featuring Princess Leia that despite the term's historical usage in political theory and activism the *resistance* arose because it was a feature of Star Wars, and Carrie Fisher had just died. You could argue that its usage in Star Wars comes from political theory and activism, but even so the real significance is muted. If you don't know something is a reference you don't fully understand it; this is the great humiliation of allusion. Anyway, the message I got in the yoga class was that everyone was going to the protest, so I, someone who actually cared, someone who had, after all, served as president of her (red-state) high school's Young Democrats of America for not one but two years, should go, too.

Whenever the march had come up in group small talk or whatever, Felix responded ambivalently, with a nodding *hm* or a despondent *yeah*, and then excused himself to go to the bathroom; I couldn't figure out what he thought of it, if he thought of it at all. I respected this; it made me want to look at him meaningfully in the eye and share an understanding, maybe one that would include a justification of the Instagram conspiracy theories. When confronted with the subject of feminism in public in general he always deferred to me or the other women around, understanding that expressing an opinion on the matter could discredit him even if he were right—he considered the territory mine and didn't feel the need to conquer it the way some men did. To avoid accusations of antagonism, envy, or mediocrity, a man discussing feminism had few options but to become a toothless sycophant, and even then he'd be ruthlessly mocked or treated with skepticism, and Felix was neither a masochist nor a person who could easily dismiss what people thought of him, including those he disliked. This wasn't the result of low self-esteem or paranoia but, I think, a desire for control. When I told him, months after the fact, that his pub crawl colleague Kasia had said he was "interesting," he swiveled from the idle reminiscing we'd been doing to something very solemn, and he proceeded to ask so many questions, about her tone, about her facial expression, about whether she had seemed mad about something, about whether the comment had been made before or after he and I had spent the entire session at the third bar talking in a corner where he had touched my arm—his memory surprising and flattering—that I had to lie and say I'd interpreted it as her having a crush on him, but because I hadn't come up with that lie soon enough, hadn't introduced the comment with the teasing insecurity it would have called for, he didn't believe me.

I sent him a message as I left the yoga class, blocking the door and then almost falling on the step outside because I was looking at my phone, saying that I thought I would go to D.C. the next weekend, and in addition to the adrenaline from almost tripping I think the announcement gave me a little thrill. I was excited to be distanced from Felix, to be able to concoct a last-minute plan that didn't involve or concern him. I'm not saying he was possessive—he was the opposite, almost too laissez-faire, rarely expressing anger or frustration or any other negative emotion about me saying I was having drinks with an ex-boyfriend or spending time with someone he disliked—but rather that I interpret boyfriends' silences and noncommittals as masculine efforts to conceal themselves and the fact that they are feeling more than they say. I try to assume everyone is working with an inventory of emotions identical to mine, and since I couldn't help taking it as a tiny betrayal when I heard about a boyfriend's plans made without me, particularly if he brought up said plans nonchalantly several days after making them, as if having plans were not important, as if our two lives were not an intricately woven tapestry but merely two lines sometimes intersecting, I imagined men suffered the same pinpricks of disappointment when I did the same. This was delusional, I knew, particularly because I obviously liked to maintain my own independence and should theoretically be able to rationalize another person's desire to do so. Nevertheless I preferred to think of everyone I'd ever loved or gone out with as existing in a constant state of devotional pining for me, sexually and spiritually, ideally not even leaving the house except to pick up necessities, and I assumed they liked to think of me the same way.

Three minutes later he replied, "For the inauguration?" I said haha no, for the Women's March, I was thinking I could probably stay with Jeremy, Jeremy being my friend from high school who worked for Booz Allen, doing work he only discussed by raising his eyebrows suggestively. In addition to being true, this was calculated to induce jealousy. Felix did not believe that Jeremy, who was gay, was "really gay," and he believed that even if he was "really gay," it wasn't as if being gay prevented you from having sex with women. In Felix's view everyone's sexuality was fluid, both a threat (to his relationship) and an opportunity (to sleep with interesting people regardless of gender). The idea of labeling yourself, even with the anti-label labels that were proliferating or said to be proliferating in progressive spaces, *pansexual*, *demisexual*, *sapiosexual*, *asexual*, *poly*, *queer*, etc., was to him just asking for confusion and angst; worse, any declarative statement about yourself would inevitably result in having to publicly revise whatever distinction you'd made, admitting you had not known yourself as well as you thought you did. I would say, So you think it makes people look bad to say they've changed their minds? And he would reply, I think it makes people look bad to make claims about themselves in the first place, because it seems as if they are not smart enough to consider the possibility that they are delusional or will change their minds. (The ex-boyfriends are rolling their eyes and shaking their heads; they never liked this guy.) If you're wondering, *Well, then, were you guys in a "monogamous" relationship? Is that not a label?* I will tell you: we weren't in a "monogamous" relationship until he moved back to the States, at which point we became "monogamous," which he would say was not an identity structure but a relationship structure. (Critically, though, both structures.) (If we said we were *polyamorous,* that could be either or both, depending on the context.) *OK, fine,* you, the reader uncommonly aware of *identity politics,* say, *but you're using gendered pronouns? Did he not use them for himself?* He did use them, you're right. Don't get mad at me. These aren't my inconsistent views, remember, but Felix's. I think they're mostly related to his reading of philosophy and the traumatic combination of being the smartest person and worst painter at art school; that would create a lot of combativeness, a lot of animosity, plus a foundation in this kind of discourse. Sexuality-wise, he had never had a gay experience, but he said he was totally open to having a gay experience if the right guy came along, and he thought the fact that he had never had a gay experience said more about how terrible men were than it did anything about himself. It's true, he had no male friends. Or many friends at all. Nevertheless, because of the demands of society, when pressed he said he was straight, which he was.

Walking down the street checking for dog shit and approaching pedestrians in my peripheral vision, I watched the ellipses appear to signal he was typing. He said he thought it would be good to go to the march. I said of course he could come too though the traffic would be awful and it would be hard for us to find an Airbnb at this point if he didn't want to stay at Jeremy's and probably the march itself would end up being underwhelming. He said no, no, he wanted to work on a "piece" he'd started recently and thought was going somewhere. I didn't think to ask what the piece was. Sometimes he'd offer me the broad strokes of it, but lately I found myself unable to concentrate when he talked about art, either his own or someone else's; my mind would turn to angry conversations I'd had with a friend years before, or to how I could style items of clothing I wanted to buy, or to what might happen if an editor at one of the magazines I wanted to work for "discovered" an article I wrote. I told him cool great and said we should see each other before I left. By this point I'd made it home and now you have no idea what the route from my yoga studio to my apartment looks like because I was staring at my phone for the entire walk.

. . .

AT WORK, THAT MONDAY, I TOLD EVERYONE WHO TRIED TO MAKE small talk with me that I had decided to go to the Women's March. "I'm a good person now," I said, dispensing peanut butter M&M's from the peanut butter M&M dispenser in the kitchen. "I'm also eating a healthy breakfast." No one laughed except the intern, a long-nosed field hockey player and the only person we interviewed who knew what the *Village Voice* was. She told me studies show that people who talk about their goals are less likely to accomplish them than people who are humble and quiet, because talking about plans makes you feel like you have done something and then you feel less like you need to do something. I liked her; she was overfamiliar, as if unperturbed by the paranoia of social media or the precariousness of her place in the world. She also had follow-through. I asked if that was supposed to mean I wasn't humble and quiet, and when she said yes I told her to do twenty push-ups. When she dropped in the middle of the aisle between our desks only a couple of people noticed; they watched bemused for a few seconds before silently spinning back to their computers. If it had happened in the afternoon the entire floor would have come over and cheered her on, phones in hand, live-tweeting the event to trick themselves into thinking that because our office was cool, not like other offices, we were not really working, and that being at work was in some ways actually more fun than being at home, alone, streaming a TV show we pretend is good while eating delivery we pretend to afford. In the process we would be advertising our website. We also had free beer, but we weren't allowed to start drinking until five, even though we often had to publish the first articles of the day from home while brushing our teeth and listening to podcasts hosted by other journalists awestruck by the beautiful nuance of everything, which should have pushed five forward to at least three. At the office mornings were spent in a hunched laptop trance, scrolling through feeds, groggily yet frantically proofreading articles that had to go up before noon to optimize traffic, fielding annoying requests, and posting possibly original jokes and observations on Twitter as they materialized.

We spent all day on the internet, and especially on Twitter, ostensibly looking for stories but mainly just looking; digital media was unionizing at the time, and a recurring joke in our meetings was that we should get the company to pay for addiction treatment. People were funny. Certain employees were bafflingly loud chewers, or shouty phone interviewers; they promoted camaraderie among the rest of us. Sometimes you would catch the eye of the coworker with whom you were Gchatting and share a look or smirk, or ostentatiously cover your mouth to stifle your laughter; by the afternoon these interactions would become less surreptitious, the disorientation of spending all day on the internet leading to outbursts that welcomely disrupted the forced calm of the open-floor office. In this way, it was kind of fun. At push-up number eight the intern asked if I was Instagramming her; I said no, I didn't want to get fired for advertising a labor violation. She said she wanted me to post a video so she could show off without having to show off herself. I said it would be feminist to post a video of herself doing push-ups, and maybe she could become a fitness *influencer* and leave the media behind. By twenty we were late for a pitch meeting and she was sweaty.

I was a blogger, if that wasn't clear. I would have liked to claim a more dignified title, journalist or writer or critic or reporter, but I didn't, because I didn't want to contribute to the rapid deterioration of those titles; I was hoping to one day claim them and scrape off some legitimacy for myself. My job was to write two to three articles per day about "culture"—items about celebrities or suggestive studies or, lately, politics—and though that may seem like a lot it quickly became totally doable, not so bad at all. (Initially they'd told me I was supposed to write four to five articles per day.) You got used to it, and because I was often just rewording pieces other people had written and adding mean jokes, it wasn't particularly exhausting. Once I developed my tone, a rote, pseudo-intellectual dismissiveness that could be applied to any topic so long as the worst political implications (ideally, that the thing being discussed was *bad for women*) were spelled out by the end of an article, I wrote fast, and I accumulated a modest but respectable number of Twitter followers, in the mid four figures. Although I didn't feel I was doing something evil, I did feel I was participating in a system that ran on panic and distraction, in which being stupid but not too stupid, prioritizing not quite the right things according to close-but-no-cigar logic, was an asset, and perhaps because it was my job to detect the gravest possible outcome in any scenario I couldn't deny that what I was doing was probably evil even if I knew, ultimately, it wasn't. Office work generally requires emptying your mind so that all the dumb shit people tell you to do doesn't meet any obstacle on its way to smooth execution, but working in online media you couldn't be too listlessly vapid because then you would bring disaster, opprobrium, and legal obligation upon the enterprise: scandal, offense, virality on behalf of something widely agreed to be unethical. Everything you said or did was meaningless and impermanent as well as potentially hugely significant; the effect was that you were both neurotically tetchy and quietly demoralized all the time, constantly justifying your acquiescence to stupidity as relatively minor and in service of a greater aim. Unfortunately humility did not help the cause, which was to appeal to a youngish audience that assumed it was smarter than it was, that wanted seemingly complicated arguments that conformed to its associative ideas about the world, but delivered simply. It wanted to learn things that it could trick itself into believing it had always known, so you had to write as if you were like everyone else, and as if everyone else were decently intelligent.

The website, which millions of people read every month, had once been good; now it had expanded its coverage so that it was, except for slight distinctions in the adjectives people used to describe it, indistinguishable from a suite of other websites that had also once been good. All these websites—in fact, most websites—also produced videos, which the company executives believed were more profitable than articles, though they cost much more to produce and it was inconceivable to me and many of my coworkers that anyone would rather watch a hand-holding tutorial about how to make macaroni and cheese with weed in it or what the Hyde Amendment was than read a short article. Facebook was widely understood to be responsible for all this and there was not much more to say about it. I had worked at the website for a few years; I liked having a paycheck, even if it was considered small, a place to go, people to talk to, and something to do that I didn't have to come up with myself. I hated the rest, especially the separate email account, the way it constantly generated, mainly press releases for irrelevant premieres, and the way my colleagues and I, knowing it could be scoured by management and used against us at any time, tiptoed around talking to each other with platitudes and jargon. Sometimes they switched out the peanut butter M&M's for peanut M&M's and the discovery was so crushing that I couldn't work for the rest of the day. I occasionally got to write *longreads*, departing from my bratty knowingness to do what my boss called a *deep dive* into some surprisingly relevant but forgotten historical figure or unheralded cultural product. I usually wrote these pieces outside the office, in the mornings or on weekends, so the dive could never be that deep; they were not seen as real contributions to the website, though my boss redeemed them by saying they boosted our credibility among "smart people." The understanding was that no one read them—I had access to the actual numbers, through a program, but I never logged in, fearing I would become obsessed, so instead I sought out people discussing my writing on social media, by searching the link to the article or my own name or any other related term, and I deduced that smart people did not bother with this website, and I didn't blame them. Sometimes I'd notice arguments or ideas I'd written show up in more popular writers' pieces six, eight months later, and I would say to myself: There are no original ideas! You're just ahead of your time! And then I'd get mad, partly because I felt I had been tricked into caring about a measure of success that I did not want to care about, popularity. Yet it seemed the only way to rise above popularity was through same. I found myself wishing someone would actually plagiarize me, lift a sentence or two, so at least I could believe I was being unacknowledged and not just ignored.

The pitch meeting was, like all meetings, almost totally pointless, except that someone at the company had created a spreadsheet of contact information for employees who were going to the march and had space in their cars or accommodation for others. In a show of righteousness the company was allowing anyone who wanted to travel to D.C. to leave the office at 1 p.m. that Friday.

I arranged to get a ride with a video producer I had never met and her former camp counselor, who drove. I showed up outside an apartment in Fort Greene and we got on the road in the gray rain by Friday afternoon, only an hour after we said we wanted to. The camp counselor, gregarious and still dressed in hiking boots and the kind of sporty fleece vest intended to gain children's trust, was now a labor lawyer working on freelance issues, with a daughter in college studying "something horrible, I don't want to talk about it"; the video producer's large, sad eyes reflected her years-long struggle to get a boyfriend and a full-time contract at the website. Running her hand through gauzy umber hair, unbothered by traffic signs or sudden stops, the camp counselor brought up both issues and offered her no-nonsense advice almost as soon as we got in the car, as if continuing a previous conversation. "You're too worn down, you can't imagine anything anymore," she said, her voice coaching. "You need imagination to get happy, and I don't mean it in a tech way, God, I mean that you can't just accept what's in front of you, and no one's going to come up with a good alternative to what's in front of you, because everyone is unimaginative, because they don't give a shit about anyone but themselves. You do give a shit, that's why you're good. But you're also trapped. You have to figure out how to keep giving a shit without getting covered in it." They shared the trendy flavored seltzers they'd brought and I offered them peanut butter M&M's I had taken from the office, which they did not accept. Everyone was feeling generous that weekend, so they refused to let me pay for gas, and though I could have I was grateful for that. In the back seat I texted with Felix and tried to think of a strategy to ease myself into an initiation of our breakup, not to break up with him then over text message but to foreshadow that all was not well; I either didn't want him to feel totally ambushed, or I wanted him to begin to dread the realization of a back-of-mind suspicion. I typed and deleted, typed and deleted, looking for double meanings, plausible deniabilities, but there was no natural way to do it. So I just said I missed him already!!! with the multiple exclamation marks I tended to use to convey a sheepish sincerity.

In the car, listening to Bruce Springsteen once we got to New Jersey, the women would periodically bring up horrible facts about Donald Trump and when appropriate I would interject references to articles I'd read that elaborated on their worst fears about his immigration policies or ties to Russia in order to seem like I was engaged in the conversation and not texting my soon-to-be-ex-boyfriend. It was always refreshing to spend time with people who weren't online all day; it made me feel like I could one day live such a lifestyle, and in the meantime I was at least a person who really kept up with the news, who was really dialed in to what was happening in the culture, even though it was increasingly difficult to say whether society was bettered by my knowing what was going on and clear that *dialed in* was a quaint anachronism insufficient for describing the desperate attachment I had to the platforms that gave me my acute awareness of the culture and the news. Felix was being funny and sending me memes I pretended not to have already seen, and I wondered momentarily if maybe I was making a mistake, if he could explain, if I shouldn't necessarily break up with him after all, depending on that hypothetical explanation. I reread an email he'd sent me while he lived in Berlin, a sweet and energetic account of his visit with a former professor that segued into a casual analysis of *Our Mutual Friend* that segued into a nice comment about my hip bones, and it occurred to me that the negative change in his behavior and attitude might indeed be, at least a little bit, the fault of my influence, something I ignited. But then I reassured myself that he was his own person, an agent, and that a comparison between his manipulative experiment and the laid-back acceptance with which I occupied my distasteful position as a cultural producer could only be made in *bad faith*. Since he claimed to eschew constant cell phone usage I'd always thought his quick responses to my messages must have been related to an eagerness to talk to me; now I realized it was because he had a secret life to manage on his phone, and my text messages happened to be there, too.

People who worked in video production always had unfathomably carefree attitudes; it truly shocked me how long this woman and her friend took at each of the two rest stops we visited. They didn't seem to want to "get back onto the road" or "make good time" at all. Both Travel Plazas were crawling with women in groups, mothers and grandmothers and children and teenagers and many in their twenties and thirties, and a not-insignificant portion were wearing magenta- and bubblegum- and rose- and blush-colored knit hats with cat ears. I heard someone marvel that the yarn store had run out of pink. I'd not cared about the Women's March so much that I'd had no idea the hats, dorky but because of the number of grandmas unmockable, were part of a plan before I saw them forming the laughably long line at the Delaware House Travel Plaza Starbucks.

Sitting around a table avoiding a smear of ketchup from our prede-cessors and eyeing the camp counselor's curly fries I told the women I was planning on breaking up with my boyfriend when I got back on Sunday night. They responded with rehearsed sincere apologies, plus slight surprise that I was revealing something so intimate to them, though it didn't mat-ter if these women knew I was going to break up with my boyfriend; they didn't know him or me and it was not something about which I needed advice, though they'd enjoy giving it. "Is that who you've been texting?" the producer asked. To add insult to injury the camp counselor then queried how old I was, nodding as she ate her fries. No particularly useful advice was given, though the strength of my conviction was celebrated. The pro-ducer said she was becoming fed up with dating apps because everyone she met wanted her to go to concerts with them or revealed only after the date had begun that actually they didn't drink; all the other men posted photos of themselves next to their cars. Yes, even in New York. In the past I'd felt removed from these types of complaints, which I recognized as probably true but had never connected with. Before Felix I'd dated a series of nice-enough people I'd met at parties or who were repurposed from college; I'd never felt I should use a dating app or even really thought about them, unless I was assigned to blog about the data collected by one. Would I now become this data? Would it not be humiliating to go from the great story of falling in love with my Berlin pub crawl tour guide to saying, "We met on Tinder"? There were people who refused to go out with anyone they didn't meet on an app, with anyone who hadn't been superficially vetted and cat-egorized as possibly romantic in advance; would I become these people, distrait from a cacophonous loneliness and so eager for a prescription that I would adopt an obviously misguided rule I'd found on the internet? I told the producer she should go to a socialist meeting, where there would be a lot of politically engaged men who loved drinking. She replied, Oh, but I'm such a Hillary girl, and I knew exactly what she meant: she believed so-cialists were sexist. I had only been to one socialist event in New York and didn't even vote in the primary, so maybe it was guilt that inspired me to begin to attempt to explain what Hillary girls were missing wrt the *intersection* of class with race and gender and sexuality, wrt I mean I grew up in . . . The women were silent as I went through all this, my eyes rarely making contact with theirs and instead looking off at the condiment-and-napkin station, so after a few gestures toward my socioeconomic background without revelation I added "but she does have to deal with a lot of shit" to make sure they didn't abandon me at the Travel Plaza. I was offered the last curly fry. All in all it took us eight and a half hours to get to the beltway, in the rain.

Resisting their dutiful objections I made them drop me off at some unknown corner so I could walk to meet Jeremy at a bar in Shaw. I wanted to sleep immediately, but we hadn't seen each other in about two years so I would have to drink a beer and listen to him talk. The bar, stalwartly dingy despite the creeping cleanliness outside, was crowded, but I got seats for us by emphasizing my natural weariness and saying loudly, "I feel like I might pass out? I don't know what it is. I mean, I definitely ate . . . ?"

Jeremy had recently started a militant group workout regimen and was, frankly, very hot to begin with; he arrived late to everything because no one had ever gotten mad about eventually seeing his face. In the past he'd occasionally slept with women, always a little mordantly I thought. Felix didn't know that, nor did he know that Jeremy and I had made out three times over the course of our friendship, each one very fun if disorienting; I siphoned my deniability from the way Jeremy had, after moving to D.C. a couple of years before, become more straightforwardly homosexual, going to gay bars but no longer any *queer spaces*, confusing fewer and fewer people. He showed up twenty minutes after he texted that he was five minutes away and immediately began telling me about how his new boyfriend was accusing him of *gaslighting* him about his (the new boyfriend's) cooking skills, by saying he didn't have any. "But he can't cook!" Jeremy said, seriously bewildered. "He even made a joke about it on Grindr! He almost *poisoned* someone!"

Occasionally he would ask me about some aspect of my life and I would say something equivocal—it was all fine—until he asked how things were with that guy and I was able to touch his hand conspiratorially and say, with a naughty smile, Bad, I'm going to break up with him on Sunday. I hadn't planned on telling Jeremy, or anyone, about the Instagram account, but I suddenly realized I was bored of trying to care about something I did not care about. It didn't have to make me look bad that I had dated such a person, I reasoned, so long as I spun it the right way; a laughing confidence would make anyone doubt their harsh judgment of my judgment. Besides, Jeremy wasn't on any social media except for his wholesome Facebook account, where he posted photos of his rescue pit bull and shared news articles several days after they had been wrung dry of any interest on Twitter; he didn't know Felix or anyone else who did. Following a compulsory moment of headshaking for the potential harm the Instagram account had inflicted on the country, the way it may have influenced voters or hoodwinked the gullible who would go on to hoodwink the more gullible, we laughed together as I showed him my favorites of Felix's posts; since we knew or thought we knew the intention behind them, we analyzed them like they were works of art. We didn't get home until one thirty, after stopping at Jeremy's friend's house to smoke a joint on the windy roof, which I resented intensely.

Felix stopped replying to my texts at around 11 p.m., when he said he was going to sleep and I told him we were going to the friend's house and added an angry emoji, and when I woke up at seven to leave for the march, he still hadn't sent me anything. I was annoyed but didn't find it peculiar— he slept late and refused to see the advantages of certain relationship best practices, like ignoring your friends and surroundings in order to text your partner constantly. I reminded myself that I should be happy he didn't text me because another minor annoyance on the pile would make the breakup that much easier.

In the days before the march, women's websites had published clusters of articles on how to prepare: what you should wear, what you should bring, what you should know. The first type of article was ridiculed: yes, we're women, so the most important thing for us when making a political statement is how we look? Very sexist. I thought the guides had a point—I spent a long time figuring out what I would wear, seeking both practicality in unpredictable weather and to give off a sense of intellectual purpose—but like almost all internet guides the articles were completely unhelpful beyond suggesting a fanny pack, which I borrowed from a friend's boyfriend. Ultimately it doesn't matter but I'll tell you anyway, because it felt a little like a disguise: I wore loose jeans, a men's work jacket I got at a vintage store, a baseball hat, the stocky Australian farm boots that had become trendy (unfortunately I didn't buy them until after this development, so I can't claim savvy), and the fanny pack. The website for the event had firmly explained that bags larger than six inches across would not be permitted and that the only backpacks allowed would be the clear kind we had been instructed to buy in fifth grade, after the Columbine school shooting. It was foggy and gray but not raining or cold.

As I made my way into a line for the escalator at the Metro station near Jeremy's apartment I saw that most people had followed the rules, which we would soon learn could in no way be enforced, as well as worn the pussy hats. There were a lot of women, even there at that insignificant stop with a name I don't remember, and as we waited under the sick mossy light favored by the D.C. transit authority we looked across the tracks at the empty platform for the trains heading away from downtown. More and more groups of women, mostly older, with short fluffy hairstyles and many-pocketed jackets, came to wait, and when our train arrived only about half the people standing on the platform could fit. Alone I was able to squeeze and once inside held onto an overhead bar, sweating, and laughed with all the people there who seemed like they had only ever used a subway on vacation, people who might have gotten lost if it weren't for the compass of the crowd squinting at maps and asking other passengers if the train was going where they wanted to go, asking even though it was clear that that was where everyone else was going, too. At station after station no one got off, so no one could get on. I could feel my face flushing; the skin at the top of my forehead along the band of my hat began to itch. A man with a protest sign folded politely in half tried to get off a couple of stops early and when he couldn't make it to the doors before they closed he could only chuckle and shake his head. Despite the large estimates and elaborate preparation, everyone had expected the city to look like it does when there's a home game or big concert, noticeably more populated and obnoxious but not transformatively so. I didn't pay attention to the names of each stop and got off with everyone else. The platform filled with women and as we glacially followed instructions by engulfed employees to keep moving, someone at the top of the far-off escalator began to cheer. Down the escalator and along the platform the feminine whoop carried, signs bobbing in the air, until the entire station was rooting itself on.

The streets of downtown D.C. were made up of lines, people waiting at coffee shops, people making their way from the subway to a square to another square, emerging from the underground at a rate that would remain steady all day. The sense of population was geometric and unsteadying: the area I was in was crowded with people, a number I couldn't hope to estimate, and all around me radiating outward were identical areas crowded equally or more so with people. Later I would learn that this thought process could be applied not just to the square blocks of downtown D.C. but to towns and cities around the world, where only just fathomable numbers of people were congregating to protest something that was so multifaceted and specific that only general, sweeping words fit perfectly. In the weeks since Trump had been elected there had been a quick proliferation of vocabulary: *authoritarian, strongman, autocracy, kleptocracy.* There were *working groups* and *organizers* and various praises and critiques of *black bloc* tactics. It was as if everyone had taken Introduction to Political Philosophy and wanted to impress the hot professor, who had grown up in the Soviet Union. If everyone in the world could take Introduction to Political Philosophy I'm medium-certain we would have been in a better situation than we were, but as it was the language felt wrong, ripped from the past and pasted on the present, its rough edges visible and curling, though I couldn't find a way to pin down *getting educated* as a bad thing.

I arrived downtown hoping to sit quietly in a coffee shop and eat breakfast before going to the National Mall, where a demonstration was being held before the march, but when I got out of the Metro I found there was nowhere viable to do this; every café was full of people taking pictures and talking and laughing. After walking several blocks I stood in a line and bought a yogurt thing with granola and a coffee and a package of expensive beef jerky they were selling at the counter; I had been spending money somewhat frivolously because I was about to do something brave and honorable by dumping my boyfriend and needed to positively reinforce my decision. I went outside and sat on some concrete barricades, used the previous day for the sparse inauguration parade, and watched in dismay as a man, a little older than I, saw what I was doing and came over to sit on another one, within speaking distance. A pair of women I couldn't name but believed I recognized as prominent feminists or intellectuals left the café and walked briskly down the sidewalk. I was asked if I was alone. I looked over right as he was taking a bite of an egg sandwich.

"No," I replied. "It seems like there are thousands of people here."

He laughed. He had ice-pick acne scars and spoke as if he had a single cotton ball inside each cheek—slightly impeded, a little wet—but his jaw was all joint and tendon, an illustration of the human body and its beautiful functionality. Since I was not yet agitated I kept talking to him. Felix would always tell people that strangers loved to talk to me, like really talk to me, not just say hey girl or whatever, and although I felt unnerved and imbalanced after most of these interactions I couldn't help but reply when approached. I never understood why the strangers persisted; my discomfort made me a drag to talk to. As the guy ate his breakfast, he told me he had driven down from Philadelphia with his sister; they both thought it was important to come because their mother had grown up in an internment camp in California from ages two to six. I offered something paltry, "Wow," and after he elaborated for a bit on how comparisons currently being drawn between Germany in the 1930s and the situation right now failed to consider the racist legacy of the United States (as well as the influence of social media), he asked what I was doing that evening, after the march. Until then I'd been happy to continue talking, impressed by his articulacy and admiring of his face, but I panicked at having to make a decision based only on what he'd told me—the mother, the sister, the deleteriousness of social media—so I told him I was going to a Planned Parenthood benefit concert with my boyfriend. Smiling with no teeth he left mid-sandwich, and I got yogurt on my pants. It took me longer than it should have to realize that I had just been hit on at a feminist protest, though I didn't mind.

Turning the corner from Judiciary Square I joined a growing pack walking toward the Mall down a street that looked like what's called a *business park*, the kind of complex where they sell cheap ideas of importance. The streets in downtown D.C. are too wide—empty, during nonbusiness hours, they looked especially too wide—but the crowd had covered the sidewalk, so many of us walked in the road now closed to traffic. The sky was watery but nonthreatening and no one seemed to notice as we passed a famous far-right conspiracy theorist shouting into an iPhone camera, sweat beading on his round tan head. I got close enough to do something to disrupt his shoot, push him or insult him, but all I did was look; I wanted to tell someone but there was no one to tell. There were many celebrities in D.C. that day, but the only other one I saw, later, was the now-former secretary of state walking his Labrador down Constitution Avenue as if he had been going about his day as usual and just happened to stumble upon a massive protest against his former employer. He smiled and waved and posed for pictures as he went, with rows of people filming from the sidelines and the most daring struggling to hold their phones aloft as they took videos of themselves walking alongside him.

The march wasn't scheduled to start until the afternoon, but the organizers had planned a rally, a series of speakers that included Madonna and Angela Davis, that was about to begin. A conservative magazine editor would later write a piece criticizing liberals' approach to stopping Donald Trump and use this supposedly alienating lineup as proof of their misunderstanding of the common man. "Look at this roster of speakers from the January 21 march," he wrote. "What is *Angela Davis* doing there?" I felt these types of criticisms were rooted in the wrong assumption that organizers had thought ahead to achieving an elegant ideological ideal when really the march had originated because in the days after the election a couple of women (at least one white and living in Brooklyn) separately decided they would host—or decided to say they'd host—post-inauguration-day protests and initiated Facebook events that gained overwhelming support. As interest grew and people began asking about permits and diversity, a group of experienced activists had had to swoop in and save them: though a protest seems like it should be unwieldy by nature, developing spontaneously and out of passion, threatening for its unpredictability, it turns out you need permits.

As I walked down Constitution, I checked my phone and saw a missed call from a California number I didn't recognize. Felix should have texted me by then, but my angst about it dissipated as I approached the Mall, where the crowd was getting denser and more determined. I felt the urge that comes at concerts to get to the front, though I had no idea what I wanted there. In the distance I could see the Museum of the American Indian, on the left, where tiny people were seated on buttresses watching the crowd form. I had no idea where it ended on any side, and several people on an elevated platform, including a young boy with a sign that said, "This is what a feminist looks like," blocked my view directly ahead.

I reached the edge of the mass and began to haltingly make my way through, weaving past groups holding hands trying to stay together, girls who had miraculously spotted friends across the crowd and were now hugging with their mouths happily shocked open. I tried to memorize the signs and slogans, many of which featured female anatomy or mocked the new president for his small-handedness, small-mindedness, use of Twitter, and secret baldness, but figured there would be photo galleries online later if I wanted them as memories. Some of the messages were passive-aggressive— "Sisters, not just CIS-ters," or "I'll be seeing you white ladies at the next Black Lives Matter march, right?"—and others presented a forced sass: "NOPE." In the days leading up to the march there had been disagreements on the official Facebook page for the event: A young black activist had written a post telling white women, "You don't just get to join because now you're scared, too . . . You should be reading our books and understanding the roots of racism and white supremacy. Listening to our speeches. You should be drowning yourselves in our poetry." A fifty-year-old white woman, Jennifer from South Carolina, told *The New York Times* that she found this unwelcoming and would no longer attend the march, adding, "How do you know that I'm not reading black poetry?" a comment for which she was mocked on Twitter. The young black activist's comment didn't seem to come from any real desire to educate except inasmuch as educating others allows one to exist on a higher plane—the idea that there was something to join, like a club or a group, with shifting gatekeepers of varying degrees of benevolence, was not an idea that men, being lone rangers, had ever had to overcome. If it seemed like there was something to join, it's because it made someone feel important to portray it that way. Ultimately, though, Jennifer from South Carolina should have let it slide, because everyone knew she wasn't reading black poetry.

I looked left and saw the misty Capitol building in the background of the sea of people, a fuchsia exhortation to RESIST a few feet in front of me. A pink and purple stuffed vagina the size of a Great Dane jounced top-heavily in the distance, apparently part of a headpiece. I maneuvered into my fanny pack for my phone—no messages, but no one had cell service, something I'd overheard more than one person say—and took a photo. To my right the Washington Monument faded into the air. The crowd was getting tighter, but I pressed forward, as if there were somewhere I had to be.

I reached an impasse near a traffic light that would cycle through its colors and signal the WALK countdown throughout the demonstration. Very occasionally I suffer from sleep paralysis; I wake up stuck in bed and have to wrench myself past some shadowy barrier and into consciousness. Besides this, I had never in my life felt so physically unable to move. Although lines of protesters were able to snake through, led by people shouting that they "had a diabetic here!" or something similarly intended to invoke urgency, this rare movement seemed to intensify the fact of the mass; we were no longer a crowd of individual people but components of a single unit that none of us controlled. On the right an ambulance appeared—we were standing in the middle of what was usually a street—and people shouted to let it through, as if we couldn't clearly see the large flashing vehicle alerting us to an emergency we were making worse. (A friend who'd found a space near the stage, which I would later learn was only about a block and a half away from where I was, told me that someone had had a heart attack.) There were no police anywhere, no barricades, no help. Later this would be determined to be the result of racism—because the march was predominantly white, the thinking went, authorities determined that a strong police presence wasn't necessary—and I would feel guilty that I had in this moment wanted some authority to appear and herd us. I'd been watching a young, attractive priest act as a leader for a group of people, attempting to ferry older women back in the direction I'd come from, and he had only managed to travel a little sideways. People started nerdy chants and couldn't get them to catch on (too many syllables, the rhythm was off); one woman tried to start "America the Beautiful" and failed, her warbly sentimentality chilling. My fears multiplied—pickpocketing, fire, broken toes, the fact that ISIS was lately encouraging followers to carry out acts of terrorism by procuring large trucks and plowing them through crowded public spaces—but like everyone around me I didn't express anything but testiness, the temporary indignation of a person standing in a particularly inopportune spot on a crowded subway car when they need to get off at the next stop. I realized that if I stood on the balls of my feet I could see screens projecting the speakers' faces, but there was no sound. A man farther ahead shouted, "Gloria Steinem is on!" and everyone cheered for minutes. Another ambulance appeared and although the mass's ability to clear enough space for it to pass was reassuring, the swarm in its wake was not: people seemed to sprout out of each other to fill the space the ambulance had made. I felt suddenly that I had to get out, escape, go to the suburbs and never return, but in every direction people were packed as densely as we were. I looked at the group lounging on the steps of the Museum of the American Indian and envied them, though they would probably stay for the entire event, unwilling to give up their position, and I couldn't imagine that—in addition to being scary it was also very boring. I reached for my phone and saw messages from a friend who had gotten on a bus in New York at 4 a.m. and was still on it, in bumper-to-bumper traffic, and I tried to send her something in return—"It's awful, trapped, can't move, can't see"—before I turned against the crowd and began trying to make my way out.

To accomplish something like this, you have to be rude, aggressive; I used my leading arm like a wedge and slipped myself between teenagers and their friends, mothers and their mothers, mothers and their children. I saw newborns wearing noise-canceling headphones the size of their heads and countless kids being exposed to nonsexual references to genitalia—images of uteruses and vulvas were everywhere, their anatomical correctness part of the political message. Eventually I followed a group that had formed a successful line back toward Constitution, though it took about half an hour to get there. On the way a woman standing on a platform encouraged people passing on their way out to come up and see how far the crowd went. At the edge of the crowd was an impressive group of self-identified undocumented women chanting in Spanish, and as I sat down on the grass in front of the National Gallery of Art Library a jogger in a McCain/Palin '08 T-shirt passed by. It was at this point that I saw the former secretary of state and his dog.

I tried to call Jeremy but couldn't get through; we'd decided we would meet for lunch at two, but I wanted to be far away from the march now, at eleven forty-five. I went to the National Portrait Gallery and used the bathroom—security guards were happy to show everyone who had come there for this purpose where it was—and considered going inside to look at paintings but didn't. Tiredness weighted my hands and feet and I thought I could feel circles purpling under my eyes. As I came out of the museum my phone received a few messages at once—the friend who was stuck in traffic saying they had finally parked, Jeremy telling me he would come early to the Belgian restaurant if I would text him when I was done—but still none from Felix, with whom I now felt furious. I couldn't wait to break up with him; I would cry a little, but I would be better off. I noticed, again, that there were no police anywhere. As I went down into the Metro and watched the up escalator bring person after person to the protest that would continue for hours, I again had a restoratively heartening experience. At the bottom of the escalator a steady and buoyant line waited to ascend, and looking at the girls in tutus and college students in homemade T-shirts I forgot about the stupid problem that I'd prolonged for melodrama and could only feel I was glad I came, to have seen it.

. . .

THE RESTAURANT WAS EMPTY EXCEPT FOR A COUPLE I TREATED with suspicion—they weren't wearing the red hats that identified unapologetic Trump supporters, but there was something frowning and conservative about them. The woman was much younger than the man and wore heels; they were both eating steaks. The night before, it had been disturbing to see the hats on gangs of boys in waxed jackets walking up and down Fourteenth Street; they had come to D.C. to see the inauguration and brought with them a sense of confused infiltration, middle-school bullies who had only just realized they were physically intimidating, and publications ran photos of men and women in black tie going to inaugural balls looking like actors who had stumbled onto the wrong set.

I sat at the bar, ordered a beer, and read the news on my phone: There were photos from marches all over the world, in Nairobi and Kolkata and Belgrade and Melbourne and Jackson Hole, Wyoming. About thirty people aboard a boat in Antarctica each held up a different-colored sign—"Seals for Science," "Save the Planet"—in a photo gallery on the *New York Times* website. All the pictures were dominated by women looking defiant but happy. The word *solidarity* seemed to belong in that category of formerly incisive political vocabulary on the fast track to overuse, but there was nothing else I could sense from those people protesting, from the overwhelmingly cheerful attitude of the turnout. The march organizers had insisted that the event was not intended to be an "anti-Trump" protest but rather a "pro-woman" rally, and although I doubted any event beyond the election of Donald Trump to president of the United States could have inspired such numbers and fervency, I nevertheless saw traces of that optimism and positivity in those photos, and in the crowd that had so recently almost given me a panic attack. I wondered if I was in any of them, in the background, captured from a bad angle and contributing to some nebulous statement I didn't necessarily agree with. I don't think positivity works, not least because it's alienating, but then again so is being a bitch.

I'd finished the beer and the bartender was asking me where I was from when Jeremy walked into the place complaining. "Definitely Trump supporters," he said in a loud whisper as he walked past the silent couple finishing their beef. All the restaurants in D.C. were clean and obvious; they looked like they were designed by someone who had forgotten until the very last minute that restaurants usually had tables and chairs. The menu had many items needlessly listed in both Dutch and English, and the waiter spent a long time telling us that the mussels were really good until Jeremy said, "We don't want mussels. We want Brusselse spruitjes and Belgische frietjes and macaroni en kaas." The waiter nodded and left.

"I used to sleep with a Belgian dancer," he said. "I always used to ask her to pick her favorite language and she really didn't like it."

Jeremy had thin lips that were always chapped and an olive tan that had inspired his elementary-school classmates to tease him about being adopted. He wasn't adopted, just tan, and it made him cry every day. After that I believe he became hardened. I told him he shouldn't be rude to service staff and he replied, "It's OK if they're white." He had a working-class upbringing that he never talked about except to refer to it vaguely and awkwardly as such, his "working-class upbringing," and again I think it gave him a chip on his shoulder.

The Brusselse spruitjes were prepared the same way they are at most trendy restaurants, and when they arrived I received another call from the unfamiliar California number that had tried before. I picked it up as Jeremy was explaining a TV show he watched but didn't like, and he immediately pulled his own phone out of his front pants pocket and slumped over it. The voice on the other end of the line said it was Darcy, Felix's mother's assistant at the production company where she worked. I had never met or spoken to Felix's mother; Suzanne, which is what he called her when he spoke of her at all, lived in Los Angeles, and Felix had not invited me to join him the one time he'd visited her during our relationship. Darcy asked if I was available to take a call from Suzanne; I said I was. I must have sounded confused because Jeremy looked up from his phone. After a short pause Suzanne got on the line and said that Felix had died.

Her voice was strained but direct; it sounded as if she had prepared how she would tell me. I had googled his mother once in the early stage of our relationship, and I knew what Darcy looked like because Felix had once shown me her Facebook page, which he thought represented what a "normal person" cared about. When I surmised that she had eleven fairy tattoos and collected photos of each of them in an album called "FAERIES," I said that wasn't normal at all. He had died in "an accident"—she kept saying "an accident" until she finally added, "a bicycle accident." I don't know what I was doing with my body or face but when I hung up I had red lines on my left hand from sitting on it and pressing it into the ugly chair. The bicycle accident, she told me, happened somewhere upstate, where Felix had gone by himself in the early morning, a detail furnished by the Metro-North ticket stub in his wallet. This was consistent with other things he did. I should mention that although it was January it was very warm, like spring but darker, so a person going upstate to ride a bike wouldn't have to be hardcore. After several long pauses backgrounded by the sounds of suffering Suzanne sniffed and said, "I'm sorry, honey," and that they would be in touch about "the plans." Jeremy probably couldn't hear the entire thing but could make out bits of what she was saying, and of course there was my distraught face. He spent the phone call not knowing what to do with his hands: He put them flat on the table, touched my leg just for a second before sensing it wasn't a natural thing for him to do, put them back on the table, ate a spruit but seemed halfway through to find it repulsive, unlocked his phone, locked his phone, ate another spruit. At one point I said something like, Did they take him to the hospital? because I felt my thoughtlessness was not appropriate and it was the only question that occurred to me. I said, Uh-huh, uh-huh, oh. The word *spruitjes* is very pleasant; the *j* is delicate yet propulsive. Jeremy was not such a jerk that he would say the obvious inappropriate jerk thing—"At least now you don't have to break up with him?"—but as he quickly paid our bill with most of the food uneaten I started thinking it, at least now I didn't have to break up with him, so I imagined Jeremy had been thinking it the whole time. We had that in common, selfish black humor, always saying things our mothers kind of gasped at, first because we wanted to test them out and then because we became more comfortable with—and better at defending—the selfish black thoughts. What can you do when something is that shocking but react reflexively? It was a guilty thought but it was the obvious thought. I think anyone in my position, not that many people would ever find themselves there, would think it.

MIDDLE

(Nothing Happens)

WHEN I WAS A TEENAGER I TOOK A QUIZ IN A MAGAZINE THAT promised to help you determine "if you're really in love or just crushing!" One of the questions was something like: If your guy hasn't contacted you in a long time, do you assume a) he's busy; b) he's cheating on you; or c) something bad has happened to him? If you choose c) it means you're in love, I learned, so whenever I had imagined Felix's death, I had always taken it to be a sign of the purity, or at least intensity, of my feelings. Having not imagined Felix's death for months at that point, I was more surprised than I might have been when it actually occurred.

I didn't cry until we got back to Jeremy's apartment, and I didn't do it in front of Jeremy, who seemed to feel as if his impenitent gossiping had somehow contributed to the situation. "I'm sorry," he kept saying in the Uber, not in the rote, box-ticking way, as if he regretted what had happened and wanted a shorthand for impossible condolence, but as if he had actually done something wrong. "For what?" I kept replying, again not to suggest the usual thing, that he had nothing to be sorry for, but as if I expected he would provide a satisfactory answer. Once I shut the door to his spare room, my tears arrived, and unlike our conversation they strained for no meaning, coming as if on schedule, reflexive, unfelt. I didn't sob, heave, weep, thrash, moan, bawl, or experience the sort of humiliating physical wrenching of face and stomach that I associate with true devastation. I was crying, just crying, as much from shock as anything else, the tears receding and returning, for ten or fifteen minutes, the amount of time one might cry after a particularly painful career failure. After I finished, I sat up in bed with my swollen nose and the bottle of wine Jeremy had brought in while I, dignified, kept my head under the blankets, holding my breath so as not to betray a sniff, and thought: nothing.

This might have disturbed me, but I remembered that I rejected sentimentality for sentimentality's sake, and that I was in the unique situation of being in a unique situation, with no burdensome expectation for my grief or lack thereof. Was there something to be sad about? I had been with a person; I had come to see him as despicable; twinges of doubt about that assessment were chalked up to memories and hormones and ultimately redoubled my certainty of his contemptibility; now we were no longer together. I had already mentally separated from Felix, who had become, I guess you could say, despite it seeming a little on the nose, dead to me. From a certain perspective, the only difference between this and a messy breakup was that now I could be certain we would never see each other again. The elimination of this possibility could only be good. What's more, my memories of Felix would be mine, to do with what I pleased, rather than subject to objection from the only person who knew them as well as I did.

Drinking wine from the bottle, which had been delivered with an opener but no glass, I felt better, and then I was hit with the force of knowledge never to be acquired. There had been an explanation for him somewhere, and now it was gone. My writing him off as inexplicable had been lazy; I had just not wanted to try. Suddenly, moronically, I understood why the cliché was "loss." Phone, wallet, *keys*—I would not be able to unlock the door. I

soon began thinking of his muscular forearms and the way he used to pro-
nounce *Slavoj Zizek* radically differently every time he said it. (As a joke.)

A woman I worked with used a photo of a pink neon sign that read
"FEELINGS" in all capital letters as the background image on one of her
social media accounts. FEELINGS were popular at the time—expressing
them was seen as a kind of feminist statement, the reclamation of an "inappropriate" femininity previously dismissed as frivolous or hysterical, and
as a result people were constantly declaring (on social media) the intensity
of their emotions: about celebrities, about television, about heavy-handedly
alluded-to romantic turmoil, about pizza, about cute animals, about dead-
lines. The seriousness of the object of the feelings was usually inversely pro-
portional to the strength with which they were announced; it was a joke,
yes, but it also tapped into the way specific emotions can swell without
warning: the gratitude for a relatable view expressed by a famous person,
the deep desire to hold a cat, the fear of disappointing an employer or being rejected by a love interest. I had identified with the impulse to express
profligately at times, though I tried not to act on it, because the people who
declared their emotions in this way were annoying, and here was where Felix's philosophy about not making public statements about yourself that you
would later want to renounce made the most sense. Now that I had actual
feelings, unlikely given the almost-laughable originality of the situation to
have been anticipated, I could say for certain the whole trend was absurd.
Feelings are nothing like a pink neon sign at all.

The ex-boyfriends are nodding. They don't know what to say. It's awful.
They're sorry.

· · ·

I STAYED AT JEREMY'S FOR A LITTLE OVER A WEEK, SLEEPING IN
his guest bedroom and eating his food from the organic supermarket and
listening to the same playlist of eight songs I'd made back when Felix was

still in Berlin and I still liked him. Listening to these sad songs of the past in the spare Ikea Malm was comfortingly abject for me; I used them to reassure myself that I once had simple feelings about Felix, admiration and yearning directed across the Atlantic, which justified the peaks of sadness that were now rising out of the mist. I was nostalgic; maybe I had always been nostalgic; maybe that's why I hadn't broken up with him immediately, because our meeting had been so unlikely and I'd wanted to hold on to its rarity. Had our connection been particularly unique? At times I'd thought it was. I never had the sense of certainty married or otherwise in-love people talked about, the coherence that came with recognizing someone so suited to you that you were forced to recognize yourself; nevertheless, he would sometimes voice so confidently ideas I felt I might have gone on to form, too, if I had been quicker or sharper. These sentiments were always external—about culture, common behavioral tendencies, politics—and not about himself, never about himself, actually, but they created what I'd thought was a clear outline of him, a very detailed negative space.

Unfortunately I couldn't let my nostalgia remain uncontaminated by awareness of my own foolishness for very long. A stupid thought: if I'd broken up with him sooner he might have been too sad to have gone upstate and would not have died, a win-win. Such a counterfactual was philosophically bankrupt, not to mention unfounded—I'd never known him to claim the kind of sadness that prevents you from doing something, and I suspected he wasn't that dedicated to our relationship anymore, anyway. But regardless I wished I'd confronted him. I could have asked him *why*, and even if he'd refused to speak and just shaken his head, I could have looked at his body language and facial expressions and tried to detect some truth in them. I could have grabbed his face cinematically and made him look at me, and even if he pulled away it would have given me something more to analyze than what I had. I often thought about the call from his mother—how she must have begun trying to call me within an hour or two after she received a call herself, early in the morning her time—and whether it suggested Felix had made me seem more important to him than I was. The oddness of it seemed consistent with Felix, who refused pathos but understood its importance to others. His gifts were always thoughtful, yet practical (and expensive) enough to transcend romanticism: a framed print of a painting we'd seen together, for Christmas; the complete set of Virginia Woolf's diaries, for my birthday; a fancy hand lotion or new record or knowing brand of candle, for no reason. I'd thought his generosity was evidence of his solidity, but speaking to his mother made me wonder if it wasn't just a quality he cultivated because he felt he had to.

I went outside three times that week: once to go to a restaurant and eat French fries, once to walk around the block (architecturally unpleasant, emotionally wearisome) because I had suddenly become very hot and sticky in the bed and had to leave, and once when Jeremy forgot his keys and I had to meet him at an "LPQ"—Jesus, I said, call it Pain Quotidien—to give them to him. It was always helpful, being outside, to remind myself that reality did not consist entirely of the single event that was redirecting me at that moment, but it wasn't enough to dissolve the dread I felt when I thought about leaving the house again. Otherwise I looked at my computer so often I felt sick, refreshing Twitter constantly between attempts at reading articles or sending emails. I googled "boyfriend died" and turned up several personal essays in which the aching sadness produced by the accident or rare cancer was always unspeakable, taking years to get over. That I found these unrelatable seemed an indictment of both me and the essays. I will not deny that there was some guilty laughter. I'm not trying to be cavalier; I'm trying to say I may have been at times a little cavalier. I could find no example of the normal way to react to the death of a semi-serious boyfriend about whom you felt ambivalent at best even before you realized he was pretending to be a conspiracy theorist online. It's not very rigorous to seek out and prize relatability, but it can calm you down, and like expensive beef jerky this was something I thought I'd earned.

The company I worked for gave me three bereavement days for the death of someone who was not an immediate family member, and after two I called my boss and quit over the phone. I didn't do it because I was sad—I was not only sad, or even mainly sad—but because I was helpless to avoid learning all those death lessons people learn and the prevailing sense I got from them was that I shouldn't work for this horrible company anymore, that the unwashed hours I'd spent refreshing various websites in bed had been no more a waste of my precious time on earth than the more hygienic hours I spent doing the same in an office. Though I had imagined her begging me to stay, offering me more money, or at least expressing dismay at the loss of my talent/gumption/etc., my boss replied to my quitting announcement with, "Oh, that's too bad. Let me know if you ever need a reference." A drunk coworker had once let me know that I'd established myself as a somewhat retrograde cynic, a *toxic* presence in the office but ultimately safe from firing because, among other skills, I was one of only two people on staff who knew how semicolons worked; my leaving was a wash. Later that day my phone lit up with congratulations from my coworkers, who had presumably been alerted. They hated working there, too, though most of them maintained they felt ultimately "lucky" to have writing jobs in media, even stupid ones, when so many were evaporating into the industry-wide *pivot to video*.

What was I going to do? It was not something I worried about, and I loved having a good reason not to worry about it. On my seventh day in D.C. Jeremy brought home champagne, cheap, and then said sorry, you can stay as long as you want but my mom is coming next week and will need to sleep in the guest room, so actually you can't stay as long as you want and should probably leave. I apologized for having been annoying and said I would leave tomorrow or the next day. I tried not to sound disappointed but I must have seemed it anyway, because when I asked him if he would come as my date to the "celebration of life" in Los Angeles I'd been invited to, he got a sad or pitying look in his eyes and said, "Darling"—to my knowledge not an endearment he'd ever affected before—"I'm *gay*." I replied, "Darling, I'm iro*nic*." Imagine me muttering: *also a marginalized identity these days.*

That night I spent an hour trying to ascertain whether sending funeral e-vites was something typically done, "Best 25+ Funeral Invitation Ideas on Pinterest" indicating the affirmative. If the bereaved finds him- or herself overwhelmed by logistics, tips for getting to the invitation step abound as well. Step 1: Decide Whether the Funeral Reception Is Formal or Informal. Step 2: Write Out a Guest List for the Funeral Reception. Step 3: Determine the Details of the Funeral Reception. I tried to project myself into the mind of the kind of person who would need such instructions but not require help with the socially nebulous and actually difficult aspects of funeral planning, and I failed.

Before my trip back to New York I woke up with, ahem, morbid curiosity about the Details of the Funeral Reception and researched flights to Los Angeles using the bus's spotty Wi-Fi; luckily they were too expensive to justify, especially for a newly unemployed person and especially because as soon as I started to envision the possibility of attending a not-funeral populated by the sort of wide-hatted culture-industry Los Angeles people I suspected his mother would invite I wanted to die myself. Everyone would be squeezing my hands and shoulders and making eye contact meaningfully, assuming they couldn't understand my complicated pain while silently critiquing my outfit. On the bus, I received another email from the realm of Felix's mother, via PayPal, telling me I had been sent a thousand dollars (by her). I'd been told many times that she was a bizarre woman as well as very wealthy, which also explained why she'd had her assistant patch her through to give me the news that her son had died, so I didn't object; I came to think of this as a refund for the remainder of our relationship. Maybe she reasoned that a thousand dollars was the amount of money Felix would have spent on gifts and dinners out for the rest of our time together. Maybe she didn't relate the sum to any pecuniary effects of Felix's death whatsoever and just thought I could use a thousand dollars. Having resolved in college to accept charity from people with more money than I had whenever it came my way, I didn't try to return it.

Back in Brooklyn I mostly lay around in my bedroom, leaving only to pick up Thai food, reading quarters of books, and staying up late portaling from one social media account to the next. The frequency with which I would find myself back at @THIS_ACCOUNT_IS_BUGGED_ was natural but dizzying, and occasionally enraging: the account itself, if taken at face value, was boring, consisting of doctored photos and lengthy captions that hinged on one thing being not quite what it appeared but in fact a link in a chain of involvement of larger and larger entities, all the way to the very top. The formula seemed too stupid to be genuine, and indeed I believed it was, so I kept close-reading for clues, fixating on some misused word or strange reference to the state of Pennsylvania as the "Cassandra of the United States.. [*sic*]," only to realize that I'd been tricked, that inspiring spun-out overinterpretations was surely the point of the exercise. I could write off any departure from acceptability as contrivance for fiction's sake, but that he didn't promote or acknowledge theories involving children—Pizzagate, Sandy Hook—seemed an ultimate indication of his intent to deceive but not harm. Still, I searched the account name everywhere, on Facebook, Twitter, YouTube, Reddit, 4chan, 8chan, Meetup, GitHub, Medium, Quora, Yahoo! Answers, forums for Berlin expats, software developers, Instagram influencers, various podcasts, cheating partners, Second Life users, home chefs. I looked, even, at DeviantArt. I sensed but couldn't be sure that I lacked the technical skills to accomplish what I wanted to accomplish, that enlightenment would remain off-limits unless I learned to code. The username only showed up on sites besides Instagram when someone else would refer to one of his posts, taking minute issue with it or, more commonly, promoting its mind-blowing genius. That I didn't know what I was looking for only reinforced my need to find something, the disappointment heightening the importance of the next session yielding fruit. Searching his actual name gave me little of what I hadn't already uncovered in the early days of our relationship, but I did find a sparse memorial Facebook page, featuring tributes by old friends I'd never met, one of which was written as a letter to

Felix that began, "Hey man." Whether this was an admirable greeting for a dead person I did not know; it acknowledged the casual nature of mortality, which can happen to anyone, but it was also plainly eerie, suggesting that Felix might google his own name in the afterlife. The message wasn't particularly passionate, but it was appreciative of his "special outlook on life," which despite the phrase's vagueness was something I understood. I clicked on the guy's profile, but it was totally private.

One of the many strange aspects of the Instagram account was that in life Felix had never tried to sell anyone a philosophy; his charms had not reached their apex in a holistic vision of the world but rather in disparate strategies for dealing with its particular circumstances. He had ideas about things, of course, and topics he cared about more than others, but in his intellectual life he didn't appear to tail principles like KINDNESS or TRUTH or MONEY or ART or even LOGIC, which he was happy to reject if he thought it was the right thing to do. Yet his smug zen was frustrating, not something that was ever going to inspire feelings of safety or long-lasting love. You could only pin him down by virtue of not being able to pin him down, his sociability entirely calculated and his flirtatiousness equal-opportunity; he was like one of those people who look different in every photo, whom you need to meet several times before you can recognize them in the street, except instead of his face it was his personality that always evaded what you'd had in mind. At first I'd found the task of interpretation fun. He had a seemingly endless supply of unlikely anecdotes and random skills, the sort of things that signal a broad and varied life but that never cohered into anything resembling a character, not even one that could be described as "broad and varied." If I ever thought something he said sounded outlandish or not quite true, he'd turn around and prove it. A photo of him with Howard Dean, the pair of them red-faced and laughing, surfaced when I expressed skepticism that he had snuck into a private dinner with the former governor and impressed him with a dirty joke. About a year into our relationship—a year!—I learned he was great at the harmonica because he got into an argument about the politics of the South with a woman at a party, who doubted he possessed the appropriate foundation to discuss the topic; when I expressed surprise at not only his talent on the blues harp but also his sudden willingness to draw attention to himself in public, particularly through such a brash, avant-garde social maneuver (the woman did not get the joke), he told me that it was all about CONTEXT: it was OK to act out at parties. That was what parties were for. Where had he learned the harmonica? YouTube. Also, he added, the harmonica was developed in Europe, with ancestors from China.

By the time this happened I was coming to see him as disrespectful of other people and their energy, especially me and mine; my time would have been better spent analyzing my own unrevealed ordeals. I often felt he lorded his patience and reasonability over me even as he abandoned those qualities when it came to his own problems (pointing this out was one of my favorite rhetorical strategies); if an issue didn't affect him directly he could just let people be plodding and prosaic without even privately ruing them, not because he had generous thoughts such as *Life is hard and everyone is trying their best*—this was, anyway, patently untrue in many cases—but because he just didn't care about other people very much. Or maybe he did care, but he didn't want to be associated with an intensity of feeling to anyone he knew, so he had to project himself into an earnest online alter ego. Late one night I found a mean-spirited archived county paper article about him scoring an own goal when he was an eight-year-old soccer player. The team was not able to turn it around by juice-box time. It made me very sad, but I didn't think this was his original trauma, the answer to the meme that goes: *Who hurt you?*

A couple of weeks went by this way until one day, at who knows what time, I couldn't stand looking at the same four websites anymore, so I went to a different website, where I bought a cheap one-way ticket to Berlin for the end of February. I hadn't thought about doing this before, but it felt like the right thing to do. As I waited for the foreign website to process my credit card information, failing twice because I had included in my address unacceptable versions of the abbreviation for apartment, I realized that the thousand dollars from Felix's mother had probably been intended to cover my travel expenses so I could go to Los Angeles to celebrate her son's life. I decided that if I ever had to answer for my absence, I could say I was so distraught that I didn't think about it, which may have been true, but I doubted she would contact me again.

For a few days I didn't tell anyone I'd decided to go to Berlin, and I was surprised at how easily I could not only keep the secret but forget about it entirely. I'd missed many protests against the new government during this time—they were held almost daily in the weeks after the Women's March as liberals and journalists warned the general population not to become *complacent* or *normalize* the situation. When I took the bus home from D.C., I arrived on Canal Street just as thousands of people were streaming uptown from a rally in Battery Park where a friend told me everyone was talking about impeachment. Who was everyone? I wanted to know. The people who spoke, she said. Great weather. Felix would have said, albeit in a wistful tone that may or may not have been perfunctory, that protests "never really accomplished anything except making people feel useful"; he could discourse about the horrors committed by any number of governments for hours, from a developed leftist position, getting angry, insulting opponents, but at the end of the day he could set them aside and say, all right, well, I have to get back to work. I was as inclined to agree with him—minus an allowance that making people feel useful is as worthy a justification for doing something as any other—as I was to be moved by the display and by the personal stories of those affected by various policies being protested. In Jeremy's guest room, distracted by feeling, following the announcement of a travel ban, a de facto *Muslim ban*, I'd looked at photos of heavy-coated people—the weather was less great than erratic—swarming JFK and Dulles and O'Hare, their signs hung over the railings of parking garages, their yelling bodies pressed up against arrivals-area barriers, of groups of lawyers sitting on tile floors in circles of urgent typing, and I'd felt very bad, and not inappropriately. Yet whatever was achieved by a group of people congregating peacefully for a cause almost always seemed too small, not so different from what could be achieved by *incrementalism*. And the group, regardless of its size or passion, could always be dismissed as not representing everyone else, a group that was always unfathomably larger.

I started going out more when my roommate's boyfriend dumped her, rendering her suddenly in the apartment all the time, too. She cried more and louder than I was sure I had ever cried in my whole life, so much so that I sought to differentiate myself from her; it's always nice to have a foil. At one point we were drinking wine at the kitchen table, weeks uncleaned, and I told her, "At least he isn't dead," and she replied, "At least you didn't love him," and decamped irreproachably to her room, taking the half-empty bottle with her. I was giving up my room at the end of the month, so it didn't matter if we hated each other, but I was impressed by the retort so the next day I acknowledged that what I'd said had been insensitive. She nodded and made some semi-ironic comment about the enduring relevance of *Sex and the City*, which she was watching on Amazon for the first time. What happened was this: her now-ex-boyfriend had found out she was sleeping with a famous journalist who worked at *The New York Times*. How did he find out? One of the now-ex-boyfriend's good friends worked with the journalist's now-ex-girlfriend, who must have done some phone excavation because one day she posted a photo of the cheating journalist on social media along with a screenshot of a sexy text message exchange, recipient respectfully blacked out, perhaps as a feminist statement, and the disclaimer "WARNING: DO NOT DATE THIS MAN. HE IS A PATHETIC UGLY LIAR AND A TRASH PERSON." This created ripples of gossip that eventually overtook my roommate. She made all her social media accounts private, not because she was being overtly harassed by strangers but because she became unsustainably paranoid that she was being judged and disparaged in private messages, which she surely was. It's convoluted, I know, but that's how these things are. It's too bad it happened when I was woozy from *grief* because at another time I would have delighted in the spectacle, and I wanted to ask her if the infamous text messages had been hers. (The language was fill-in-the-blank, huge cock, cum on face.) Instead I silently connected the incident to the social media pursuits of my own ex-boyfriend and peered into a horrifying future for us all. I envied the recklessness of the journalist's now-ex-girlfriend, her willingness to sacrifice appearances to both personal and professional contacts for the quick hit of petty vengeance. I had fantasized about several brutal lines I might post online about various enemies, including Felix, whose anti-eulogy might even be appended in my savage alternate internet reality with a sardonic RIP, but I always resisted, assuming being *messy* would cause me harm in the long run and also knowing deep down that it was just not the right thing to do; some people on Twitter seemed to believe every problem could be solved with publicity. I even began to pity my roommate, who ordinarily annoyed me to the point of searching for new apartments on Craigslist and whom I'd advised several times to make some kind of choice, break up with her boyfriend or stop seeing the journalist, before things ended badly for her. She'd been hopeful that the journalist would help her get her pitches accepted at a big publication, if not the *Times* itself, but she wasn't a very good writer, and now that her name was circulating as that of a home-wrecker it drew further attention to her bad writing. What's more, my roommate's now-ex-boyfriend, a normal guy who worked in comms and who she'd always insisted would forgive her if he ever found out about the journalist because they were soul mates, "just couldn't" speak to her, which made her feel that she'd squandered three opportunities, one professional, one passionate, and one enduringly personal, though really she'd only lost the last two, and I questioned the mutuality of the second. "He said we should start a podcast together!" she wailed of the journalist at the kitchen table, and I thought, He probably says that to all the girls.

When I finally did mention the ticket to Berlin, my friends, their minds narrowed by therapy, urged me not to go. They said I was repressing, no not repressing, mishandling, denying my feelings about Felix's death. They didn't understand why I would travel open-endedly to a city where I didn't know anyone or speak the language; it only made sense if I needed, like, in order to fill some absence, to do some kind of subconscious investigation? They believed the subconscious investigation was being mapped onto the city of Berlin, and they believed this would not work because if I had no one to talk to I would kill myself. I told them that actually the choice to go there had little to do with Felix and more to do with what Felix had made me realize. The people in New York were petty and hypocritical in a way that made me feel isolated no matter how many I spoke to, I said, citing the journalist and the roommate. Everyone I knew suffered from vicious bruxism because of stress and all the dentists exploited this by failing to mention, when recommending mouth guards, that you could purchase one for $30 to $40 at the drugstore rather than pay $350 to $700 for a custom dentist-produced version. I don't want to go into more detail about the healthcare system because it's far beyond the scope of this discussion. "Also, the subway is terrible," I said. "It's an insult. And you can't even flirt with people on it anymore because everyone is looking at their phones." I could have gone on and on. I'd never really cared about New York the way other people did, never romanticized fire escapes or exposed brick or the days when you couldn't get a cab to take you to Brooklyn. I had only seen three Woody Allen movies, and I couldn't even tell you what happened in them. I got lost almost every time I went to SoHo or the Lower East Side; I could never remember the order or direction of nonnumbered streets and avenues. Felix would tell me to meet him at bars or restaurants and I would always underestimate how fast the subway could get me there, because I believed on principle that it should not take forty-five minutes to go two miles, and he would get annoyed that I was late.

No one cared about any of this; it was all acknowledged unanimously as true and therefore considered irrelevant to even bring up. My friends demanded more reasoning, something concrete or legitimate; to have pragmatic or ideological gripes against New York was not unique. Who was I, they wanted to know, Joan Didion? I lied that I had been thinking about going to Berlin for a while and at this point felt that stopping those thoughts was a good enough reason as any to go. What is the point of being middle-class in the twenty-first century if you can't do things whimsically? I asked, and they shook their heads. Millennials aren't middle-class, they replied, ordering another thirteen-dollar cocktail. Having been informed of neither the deceased's duplicitous Instagram habits nor my (admittedly shaky) intention to dump him, my friends also didn't understand that perhaps what they saw as my need to get over him through active purging of emotion was healthier than it appeared. Exasperated, I asked if they wanted me to wear a veil or something? Did they wish I'd married Felix so I might adopt a clearer public framework for my grief? They didn't laugh. All jokes to them were transparent attempts to mask my pain. I said something I'd been saving up for a while, that, you know, it's kind of like he *ghosted* me, and they made maternal *tsk*-ing sounds of nonamusement and cocked their heads like sweetly confused dogs. One (me) wonders if they would have been so aggressively naysaying if I'd said I was, oh, I don't know, pregnant and keeping it.

The ex-boyfriends say they are on my side, and my problem is that I'm giving the friends too many opportunities to object. People like a single explanation. Concise. Simple. Direct. I'm always proposing too many possibilities, which makes it seem like I'm lying. I should have said I wanted to learn German.

But it was too late for that. The friends' attempts to thwart my plans intensified as my departure approached. They began to appeal to vanity. Wasn't it kind of tired to withdraw to Berlin? Hadn't moving to Berlin become a toolish popular fantasy among New Yorkers in recent years? If it weren't for L.A. would it not be even more so? Was the influx of upwardly mobile English-speaking foreigners not a serious problem for German society, not to mention rents, and did I not see that I was going to appear stereotypical by participating? I told them I wasn't necessarily *moving* there, I was just *going* there, and at least for now L.A. does exist so I don't have to worry about beach people bothering me; they will have been weeded out. The friends asked me if I didn't feel a little guilty abandoning this country at such a monumental political moment; I said no, that was ridiculous, and shouldn't they feel a little guilty acting like the United States is the center of the world?

As a last resort, they made an appeal to practicality: How would I afford to gallivant in Europe for an undetermined amount of time without a job? Though I'd saved enough money to last several months after I quit my job, it's true that I sometimes woke up in the middle of the night with anxiety resonating in my chest, about money, and that to go back to sleep I would eventually succumb to fantasizing, mainly involving Felix being there next to me, spooning largely and firmly. I didn't like this and I don't like to mention it now. To my friends I replied that I had an amount of money in savings because I lived with a roommate in a rent-stabilized apartment in Bed-Stuy and wore shitty clothes even though I'd earned enough to buy oddly proportioned fancy ones. I never took cabs or paid for my own drugs. I'd had a couple of small student loans and paid them off doing freelance work I never told anyone about because it was embarrassing. (Copywriting, not sex, which I at least might have written about later.) I also pointed out that Felix usually paid for me at restaurants or bars or movies, and that I had always let him because I felt he deserved it for complaining to me about how much money he made, so in fact for the last year or so my overhead had been extremely modest. They said I was overcompensating for my despair with snark; I didn't have to be so clever all the time. One of the rich ones asked why I didn't get a new job I liked and then invest some of that savings instead, and I said, "Probably because I've been quietly preparing to flee the country and write a novel [NOT this one]." He rolled his eyes. I said he was obviously trying to sabotage me; it was a bad time to invest; the market was up. He said he knew I knew I didn't know what I was talking about. I said it was unfair that he knew I knew I didn't know what I was talking about, because I was still right, but the fact that we both knew I lacked the background knowledge to prove it meant my rightness could be easily denied. He said why couldn't I just write my novel in New York? I said, My *boyfriend* just *died*, and I narrowed my eyes forlornly. There, I had hit on something useful: while *grief* meant to them that I could only have one justification for my actions, that justification could be applied to anything, so long as it emphasized my prerogative to *feel my feelings*. It was not that I was running away from my sadness, or from myself; it was that I was running away from all the pressure my friends were putting on me to deal with that sadness in a way that was recognizable to them! Aha. My friend said nothing and paid for my drink. They all knew I'd hated my job, so if I did a kind of reverse analysis I could make myself feel insulted that they weren't supporting my decision, which was clearly the right thing for me, as a person who had recently experienced loss under disorienting conditions.

Nevertheless when I left my rich friend I felt adrift, bereft. I wrote a text to my spiritual friend, Mila, asking what is my problem??? She replied that the recent solar eclipse in Pisces had made everyone sensitive as hell and having endured a lunar eclipse in my sign just two weeks before I needed to give myself space to feel and heal. "your bf just died," she added, helpfully. "get a manicure." I said I didn't like manicures because when they chipped after two days I felt I had wasted money. She said that was the wrong attitude but regardless the manicure was not meant to be taken literally. "the manicure could be a haircut or an expensive salad or trip to an art gallery. it just means something nice that you don't have to think about!"

The ex-boyfriends are shaking their heads—they are on my side, truly, but the outreach to Mila made them suspicious. Mila is for light problems and trivial grievances only, they reminded me. Now they too think I'm protesting too much.

As I was forced to defend my half-baked decision it began to firm up and set. I was certainly not stunted, but I was still at an age when doing things like changing a light bulb planted in me a seed of pride; moving to a country where I did not speak the language, even one where speaking the language wasn't really important, would force maturating behaviors. Abrupt relocation abroad existed on the spectrum of normal behaviors, but it was on the courageous end of that spectrum. Though I'd been to Berlin twice, the time I met Felix and then a second time to visit him for about a week before he moved back to the U.S., I had only seen three landmarks, no museums, several terrible basement galleries, and a damp movie theater on the sixth floor of an apartment building. I'd mainly hung out with Felix's American friends at an Australian bar that charged fifty cents more for beer than equivalently hip German places. I didn't want to go to relive my fond memories of first-stage love but to be better at being in Berlin than Felix, who had almost certainly squandered his time there. As I was studying a German-language book, I realized that for the entire time I knew him he had pronounced the name of his neighborhood incorrectly.

About a week before I left, I met my friend Jane for dinner, and her dazzling example of a truly successful New Yorker, someone who belonged in New York, who flitted around and went to meetings and had to take taxis because otherwise her shoes would get fucked up and she would look bad at the meetings, seemed to confirm that it was time for me to go. I didn't resent her—she was always laughing at her luck when she showed up to lunch or coffee wearing the kinds of things rich people own and appreciate, shapely leather bags and blouses in delicate fabrics, which she would beckon me wide-eyed herself to JUST LOOK at. I know I keep making oblique reference to a lower-class childhood but being completely honest with you it was for most of my formative years more like lower-middle, and for one brief period in the late nineties even approaching hard middle. I'd never experienced anything like Jane had, never been *locked in a basement*, the basement where my *parents* before they were *arrested* for *grand theft auto* had *cooked meth*; I had never had to endure and overcome anything actually *bad*. But it just didn't seem like it was going to happen for me in New York, it being *it*, resounding, highly publicized success, or rather I didn't care to do what was necessary to make it happen for me—work very hard, for example. At dinner I told her I'd been on the verge of dumping Felix when he died—I didn't mention the conspiracy theories, but I said I'd looked through his phone because he'd been "acting really weird" and I hadn't found anything—and I now felt an amalgamation of guilt, sadness, relief, and projection.

She told me about a new novel with a plot that resembled my situation: A woman who has been secretly separated from her unfaithful husband for about six months receives a call from his mother asking her where he is. When the woman has to admit she doesn't know, her mother-in-law informs her that he is in a Greek village and that she (the mother-in-law) is going to pay for the woman's flight and hotel so that the woman may go to the Greek village and find him. The woman doesn't want to reveal to her mother-in-law that she is separated from her son, so she goes. She does not find her estranged husband until he's murdered and left in a ditch. His parents come to the island to deal with it and she has to pretend throughout this strange and agonizing period that she is a grieving widow and not a grieving ex, though she is certainly grieving perplexedly. She also receives a large sum of money.

I told Jane that it sounded like an interesting book but it made my pain feel less significant. What's more, I "only got a thousand dollars!"

This was where the evening began to turn bad. Jane leapt into earnest apologies—oh, no, she said, it actually wasn't less significant, because the situation in the book was fictional and mine was real. So then I had to say no no no, it was just a joke, and besides things indeed could be a lot worse; mainly I was excited to go to Berlin. I'd thought using the stilted phrase "my pain" would be enough to signal that I was just teasing, but her continued look of concern concerned me. I could see her straining for niceness and sensitivity, but niceness and sensitivity were not what I wanted. This was a person I had known for several years, since college, whom I had seen vomit, whose life-changing cover letter I had basically rewritten. Once, a couple of years before, she had come to my apartment and made me shower because I had not gotten out of bed in a week. She had returned for the next three mornings to make sure I had food and coffee, and on her way out one day had yelled at my roommate for her pathetic inability to notice what was going on around her because she didn't give a shit about absolutely fucking anything except the shape of her own fucking eyebrows, which by the way only looked good on fucking Instagram. This was a person who got it. Yet now she was looking at me as if she did not know me at all, as if I had not given a single indication of what was actually going on in my head, as if I had not earned interpretation. I got the sense that she, like everyone else, expected me to offer some burst of tearful confession, one that was apparently spontaneous but still clearly outlined all the conflicts and qualifications of my emotional position, which she could then graciously accept and reassure me over. When I offered nothing of the sort, she bought my dinner, and we hugged awkwardly goodbye.

I was about to start crying walking home across the Williamsburg Bridge when a cyclist in expensive mechanical gear passed too close on the incline and because I was depleted of force my screaming response to his vanishing form was uncreative, not Shakespearean at all: fuck you. I didn't even get to call him rich. I walked the rest of the way home angry and did not look at the skyline. Rudeness was a New York trademark, once charming for the way it implied a collective acknowledgment of the struggle of everyday life, a gently reciprocal buzz-off, yet it had taken on in recent years a ruthless antisocial edge. A broad awareness of how things used to be had severed these things from history, so that they were now only pleasingly abstract ideas, repeated and exploited for all purposes: the rudeness now was unearned, just convenient. What was the fucking point of making fucking jokes, I wondered, frustrated and teary. No, it didn't make sense, but what was the point in making sense? Felix had been right. I had known since I found the account that his manipulative insincerity was a fair response to the way the world was. But since I had no one to admit that to, I was going to keep it to myself. The temperature, too warm not to worry about, dropped sharply as I stomped down Lee Avenue, deserted except for the occasional wool-suited man. When I woke up late the next morning it was snowing. Donald Trump had declared at a conference that he had been proven right about Sweden and no one knew what he was talking about.

. . .

THE FORTHCOMING CENTRAL BERLIN AIRPORT HAVING BEEN IN the works for decades and Germany's second-largest airline having reduced operations en route to bankruptcy (to be filed a few months after this narrative concludes), the options for getting to my blank slate were uncomfortable and long. Dazzled by the low low price and also a little drunk, I'd bought my ticket noticing but not really understanding the layover and its implications, only realizing when I got off the first flight and walked through the terminal's assemblage of multicultural food trucks that I was about to spend seven hours in a place where a single beer costs upward of fifteen dollars and a meatless hard-breaded pre-packaged sandwich about ten. To achieve the low low price, the airline didn't serve you a meal, though after a raft of complaints a few years before they did provide free water. I'd abandoned my snacks when the woman at the check-in counter, Juana, weighed my carry-on + personal item and with pity in her eyes offered me a deal: fit it all in the one already-just-slightly-too-wide carry-on suitcase and I could take it without paying the $125 same-day checked bag fee, determined by consultation with a chart involving length of flight and whether there was a layover. (Checking a bag online, before your flight, cost merely fifty dollars, which I had already paid; that bag was half a kilogram too heavy but was given a pass.) I will be telling this story until I die, so indicative is it of the kindness of strangers, so useful is it for contradicting my relentless negativity.

In Oslo, all the airport employees were friendly; they had nothing to worry about. As every minute moved me closer to the purchase of egregiously priced bad food, I gazed out the windows onto a solemn ice-scape fringed with evergreens, dissociated from my past frustrations, and aided by the empty stomach achieved a pleasantly empty mind. I found the layover a helpful temporal/geographic/spiritual buffer zone, by which I mean all of these things—time, geography, spirit—stopped carrying meaning as I sat and sipped an IPA the price of two IPAs at elevenish in the morning that was in my mind fiveish in the morning. On the flight, the woman seated in front of me seized the opportunity when both flight attendants had to attend elsewhere to pilfer a bag of chips from the food cart. Life was so full of possibilities, modeled by the seemingly regular people all around us. Stealing chips never would have occurred to me.

My sense of generous porousness did not last long. I had no real problems. Nothing pressing logistical or financial or governmental or even really at that point emotional (she insisted) held me back. Usually when you have these sort of searching bourgeois-white-person narratives you have to offer a disclaimer, *I know my problems do not rank in comparison to the manifold sufferings of most of the world's people . . . but,* but this preamble isn't meant to be perfunctory, a tick on a checklist; I really mean it as a point to be made in itself. Nothing was wrong. I had no problems. And yet I had problems.

A few days before I left the U.S. I found a place to live in Berlin, against all odds. There were many blog posts about the best way to go about it, and they were mostly written in an aspiringly sassy, exasperated tone that I recognized because it had been popularized by the website I used to work for. Craigslist was not what they used in Berlin; you might find something there, but the site was mostly populated by ads for obviously nonexistent glowing living rooms and stainless-steel kitchens sparkling with bad Photoshop. Many landlords were incensed by subletters, so discretion was key. If seeking accommodation on a website called WG-Gesucht, one must begin by apologizing for not writing in German, then offer little tidbits about oneself, and, if seeking a room in a shared apartment, acknowledge the importance of collective living and respect for others. I hadn't anticipated having to interact with anyone in Berlin—I had imagined myself walking around thoughtfully; getting lunch at the Turkish Market along the canal, which Felix had always talked about but never taken me to; and overcoming my inner turmoil through the delightful surprises and surmountable obstacles of living abroad. The thought of having to pretend to be excited by the idea of cooking dinner with a withdrawn physics student or moony performance artist filled me with dread. I particularly did not want to live with Germans; the presence of another sad, young American was overkill in their country, and I wanted to be able to occupy it quietly, without having to admit that I didn't speak the language and had no plans to.

At first, I was casual in my approach, responding only to posts including notes about high ceilings and renovations and wood floors, but the blogs warned that I would show up at Tegel with nowhere to go if I continued on this path. I said since I had a layover I was flying into the other airport, Schönefeld. The blogs replied not to be pedantic—this was serious. I needed to be sending ten to twenty messages a day. I said that that couldn't possibly be right; if that was right I should go to Budapest instead. The blogs said, "Honestly? Probably. Berlin is so tight, though."

I sent more messages and endured three nodding video-chat interviews for short-term sublets in what a former colleague told me were "not ideal" parts of town. (I asked him if this meant they were dangerous and he said, "Oh, no. Just that only Germans live there.") The people in the apartments picked up their laptops and walked me around so I could see bumpy visions of the living quarters: long, skinny bathrooms and capacious bedrooms with sofas and balconies, afterthought hallways lined with shoes and the occasional bike. No one had living rooms but everyone had washing machines. They explained the concept of rotating cleaning schedules in excessive detail. Smoking tended to be allowed in the kitchen. As soon as we got off the phone, I would send an email to say I would like to take the apartment, if they would have me; no one would email me back. I began to worry as I considered plan B. The point of going to Berlin, a subconscious line of reasoning went, was to introduce into my life difficulties I could understand and conquer, but not this kind of understandable and conquerable difficulty. I did not want to stay in a hostel and then have to leave the hostel once I found somewhere to live. I did not want to stay in a hostel ever again regardless, but the hypothetical logistical finagling represented more commitment than I was willing to make. I might sink into the cost and wake up three years later eating a five-euro schnitzel under the Oberbaumbrücke thinking, This is not the way my life was supposed to be!

Eventually I found and signed up for a popular, long-running email list for North American academics and miscellaneous intellectuals in Berlin, though the tone of the information about it suggested membership could be more trouble than it was worth. The person who ran it no longer lived in Berlin, and in her About the List section she twice reminded the reader that she no longer lived in Berlin but nevertheless kept up the panlist from her home in Indiana out of the goodness of her heart and her support for the Berlin expatriate community, deserving as it is of support especially at a time like this, when diversity and inclusion are vanishing, when greed and capitalism (developers) seek to destroy all that had drawn us to the Hauptstadt in the first place. You had to fill out a questionnaire to apply to join, and I worried I would be denied because of the flimsiness of my answers—occupation, interests, why was I in Berlin, how long was I staying, did I speak German—but I was accepted the next day and began receiving several emails about furniture for sale and divorce lawyers who speak English and the importance of promoting academic freedom by attending certain lectures. I joined in the middle of a debate over the concept of a young woman's reading series; the reading series focused on writers under thirty, and another woman had replied to her post promoting the inaugural event with accusations that the young woman was ageist for focusing her resources on the one age group that was interesting enough without needing a reading series to convince people. The young woman replied that there was no money or stakes involved in the reading series and that age was just an arbitrary organizing principle. There was nothing preventing the older woman from starting her own reading series, the young woman pointed out, given that neither performance spaces in Berlin nor the older woman's own apparent bounty of free time were limitations. I decided to never advertise or protest anything advertised on the list.

After a few more interviews—one in which I suspect I was disqualified for not being a vegan; one in which a girl promised to take me to the drugstore to pick out German hair products after I joked that I would have no idea what bottles said and would probably end up putting foot cream or something on my hair; another in which I was lectured for bringing "false tourist money" to the city by a man who owned a wine bar—a woman spending March and April on a residency in Portugal agreed to rent me her room because she looked up my writing and liked an article I'd written called "It's Harder to Sleep if You're a Woman." I barely remembered writing the article, which aggregated a bunch of information about how women have it bad, sleep-wise, mostly because of stress and circumstance but also because of hormones, but I pretended like it was one of my favorites and said the sunny corner of her kitchen looked really nice for writing, though I doubted very seriously I would write there. Near the end of the call the roommate who would become mine entered the frame carrying several tote bags of groceries and after introducing herself as Frieda with a jaunty little wave asked, "So, why are you going to Berlin anyway?" to the airy laughter of the woman whose room I would be taking, who, ha ha, had forgotten to ask such a basic thing.

For some reason—or perhaps no reason, but given the trajectory so far it's going to be pretty difficult to convince you there was no reason, the reason being obvious even if it may need unpacking, the reason being like a giant suitcase in the middle of the room with one of those locks on it that legally the airlines have to be able to open with minimal effort, the reason being an insult to people who spend years in therapy trying to understand their own reasons, the reason being nevertheless something I did not think about until later, at which point I felt ashamed and obvious, which I guess is where the transition "For some reason" comes from—I replied, as if I had grown up hearing stories about it my whole life, that my parents had lived in Neukölln before reunification working as English teachers and I had always wanted to learn more about that period of German history. Frieda said, "Ah, cool," and told me the bus from Schönefeld would drop me off right around the corner from the apartment. Then Frieda's brow furrowed, and she said, "But you don't speak German? I don't care, I want to practice English, but just because your parents, you know . . ." and I said no, and my parents didn't speak it either. That much being true.

. . .

A WET LATE-WINTER CHILL HAD SEEPED INTO THE STONE OF MY building's entryway and it often felt colder standing there than in the street. The apartment was in Neukölln, referred to in the literature as "the hipster neighborhood," off Sonnenallee, near Richardplatz. My street was uglier than others in the area, which was historic and every year hosted a Christmas market with donkeys. On the street were two buildings racked with scaffolding and other facades flat and peeling, and a storefront that, though the space beyond the display was always dark like an office on the weekend, featured a collection of objects that changed frequently: arrangements of beads and copper wire that someone else might call sculptures; a yellowed deck of cards; a wig splayed on a table; cacti; a broom that had been altered to look like a man who was wearing sunglasses with his hair sticking straight up. Next door to my building was a café with a bright AstroTurf welcome mat out front, and on Sundays it was packed for screenings of *Tatort*, which I was told was the German version of *Law & Order*. A bakery around the corner sold anemic croissants and pains au chocolat that looked like a child's finger paintings of pains au chocolat. Across the Sonnenallee were a Turkish grocer, where I bought nuts and fruit; a hut selling Wurst and fries, plus its tables, where men sat alone and stabbed at their sausages with tiny plastic forks; and an old, cheap, German bar with frosted windows. I did not feel I was allowed to enter this bar, particularly not before I mastered how to say "one beer, please," having rarely ordered for myself on previous trips and blithely asking for what I wanted in English if I did.

It took about seventy-two hours for the pleasant emptiness of my jet-lagged mind to morph into discomfort. I'd always believed it was foolish to enter situations without preparing as much as you can, developing expectations and fortifying yourself with realism, yet with this Berlin thing I had for the first time in my memory done just that, gone with the flow, indulged dull impulses without weighing possible outcomes or assessing risk. Now I was facing the consequences, namely aimless despair. I spent my first week in town thinking *I should buy a bike* and *I should take advantage of a world-class museum* and doing neither, choosing instead to stay in bed until noon scrolling through social media, looking at the same old posts on Felix's account, keeping track of the comments from his followers, which I found more interesting than the hopeless captions he'd written or collaged himself. That he hadn't posted since Trump's inauguration was cause for alarm. Did that mean, the followers wondered, his mission was complete? Where had he gone? Had he been subsumed in a deep state plot? Was he himself part of a deep state plot all along? Wherever he was, they missed him, though a few thought maybe his absence indicated he was living a better life now, the kind that didn't require the constant updating of social media. Frieda's showering noises began around nine, when she got up to go to her internship, which she had despite being, I guessed, around thirty-five years old. She was studying for a master's degree in something very specific within the realm of sustainable urban development and if she didn't get a job after she finished she would go on public assistance, which she told me was very good in Germany. I already knew this so I said, "No way, really?" and as she began to explain how the welfare system worked, nodding her sweet accessorized head, I realized I should abstain from knee-jerk sarcasm for a while. Having studied the German numbers up to twenty on the plane I recognized that when Frieda said "Hartz IV" she was not making reference to some Teutonic coinage for the nuanced anxiety induced by joblessness, though I'm sure they have a word for that, too.

My room was long and skinny and faced the courtyard. It only got light in the morning, when the sun came in through the curtainless window directly onto my face, so I started sleeping with my head at the foot of the bed, symbolically. The mattress was as thick as a copy of *Infinite Jest*. If I opened the window, I could hear the occasional clank of my neighbors unlocking their bikes from the racks below; otherwise it was very quiet. Because of the time difference, looking at the internet on my phone in bed in the morning in Europe was functionally equivalent to looking at the internet on my phone in bed at 3 a.m. in the U.S.; no matter how much I scrolled, it wasn't enough to rouse the people I knew to post on Twitter or, more to the point, read anything I might have posted. They were asleep! How stupid not to have considered this technicality, that relocation to a new time zone would make it harder for me to access my method for coping with difficult things, such as relocating to a new time zone. The British journalists I followed were funny, but I never had any idea what they were talking about. In the past I might have also sent Felix text messages through periods of inner turmoil, e.g., "Help I'm trapped in my body!!" He would usually respond with something I interpreted as tough love, telling me to read a book, or write one. "What are you doing" I'd always ask afterward, no question mark, because I didn't want to seem more desperate than I already did, and he would reply, lying. The internet is always on, interaction always available, but it could not guarantee I would be able to interact with someone I liked and understood, or who (I thought) liked and understood me. I'd gotten used to using people I'd never met, or met a few times, to muffle the sound of time passing without transcendence or joy or any of the good emotions I wanted to experience during my life, and I knew the feeling was mutual, and that was the comfort in it. It was compared to white noise so often for a reason: so many people, talking, mumbling, murmuring, muttering, suggesting, gently reminding, chiming in, jumping in, just wanting to add, just reminding, just asking, just wondering, just letting that sink in, just telling, just saying, just wanting to say, just screaming, just *whispering*, in all lowercase letters, in all caps, with punctuation, with no punctuation, with photos, with GIFs, with related links, *Pay attention to me!* Saying something as irrelevant to the wider world as "I'm in a bad mood" or "I can't get out of bed" elicited commiseration, and offering commiseration to similar expressions made me feel I had participated in a banal but important ecosystem. There were so many people in bad moods at any given time; all we had to do was find each other. We could pretend something good, *connection*, had come of our turning to technology to deal with boredom, loneliness, rejection, heartbreak, irrational rage, Weltschmerz, ennui, frustration with the writing process. We were all self-centered together, supporting each other as we propped up the social media companies. Suddenly finding myself ahead of everyone, spinning my wheels, with no one to acknowledge my existence at the customary intervals, I entered a state of twitchy, frantic boredom, fixating on what I could not stop considering the "real" news, from the United States, though when I was living my "real" life there I had insisted social media was not part of it but rather some aberration, new, ephemeral, a phase passing too quickly to warrant serious inclusion in a summary of my world. It fit in a summary of *the* world, certainly, but it did not reflect the lofty perch from which I gazed upon it, the world as I thought it should be. In the oddly shaped room, thinking about how I should get out of bed, about the permanent damage I was doing to nerves in my hand by holding my phone above my head in the way I did, my torso at forty-five degrees against those square and illogical European pillows, my pinky occasionally going numb, I had to finally admit that Twitter was not a distraction from reality but representative of it, a projection of the human drives and preoccupations that with free time and publishing platforms had been allowed to multiply and evolve. The superficiality this encouraged—pithiness and oversimplification were rewarded—felt appropriate not merely because it mimicked the way most of us choose to move through life but also because it had compounded those aspects of life that felt so desperate and precipitous.

Time spent this way was worse, but at least it was faster. Spending three hours on Twitter does not feel like three hours; that's the danger and the appeal. In New York I'd downloaded programs and installed plug-ins with names like StayFocused, Chrome Nanny, SelfControl, and Freedom, which were designed to block you from visiting particular websites for a set amount of time, but the problem with those was you had to turn them on, and besides I still had the phone, on which I had never downloaded any of these aids because I suspected that any day now I would throw it out the window. When the possibility of approval and validation I found online was eliminated I did not miss it as much as I would have assumed; I liked the approval and validation, a lot, but deep down I had always known these affirmations were unstable, not indicative of anything but passing recognition or, in the case of the reliable cadre of anonymous men who responded to everything I posted, sexual attraction. Even the come-ons were illusory, inspired by my virtual persona and not myself, which rendered the paranoid analysis initiated by each private message even more ridiculous, a whole person analyzing a composite's response to a composite. What I missed, now, in bed in Berlin, was not the attention but the pursuit of it, having even a pathetic project to distract me from the slowly passing minutes. No joke or complaint or article or breaking news would have sated me, but each fragment would have distracted me for a moment, and those moments would have been strung together by waiting, not only for more moments but also for news of something large and encompassing that would shift us out of this place and back where we belonged. If there were going to be such a large and encompassing shift we'd hear about it first on Twitter. Throughout my childhood I'd been warned that I'd grow up to spend a significant portion of my time doing something I could barely stand, but I'd been led to believe

I would be paid for it. When I worked at the website, I would often have the distinct thought, appearing in my head as a full sentence visualized, that *I want to kill myself.* By this I didn't mean that I wanted to actually end my life but that I wanted to enact something drastic that would eliminate all my tedious problems and erase any obligation that I was not enthusiastic about fulfilling, and also make a statement to those around me that I meant business. *I want to kill myself* was a sudden expression that recurred discretely rather than developed. Now, in Berlin, on the internet, with no obligations yet nevertheless somehow trapped, knowing that my escape could only be achieved through purposeful examination, the purposeful examination being itself the escape, I felt a strong desire to no longer have anything to do with anyone, but I didn't want to have to take any action to achieve that.

The ex-boyfriends think I need to delete my Twitter account and go to therapy. It has really helped them. One of them—my favorite, actually—would like to add that perhaps the attention I command on the platform has something to do with my Twitter profile photo, in which my hair completely covers my eyes and nose, representing me as a poutily sexy girl without a face. I point out that I don't want to go to therapy in a foreign country and that nothing is stopping him from using a photo of a hot woman as his own avatar.

Not being much of a grocery-shopper even under ideal circumstances, I would eventually be driven outside by hunger, where I replaced the anxiety of the phone, which did not work where there was not Wi-Fi, with a tortured fixation on the question of what to eat. I walked around. Many people, when they experience a bad phase of life in a particular city, associate the bad phase with the city. I understood that this had little to do with Berlin and everything to do with me. Nevertheless, the setting was fitting. The light turned everything an eerie slate, no matter the time of day, like it had always just rained, or you had just cried. Once my sense of time and space returned to me, the atmosphere no longer produced a sense of pleasant absence but of being a small and insignificant part of an endless sorrow.

Monuments commemorated dark events and challenged one's sense of self. In New York if you walk down a street and no one's on it you feel like you're getting away with something; in Berlin you feel like you're interrupting. I remembered the ponytailed daytime tour guide I'd had two years before, and the solemnity he'd assumed as he explained, sweat glistening at his temples, polo shirt square and unyielding to his form, that some people felt offended by the design of the Memorial to the Murdered Jews of Europe, which allows visitors to walk through and in recent years take oblivious smiling photos for their online dating profiles. That had been in the summer, when the scene had been bright and forgiving. Now sadness seemed to drip from the buildings, despite the apparent contentment of the people I saw in the streets, walking their strollers and freakishly obedient dogs, usually off-leash.

I became hyperaware of situations that required small talk or brief exchanges. I tried to avoid them because they necessarily resulted in humiliation and anguish; though I had been an apologetic English-speaking tourist in several countries, including this one, I was now unable to rationalize the shame of not speaking the language as a worthy trade-off for the wonders of international travel. The German word for "excuse me" was cruelly syllabic. Most nights I went to English events where I didn't know anyone, or to a collectively owned café a few blocks up from my apartment where they sold dry cakes and you could bring in peanut-sauced falafel sandwiches from the Sudanese place next door. There I overheard many conversations in English, though they seemed to pain the frowning staff; according to Frieda the cafés on Weserstrasse were quickly becoming more expensive and sleeker, like what I assumed cafés were like in Australia and Sweden, and the grungy politics of this one were under threat from developers. Before I left New York a colleague had sent me a ten-minute video rant conducted in accented English in which the speaker creakily denounces Neukölln's gentrification, and one of the points he mentions, confusingly, is that the neighborhood's "dirty dog shit" had, back when the video was posted, in 2010, been replaced by "nice baby buggies." I did not necessarily find that to be true, nor believe that this point was selling his argument, but despite having neither dirty dog shit nor a nice baby buggy, I felt unease about being there. Later someone told me that the speaker in the video had opened one of the first "hipster bars" in the neighborhood and it had closed a couple of years before.

I had been to Neukölln with Felix, and I was familiar with Berlin's happening energy, but now that I was living there its self-sufficiency seemed heightened, its communality idyllic but impenetrably baffling. You saw people running into each other and saying hi constantly. Nontourists lounged at cafés for all hours of the day, few with the intensely eyebrowed focus on their laptop screens that characterized the patrons at cramped New York equivalents. Many people seemed to have no schedule, or responsibility to anyone, even those who worked at bars or cafés or shops. This was, I guess, what Felix liked about living there: that you could come and go from life as you pleased, that you were not obligated to act a certain way or at all. He would say, approvingly, that it didn't feel real. (I guess you could say that reality requires some amount of acting, and authenticity requires some acknowledgment of pervasive falseness, but I think those are obvious points made more than enough.) Wary of making assumptions about foreign cultures I'd always told Felix that I was sure Berlin felt "real" to Germans, and he would point out that the low cost of living and robust social safety net meant every burden was more of an option to them than to us in New York, and was not having options like that the definition of freedom? But the rents were rising, I said, somewhat helplessly, aware that I could not prove a fact that was as straightforward as this. You said so yourself. It was hard to find a room in Berlin and harder to find the money to pay for it, and when you lived there you felt your world shrinking, the possibilities squeezed. He would say yes, but it's still not as hard. At this point our conversation would shift to other themes, the thing we were talking about being too nebulous to speak about cogently and extemporaneously; if we tried, we got into circuitous arguments in which it was as clear to both of us that we were *talking past each other* as it was difficult to say, "It seems like we're talking past each other." Anyway, it seemed I was now in the process of proving Felix right, that you could come and go as you pleased, though I tried to remind myself not to feel too bad about my privileged wandering; if the Germans wanted to abscond from reality they could move to various "new" Berlins perennially announced throughout Europe, Lisbon being a sunny option if the worsening political situations of Athens, Budapest, Belgrade, and Warsaw were not appealing. And there was also Mexico City and Southeast Asia. But all these places required a certain change of lifestyle, learning of language basics, and adjustment of perspective, particularly those where you couldn't drink the tap water, that Berlin did not. If you wanted to have a cultural experience—read that as "cultural experience," consisting of 70 percent sarcasm—in Berlin, the city would not force you; you'd have to seek it out.

. . .

AFTER ABOUT TWO WEEKS I WOKE UP ONE MORNING AND DE-cided: I needed to meet people. I grabbed my phone, bypassed the usual apps, and searched instead for EVENTS and WHAT TO DO THIS WEEKEND. At first, I found only club nights and theater productions, but then I came upon a blog post from 2011 about a weekly dinner held at an English bookshop. This rang a bell: I remembered one of Felix's Australian bar friends ranting about how this dinner was always full of dorks and the food sucked. At the time I had accepted this as the hard-won wisdom of experience but now that I thought about it, it was mean. I liked the idea of eating in a bookstore; though twee, it seemed like the kind of thing that would never happen in New York, both because too many people would want to come and because the bookstore would be fined for not having the appropriate licenses. Regardless, the bitchy carefree days of late 2015 had since given way to something much darker, and I thought the pure-heartedness of twee and the originality of dorks might be welcome.

The bookstore was on a side street in a bourgeois neighborhood, and when I arrived a group of people was outside smoking and talking about theater. A man was wearing fingerless gloves. Part of the building's facade was covered in black and white tiles, and the window frame and door were the same cherry red as the bookshelves inside, which were chaotically assembled. The door was partially blocked by a couple of wire racks used to display paperbacks and by a cluster of metal chairs with mismatched cushions, all of which were occupied by men who seemed proprietorial, like they hung out there all the time. A man with a thick northern English accent and round watery eyes presided over a desk covered in papers and books. There was a metal cashbox and a computer that was the color of old newspaper and the shape of two cinderblocks. He shouted as I opened the door, "There she is!" and a woman emerged from an open doorway in the back carrying a glass casserole dish with the same Ikea towels we had at my sublet; she didn't acknowledge us as she carefully descended the steep stairs behind the desk. I stood dumbly in the door, which I had not closed all the way and was letting in cold air. The man behind the desk told me dinner was five your-ohs fifty, love, downstairs, and about to get started. One of the men in the chairs got up and shut the door behind me. If I liked anything to drink the beer was just there in the fridge, two your-ohs, and a bottle of wine was five. I include the prices, obviously, because they were remarkable.

Downstairs the crowd was evenly split between chummy regulars and tourists who'd heard about the bookstore from a recent article published on a travel blog. The room was large and asymmetrical, rimmed with bookshelves, and crowded with tables of varying sizes, including a long, intimidating one in the Last Supper style and a round one on a platform in the back. Food was arranged in the corner, steaming in slow cookers and casserole dishes with shabby oven mitts and dish towels still on the handles.

Grocery-store cheeses were displayed on a wooden chopping block next to utensils, and although no one had yet made the first move a group of people seated at a small round table near the staircase was questioning the meat contents of everything on offer. I put my jacket at the circular table in the back, next to the science fiction section. The regulars seemed slightly predatory as they chatted with the tourists, several of whom were from Canada and so seemed pure and undeserving of the interrogation. I watched a man in a cabby hat pull out a pouch of tobacco and then take a small baggy of weed out of it before being admonished by the woman sitting next to him that they weren't allowed to smoke down there anymore. She wore a long skirt and rugged boots with several buckles and many silver rings on her bony fingers; a few sections of her long curly hair had fallen out of the frizzy sculpture on her head; crossing her legs she flashed patterned tights featuring little cat heads. The man said something about the place having really changed and got up to fill his plate. Next to my table was a refrigerator filled with soda and Club-Mate, popular in Berlin for the way it, as Felix said, simultaneously sobered you up and made you feel more drunk. On the door a ripped, handwritten sign read, "Honor system!! Pay for yer drinks upstairs!!!"

As I was sitting awkwardly alone and wondering if I should approach the buffet the men came down the wooden staircase and, seeing that the only free seats were with me in the back, swarmed and sat down, effectively trapping me in the corner. I'd chosen my seat because it allowed me to observe the room, but combined with my unfamiliarity and apparent newness to Berlin it had turned me into a target. There were four of them, and they vacillated between issuing me a mocking level of intense attention, exaggerating their responses to every mundane thing I said, and talking among themselves about a book one of their friends had written about the GDR. They asked me my name and where I was from and how long I'd been in Berlin; when they heard my answers, a smiling knowingness washed over them, especially a bald one who I soon learned was from Scotland.

That week Republicans in the House of Representatives had proposed a new healthcare bill to replace the tepidly more socialist version installed by Obama, and it represented a disingenuous faith in the free market—not socialist at all—and the men brought it up. After acknowledging in sad tones that, yes, the American healthcare system was reprehensibly terrible and, no, it didn't make any sense that they believed the government shouldn't provide healthcare services to its citizens, I became suddenly indignantly aware that these people were being rude. To be teased for being American seemed so 2004, not to mention that I might have had some chronic and financially crippling illness, that my family might be bankrupt from medical bills. Their glib attitude might have been triggering in me deep feelings of despair and thoughts of my impending death. The man from the desk smugly bobbed his head when he said something he thought was funny. "Why do you all—excuse me, *y'all*—why do *y'all* vote for these people?" he asked. He who had so recently called me "love." "I had thought America was all right, with that Obama bloke," he said, "but." He had a soft, uneven voice that despite his antagonism was difficult to hear; he would emphasize certain syllables unexpectedly and then pause, as if his voice were tiptoeing across a hardwood floor in the night, interrupting its journey following an errant step on a creaking board to assess whether it had caused a stirring in the bedroom. To the question of why we all voted for these people my reply might have parroted the factors I'd seen cited by writers I thought were smart—the white working class's feelings of alienation from society and unemployment, the failure of Hillary Clinton to campaign or connect, the fear of the other, few educational opportunities—though I also thought these talking points missed something that I wasn't about to try and communicate for the first time then. Tidy structural explanations tended to make out the conservative voter as impulsive and stupid even as they sought to emphasize his/her explicable humanity. *Would we all not be stupid if we were in these circumstances?* they seemed to ask. That's the thing about political people: they always have to have a narrative. Every effect must have a specific cause to be discovered so it can be manipulated. Even when they're wrong—which they always are—the idea is that the cause is merely elusive, a code to be cracked, not so diffuse as to be nonexistent. I knew anything I said to the chuckling men at this point would be used to taunt me, that they would support each other's claims in order to push me closer toward embarrassment, alternately patronizing me with exaggerated agreement and through more traditional teasing. But at the same time I hated them and wanted them to know. What would Ursula K. Le Guin do? I had to admit I'd never read her. The last time I'd read a science fiction book was probably in fifth grade, *A Wrinkle in Time*, but I didn't know if that counted because I'd recently become aware of delicate distinctions between the "science fiction" and "fantasy" genres and I couldn't remember the themes or motifs of *A Wrinkle in Time* at all. Making a reluctant nod of exception at the Scot I said the U.S. had probably done what we did for the same reasons you guys had voted for the United Kingdom to leave the European Union. Head still bobbling, the man from the desk sat back in his chair and said he had been rid of those twats for twelve years. He stood up to get food and because he seemed to be the leader of the group the other men followed.

I took out my phone. There was no Wi-Fi in the bookstore, so I tapped around on it fruitlessly, scrolling through the stuff that had loaded on Twitter three hours ago, the last time I'd had the internet, and looking at my text messages as if a new one might be hiding there, some reminder of my life beyond jarring interactions with incompatible strangers. No one had texted. I got the occasional messages from my mom, Jane, and my favorite coworker, but besides them I hadn't really been checked up on as much as I'd hoped. Though at first he'd been attentive in a daily and touching way, even Jeremy's texts had evaporated over the last few weeks. Moving to a country where you don't know anyone or speak the language sends a message of competence. I had wavered more on the question of getting bangs. Before I could allow myself to become depressed about both having made a mistake and having no one to console me about it, I decided I should find a more hospitable group to sit with, so I stood up and tried to maneuver out from the table, but hovering there between the fridge and the Scottish guy's pulled-out chair with my jacket in one hand and my phone and purse in the other, looking, I imagined, pathetic and persnickety, disrupting the convivial atmosphere on behalf of some irrelevant offense or neuroticism, I saw there was nowhere else to sit. I considered leaving, but I thought it would give the men satisfaction to have scared me away. I know this is narcissism, that no one noticed me at all, and even if they did they wouldn't care, yet this kind of self-centeredness can be fortifying, particularly when one is struggling to pin oneself down. Besides I'd already paid for the dinner and the prospect of doing what I'd done the three previous nights, eating Vietnamese food alone, was so unappealing it seemed impossible. I put my things back down on my seat and got in line.

In front of me was a girl of luminous complexion who turned around and introduced herself as Nell from Los Angeles. About my age, very thin, and in Berlin for a three-month artist residency, she had arrived two weeks ago and was staying in an apartment a few blocks away that was, in addition to being on the sixth floor, "totally wild." Before she arrived she hadn't noticed the most important sentence in the email she received about the accommodation: There was no shower. Not even in the kitchen, as some of the really old Berlin apartments had. A tiny WC next to the front door was literal, containing only the toilet, but if you were taller than, say, five foot six, you had to hold the door shut and sort of spread your knees apart while you used it. She offered me all this without my having to ask, which I appreciated. Nell did not smell bad or have hair that was dirtier than any other hip young woman—as I'm sure you know by now, washing one's hair too frequently strips it of vital natural oils, etc.—so I asked her how she was so clean. She told me she had had to get a gym membership so she could use the shower. Thankfully, everything here was so cheap, and anyway it forced her to go to the gym (almost) every day, so actually it was kind of good. Plus, the stairs worked out the butt, she said while doing a little shimmy. "Butts

are in now!" she added, beaming as she spoke, as if on the verge of uproari-
ous laughter. She managed to convey all this as well as a confident summary
of her artistic concerns—refraction—before we reached the cheese, which
she ignored in favor of lasagna-type dishes. Without saying goodbye or nice
to meet me she bounced over to her table, where two elaborately dressed
people were drinking wine and picking apart a shared slice of casserole with
their hands. She seemed like one of those people for whom the world just
made sense and would never cause insurmountable worry, though I couldn't
know; maybe she hid dark secrets, medical or familial-historical or romantic
or criminal. Nevertheless, I suspected the comfort she and her friends felt
eating a sloppy, multifaceted food with their hands reflected their comfort
with the world as it was. She had never asked me about myself; I don't remember telling her my name.

I took my own slice of casserole and smears of Brie back to my table,
and because I was the last to return the men all shifted down to let me take
a seat on the outside, so that I had my back to the room and was facing only
them. This made me feel more secure, like I was a representative for the rest
of the people in the shop, who were not jerks. When he was handing me
back my purse and jacket, the Scottish one attempted to joke, withholding
the bag as he smirked like a third grader with a crush on me, and I played
along, saying, "Give it!" in a babyish voice that made them laugh because
they saw me as a child, naive as well as a potentially lovable pain in the ass.
After this they acted for several minutes as if I did not exist, the conversation
going back and forth between UK politics, of which I had a very superficial
understanding, and a rant published in the expat newspaper about the importance of learning German to live in Berlin. I tried to interject—did this
editorial not have a whiff of anti-immigrant sentiment?—but was rebuffed.
No, the Scottish guy said, it's about you. I kept looking over my shoulder to
see if Nell and her friends had left; they had finished picking at their plates
and were talking among themselves, ignoring the couple seated across from
them who were going over a guidebook. One of the men, maybe attempt-

ing to make up for the others, asked me if I spoke any German, and when I said no but that I didn't really live in Berlin, he turned on me and said, well, that was the problem, wasn't it, and added that he suspected he would show up to a bookshop dinner six years from now and see me there, chatting with the owner, in possession of more or less the same level of German I had now. "Ein Bier, bitte?" he mimicked, scrunching up his muffinish face as he attempted a nasal Valley Girl accent, drawing out the last syllable. I didn't know how to respond to this, so I stood up to get another beer. The man from the desk asked me to bring him one and I said no; I assumed he thought I was joking and would do as he said, and I took pleasure in thinking about how surprised he would be when I came back down the stairs with only one bottle. On my way out, Nell asked me to type my email address into her phone. She said, "You're a writer, right? We can do a writing group! I also write." I didn't think I'd said I was a writer; I wondered if she had intuited it from the fact that I had listened to her.

When I came back down without a beer for him, the man from the desk was nonplussed. He asked the Scottish guy to get him one, took his seat next to me, and asked me what I was doing in Berlin. I told him my boyfriend had died and I was on a soul-searching journey to understand our relationship because we had met here about two years ago. He looked surprised and said he was sorry; I paused, looking soberly at my plate, before laughing and saying I was just kidding. He leaned back in his chair, to illustrate he had been blown away, and put his hand on his heart. He was in his forties, probably, and wearing a ratty flannel with the cuffs unbuttoned and flapping around and beat-up dress shoes. He asked me again why I was in Berlin. I said I didn't know, really: it was just something to do, and as a dancer I thought it would be interesting to try dancing in another language. He undertoned that I looked like a dancer, and as if possessed I collected my hair, which was hanging around my shoulders, and twisted it into a bun with an elastic I had around my wrist. I then raised my arms in an elegant oval above my head before lowering one to the side, keeping my elbow and wrist in the soft curves I still occasionally employed in yoga classes in order to pretend I wasn't doing yoga but something more elevated, less accessible to amateurs. I often joked that I had practiced ballet long enough to be graceful; I stopped when I was fourteen and the rest of my class was moving to pointe shoes, which I too had bought, as if I'd had any chance of success. I have flat feet, and the teacher hated me.

"Oh, so you're a *real* dancer?" the man asked, his peaky accent rising on the *real*. "Not one of those modern ones." I wished that only the people I wanted to talk to me would talk to me, and only when I wanted. I easily rustled up offense to this and told him I guessed I was a fake dancer with classical ballet training, like most modern dancers. I stopped myself from saying *professional* modern dancers because I had no idea how one reached such a distinction; leaving it assumed seemed safer. Abruptly, as if he had not just insulted what I had led him to believe was my art form, he said he would love to see me dance, and I replied, "Why? You don't know me. I might be terrible."

For the rest of the evening, which I hate to say for me went on four more hours, he did not stop looking at me, a purposeful, disturbing stare. There was something about the room—that it was warm, that it was subterranean, that at 11 p.m. people brought out their packets of tobacco and weed and started smoking, that we all knew it was cold and raining outside and were putting off facing it—that made me stay much longer than I intended, until around one in the morning, when the proprietress came downstairs to ask us to help her clear the dishes, at which point I received a vision of myself as part of this group, a weekly attendee of dinner for socially unconscious adults seeking English-speaking companionship among theater lovers and science fiction paperbacks, and I knew I had to escape.

But before that, after "I might be terrible": The Scottish man came back down from his beer-gathering venture after what we realized then was a long absence. He had with him not two but six beers, one for everyone, and announced upon his return that we would be getting "rowdy." I think in the past this would have alarmed, or at least annoyed, me, but I had no thoughts on it at all. As soon as I began operating under a false pretense, even one as dull as a swapped profession, my head was empty of concern or consideration for anything other than tasks or questions immediately presented. I accepted my beer only to realize I had no bottle opener; I held it in my hand and looked around, thinking there might be one on top of the refrigerator. The man from the desk took the bottle from my hand, pulled a scuffed green lighter out of his pocket, grasped the neck of the bottle, and paused: He held his hand toward me so I could see the proper position, his pointer finger and thumb hooked around the lip of the bottle, forming a tight space into which he wedged the wrong end of the lighter and used it to confidently pop off the cap. People, including me, did this in New York, but he nevertheless claimed it was "the Berlin way" and gave me his bottle to try. I waited for his approval on my fingering before setting up the lighter totally incorrectly; I warped the edge of the bottle cap and said fuck when it hurt me. He told me to try again with my hand a little lower, so the lighter could cover the maximum area of cap. I twisted the bottle around to give myself a fresh start and did it, though with a much less satisfying popping sound. I handed him his beer and asked what he had said his name was again. He said it was Paul.

Given that my knowledge of modern dance came almost entirely from watching the reality show *So You Think You Can Dance?* in high school, I was a surprisingly fluent discourser on the topic. I explained the difficulties of being a freelancer with bad health insurance whose job basically required some level of injury; snapping hip syndrome; eating disorders; the frustrating public dismissal of modern dance as less difficult than ballet (not that anyone cared about ballet either) (he apologized); how to fling oneself unlooking into a kind of spinning jump, the scar from a long-ago failed attempt at this proof on the bottom of my chin, not that he had any reason to doubt me. I had sat up immediately after falling, saying it was fine I was fine, ha ha, ha ha, only to look over and see the only boy in our class, an unfairly good tap dancer, with his eyes fixed on me as the first drop of blood fell onto the waxy hardwood floor. Only three stitches, but I never went back. We talked about the budget airline I had taken to Berlin. We talked about New York, where Paul used to have a girlfriend. We talked about porn, which I estimated I watched about once a month. I was careful to maintain my posture. Periodically I looked around for better company and, finding it lacking, obviously, turned back to Paul and encouraged him with nods or smiles or facial expressions that suggested I was finding him interesting. He had a number of different jobs, apologetically, and one of those really old rents. At one point, another man interjected to ask whom I would rather have sex with, Justin Trudeau or Barack Obama, and I just frowned and stared at him. Paul took it upon himself to defend my honor here, saying hey hey and reminding the man that I was new and what's more a lady. I shook my head and rolled my eyes as I put a flirtatious hand on his bony upper arm.

After we brought the heavy serving dishes upstairs and set them on all available counter space in the dirty kitchen, not thinking of washing any of it ourselves, we bade goodbye to the owner, who for all I knew had spent the entire evening sitting at the desk playing solitaire, and we were about to go outside when Paul asked for my phone number. I felt then that my procrastination had been serendipitous, because I was able to tell him, truthfully, that I didn't have one. I could have given him my American number, but of course I didn't want to and didn't mention it. He wasn't shocked at this because as I would later realize many expats, especially those who'd arrived when it was normal not to have a smartphone, had small or nonexistent cell phone plans that required the rationing of text messages and the elimination of calling as a possibility except in extreme circumstances. He asked for my email address.

I was able to dodge this request for about a minute until my impulse to pity overwhelmed me. The desperation in his eyes, the way they shifted from mere attachment to clinging. Something was off in this man; it was not a normal come-on, not obnoxious or inappropriate so much as scarily direct.

He said it again: please, I'd like to send you an email. It was so simple; it wasn't requesting anything in return. He had not done anything wrong except produce a strange *vibe*, and indeed it was a strange situation, among strange people, so I didn't know if he could be fully blamed. I rationalized that emails were the easiest form of correspondence to ignore and, relieved that I hadn't lied about my name, wrote my address on the back of a flyer for an English-speaking babysitter looking for work. I walked away from the bookshop quickly and in the wrong direction and ended up on the edge of a stone-walled cemetery, no one around, and had to turn on my data plan to navigate home, which would end up costing me fifty dollars. Drops of water appeared on the screen as I located the nearest U-Bahn.

The next day I bought a flip phone and a ten-euro-per-month plan and canceled my American contract, exhilarated by my cool willingness to forgo the internet. When I got back to the apartment, I saw that Paul had emailed me, asking if I would meet him at a bar the next day, Sunday. He apologized for being forward the night before; he said he had been "destabilized," the implication being by my beauty and wit. Thankfully it was not a long email. Though I got a little buzz at the unconcealed interest in me I was mostly in awe of the scheduling; in New York, plans were made weeks in advance and then rescheduled because one or both parties were having mental health issues. I knew I would regret it, but within the hour I replied to accept, thinking that a strange or upsetting experience would be at least different, and more importantly that it would give me something to do, keeping me from descending entirely into self-pity and ruminations on time death love solitude identity etc. I enjoyed the freedom from thoughts of Felix that a man being interested in me created. I looked up the place Paul suggested; photos people had posted online suggested it was like all the other bars in Berlin, mismatched furniture, dark, unevenly painted walls, candles stuck into empty liquor bottles disfigured by wax. I said I would meet him there at eight.

. . .

I ARRIVED AT THE BAR FIFTEEN MINUTES EARLY IN ORDER TO buy my own drink. I was antsy with guilt, as if I'd waited until Tax Day or woken up after drinking too much: something bad was going to happen and it had been entirely preventable by me. I worried about what we would say to each other, whether he would begin with some comment about my looks to which I wouldn't know how to respond, whether he would tell me sensitive things about his childhood that would make me feel sorry for him and hesitate to leave without an apology. I couldn't remember any redeeming qualities he'd exhibited on Friday that might have shone through his creepiness, but still I was there, apparently willing to see him again. Besides his forceful interest in me I guess I had liked the look of his face—the light, round eyes against his skin tone, the tired circles around them—and the fact that he was older. But the city was surely full of men with good faces who were born before 1977, and I had made a tactical error by not forcing him to convince me; I should have suggested I was unsure about further interaction and therefore required the work of kindness, gentleness, and the appropriate level of flattery before I would agree to it. Instead I had encouraged him, by exposing my neck, by listening and responding to his conversation without easing myself away, by accepting his invitation to see each other so soon after we'd met. If he became aggressive or grotesque in my presence I had relinquished my right to the feelings of unease that would linger after our date; he had been aggressive and suggested potential grotesquerie at the bookshop and in his email, yet I had still agreed to see him. I considered downing my glass of sour red wine, getting up, and leaving, but then I imagined passing him on my way out the door, having to come up with some excuse, an emergency with my family, a problem at an imaginary dance studio for which I could pretend I held one of the only keys. But I sensed I wouldn't be able to do it if I had thought about it in advance. I would stutter; the lie, my irresolution, would be obvious. No—I had never stood anyone up before and I didn't want to start now; though Paul had shortcomings they didn't (yet) justify his being stood up. It was not this man's fault that he had a bad personality, but I was totally responsible for leading him to believe he didn't. I wished I had a pack of cigarettes—you could smoke inside—but I had yet to master buying them. Every time I approached the counter at my local Späti my will to speak either abysmal German or rudely presumptive English floated away, and I had to pretend I was there for gum.

Eight p.m. also floated away. I began to feel less nervous; every minute he was late added a point to my tally. I had been very strategic choosing my seat, in the corner, from which I could monitor the door as well as watch a couple kiss on the couch, their hands in suggestive but not yet scandalous places. Felix kissed with his eyes open, unnervingly, and when I asked him why he said it seemed fake to close your eyes just because people did it in movies. I said I thought it was the natural response to having something so close to your face, intended as a hint that I wanted him to stop, but he kept doing it; concentrating on keeping my eyes closed while kissing him, to avoid seeing his open eyes, only made me think about how his eyes were almost certainly open. Each table had an empty bottle of gin that served as a candelabra, and though little slivers of gunk were wedging themselves under my fingernails I was finding it satisfying to pick off the long thin pieces of wax that clung to the neck as the upper hand recalibrated via Paul's lateness. I was transforming, from foolish attention-seeker to generous soul who had put herself out there only to have her time and energy abused. What I was doing was not a big deal; whatever happened between us was the result of my open-mindedness, which should be celebrated, and it wasn't as if I'd shown up to a dark alley or his apartment. People go to bars all the time. I sipped my wine and thought about how Felix always hated sitting at the bar. He said it made your conversations fodder for the bartender's workplace-annoyance stories; he didn't like his conversations being overheard. I didn't mind this as long as the people around weren't part of a scene or clique I was denouncing; it reinforced the ultimate irrelevance of whatever I was talking about. No one cares about your little theories, I'd told him once, unaware that thousands of people online did. I also liked the sense, sitting at the bar, that I could leave easily.

After twenty-five minutes I began to wonder if it wasn't I who was being stood up. At eight thirty I decided it would be appropriate to leave. I waited five more minutes, returned my empty glass, the bartender saying something to me that I couldn't understand but at which I shook my head anyway, and left. The couple on the couch was still there, no longer making out but simply gazing at each other, their glasses of beer half full. I was able to transition smoothly from embarrassment to indignation. I walked home along the canal until I reached a section next to a playground that was fenced off and under construction; I had to turn and walk to the street, passing another crowded bar, its windows fogged. I woke up to an apologetic, almost stream-of-consciousness email, an excuse about a "work call that extended almost beanstalk-like into the minutes of our date which I was so looking forward to." He described my beauty briefly and then explained: "I finally got away at 2045 but by then you'd gone of course as I would have done and I'd like to make it up to you but of course if you don't want I understand." I didn't reply, but that afternoon I did make a profile on a dating app.

. . .

FIRST I HAD TO DECIDE WHICH PLATFORM TO USE. I KNEW SOME people who did all of them, casting themselves a net across the web, the idea being that while there may be plenty of fish most of them had weird facial hair, and you couldn't find quality without quantity. But I didn't have the energy for diversifying my portfolio; this was not a serious endeavor but a lighthearted experiment; I needed a project, not a boyfriend. When I asked Frieda if a particular service was popular in Germany she said she didn't know because she didn't need dating apps. Fair. She was beautiful and seemed to have polyamorous friends in the art scene, or to be a polyamorous friend in the art scene. I was tempted to defend myself against the suggestion that anyone who used dating apps *needed* to—I, for example, was just bored!—but reasoned this would sound more defensive than saying nothing.

I thought I'd join Tinder, which was the most popular platform and so seemed most likely to yield positive outcomes, though really so many people were on all the platforms that positive outcomes could be found anywhere equally. I'd heard Bumble, the "feminist Tinder," had "better people," but I dismissed it immediately because of the requirement that women message first. I disliked being told what to do—I made a mental note to add this to my profile, a sexy but meaningless declaration—though the elimination of at least one level of indecision was probably part of the platform's appeal, its unromantic directness thinly veiled by the cute haplessness suggested by the name. No, where the people were was where I should go, I thought, until I spent a couple of hours on a desperately search-engine-optimized blog focused entirely on How to Get the Most Matches on Tinder and How to Write the Perfect First Tinder Message and Rules for Taking the Best Tinder Profile Picture. I knew such ingenuous cunning existed, but I hadn't wanted to think about it.

Tinder ranked its users based on popularity, I learned, another fact I could have deduced if I'd ever thought about it. Your ranking determined how frequently your profile appeared for others to be judged, judgment being famously enacted through a swipe on the phone left (not interested) or right (interested). You can only attract by being attractive, and you can only talk to a person you're attracted to if they're attracted to you, too. I discovered a forum where women critiqued men's photos before they posted them; think of it, one poster wrote, as a sisterhood, women helping women. No, I would not think of it that way—there was no room for slant interpretation here. The most banal observations were the most accurate ones. The scale of the obviousness overwhelmed. Tinder's algorithm merely reflected what we already know, that everyone loves hot people, and that hot people have it easier, in romance, in career, in any situation into which they can insert themselves. Active users, even very successful ones, noddingly obliged that the apps were creepy and depressing, that they produced the upsetting feeling of flipping through faces like they were flannels at a thrift store, and of knowing you were facilitating the conditions to be treated like a rag yourself. Couples who met on the app were defensive, assuming you thought there was something essentially unnatural about them, though they also knew the app had introduced them precisely because they made mathematical sense, that the likelihood they would have met in person, at some place of mutual interest, was high. Meanwhile the hours they'd spent swiping through profiles could never be recovered; what use did they have, now that they'd found love, for the information they'd gathered, about how humans respond to an indisputable context? Yet dissenters still seemed hopeless—millions of users, but they couldn't find anyone they liked, or who liked them? I remembered all the articles I'd skimmed about antisocial trends in romantic behavior, arisen, the implication was, through the attitudes promoted by Tinder: *ghosting, breadcrumbing, orbiting.* I'd watched a guy *phubbing* (too gross to really catch on) at a house party the year before, his head almost perpendicular to his chest, thumb expertly moving horizontally across his phone as he appraised photographs of singles in his area while our mutual friend was trying to talk to him about the (literal) pond-scum research she was doing upstate. She thought he was addicted, she told me, to the spark of promise each profile offered and to the power the app gave him to quickly dismiss not just women but futures, to act as if he had endless reserves of time and energy. Sitting hunched over my desk, I couldn't abide it. I imagined a lottery ticket illustrated to look like a smartphone, promising a jackpot if you scratched off the surface to reveal "looks," "personality," and "job." (Uncover three "looks" and win five hundred dollars.) Although I knew by this time my intention was to use my profile for casual deception, a hobby, I wanted to allow for the possibility of falling in love with a man so immediately wonderful that he would break down my mendacious defenses romantic-comedy style, and I felt Tinder was not designed for this. Though my profile would have to circumvent the expression of a personality, I didn't want to go on even fake dates with people who would concede to a system in which personality was secondary. I decided to use OkCupid.

The ex-boyfriends think my willingness to use the same analysis to arrive at either one of opposing outcomes is disturbing. Don't go on dating apps, they say, all having been on dating apps. (Their fates were mixed.) You're too sensitive for them.

I wish they would stop saying that. The rules of OkCupid said I had to use real photos of myself, which wasn't a problem. If I planned on going on actual dates, which I did, I needed to be theoretically forthright about my appearance. Real photos were deceptive, too, as everyone acknowledges; they fabricate trust where there is none, even or especially when the beholder knows that photos cannot be trusted. Of course people post their most flattering; I would do that, too; that's not what I'm talking about. What I'm saying is that you hear so many stories of *catfishing*, of people luring others into interminable online relationships with photos of not-famous models they've plucked from Google, that natural photos, taken in a variety of settings, were considered the ultimate verifiers of identity in the realm of virtual bullshitting, though looking like your photos didn't mean you were telling the truth about your occupation, interests, age, history, or unique enjoyment of coffee, food, and travel. To prevent my suitors from searching the images and figuring out who I was, I took two new pictures of myself, one by the canal in a nice sunsetty light and one in my room, both at self-portrait distance, my head filling too much of the frame. I selected a third full-body shot from my computer that I'd never posted on social media. I came up with a username that didn't make reference to my own name or any book or movie—if only I'd known I'd been living through a golden age: now they make you use your first name—and filled out the eugenicist sidebar about my height, body type, eye color, ethnicity, languages spoken, at what level

(??), religion, education, use of controlled substances, and diet. Each had a drop-down menu of responses to choose from, not customizable. Then I moved on to the fun part, the getting-to-know-you questions.

I wanted to express an alluringly evasive personality, and I knew I would have to do it through voice rather than content. In eighth-grade English, with Mrs. Hayden, who humiliated students who didn't cover their mouths when they yawned, we were required to keep a journal five days a week, responding to specific prompts. The notebook I used was painstakingly chosen, from Target, with pink and orange stripes, college rule, lines also pink and perhaps even composed of very small dots, and I wrote in it with unfiltered enthusiasm, mainly while sitting on the floor of my closet, fascinating myself with ideas I couldn't believe I was having, the person I became once I started to explain myself, the voice that emerged from thoughts and feelings. This was who I was! Now, though the OkCupid prompts were more juvenile than what Mrs. Hayden had assigned her eighth graders, I would try to become the inverse, a person whose voice determined her thoughts and feelings, whose thoughts and feelings you could only figure out by interpreting her voice. And even then, you would be wrong.

A bold prompt: Most people that know me would say I'm:

In light-gray font, in the box where you were supposed to fill in the sentence, an explainer: (How would a friend describe you?)

An idiot? No. *The Idiot*? I hadn't read it, and I didn't want to get myself in hot water with literary types, who love to quiz. Unassumingly beautiful? Too cheesy. (And redundant, with the photos, ha ha.) "difficult but worth it."

That was the tone: a cliché of characterization, apparently saying much but actually saying nothing at all, but actually saying something true via the inaccessibly flirty style. Who wouldn't want to be difficult but worth it, self-centered but valuable to others? Valuable to others through one's self-centeredness?

Current goal (What are you working toward right now?): ". . . ok, mom"
I could probably beat you at (Go ahead and brag a little, champ): "talking about myself"
My golden rule (The thing you live by): "never assume"
A movie I've watched over and over and over again (OK, you can put two if you really can't choose): "persona"
I value (Share what matters most to you): Time for a quirky list, a mix of serious and joke interests, specific yet believably belonging to many fields and types of people: "modernism, guacamole, browsing but not buying, the low season, roller coasters, travel"
The last show I binged (This could lead to a cozy couch date in the future): "don't watch TV"
A perfect day (A day you'd feel great about): "i'll know it when i see it"
If I were sent to jail, I'd be arrested for (The crime you're most likely to commit): Though I was tempted to say something pious and political—"disturbing the peace," "assaulting a police officer"—I went with "tax evasion." Could also be political.
What I'm actually looking for (No judgment: What do you want from this whole dating-app thing?): "i'll know it when i see it"

Next came a box labeled Match Questions, which would be used to determine my personality traits in relation to other OkCupid users and calculate matches, measured in percentages of compatibility. Reading this I felt betrayed. Percentages! I thought this was supposed to be the wholesome dating app, pure, simple, devised by people like (the real) me, unwilling to rely totally on insipid technology just because it's there. I wanted to abandon my project and go out drinking, but I had come so far already. I left my computer glowing in the now-dark bedroom and went to the kitchen to get a beer. Frieda wasn't home, but the remnants of a vegan stew she'd made earlier conjured her memory. She cooked with an impressive frequency and always offered to share; she said she liked to cook for other people because it helped her deal with her bipolar disorder, dropping this information so casually into our conversation that I thought she must have mistranslated it. I repaid her generosity of supply and spirit by using her Q-tips and never cleaning the kitchen.

It came to me as I was contemplating a good deed, any good deed, wiping up the orange soup dotting the counter, putting away the half onion, maybe even spraying the area with Öko Allzweck cleaner. I rushed back to my room, turned on the light, and sat down at my computer renewed: This was no longer a personal project, a dalliance with earnest dating-app usage, but a purposeful critique of the system. I could be anyone I wanted (or did not want, as the case may be), and my deception would not be selfish, cruelly manipulative of innocents looking for love, but a rebellion against an entire mode of thinking, which was not really thinking at all, just accepting whatever was advertised to you. Dare I say: it was *political*? If I ever wrote again, I could write about it. People who took themselves very seriously would get mad at me.

The website told me I could answer as many Match Questions as I wanted, but that the more I answered, the more accurate my matches would be. That's what *you* think! I answered one hundred. I'm not going to list them here. You can go on the website and answer some if you want to know what they're like. It's fun because it's designed to make you seem interesting.

Just before I declared my profile complete, I added "in the mood for love ;)" to the question about my favorite movies; *Persona* was doing too much work there. I read back over my answers: Would I date this person? Absolutely not. I was so frustrating. I seemed combative, wily and unyielding, immature and in denial about it, yet also typical, typical, typical. I would probably insult you in bed and call it feminist.

. . .

I STARTED RECEIVING MESSAGES WITH SUSPICIOUS IMMEDIACY, and they were written as if I had already met the sender. "Hey you." "Hey ya!" "Hey! How's it going?" "hey, just wanted to say hi." "Hey what's up?" "what's going on it's Marc." "If we could both travel around the world tomorrow, where would we be heading? Let's get some ideas on the table!" "Gun laws in America: discuss." "my fav thing is to provide oral pleasure to one woman—just one—in every city to which I travel to." "I would go down on you until the sun cries." "so what's your take on feminism then?" Men in India looking to talk. Men in Pakistan looking to talk. Men in Bangladesh looking to talk. Men who expressed wonder at our 76 percent compatibility, as if no closer match existed for them. "u kno what they say about ppl who assume..." One man asked what other Bergman films I liked. One man had a very bad hangover from partying until 8 a.m. that day lol! Some asking wie geht's, but not many. I sent an email to a friend expressing shock-but-not-shock-at-all about the state of affairs and she supplemented her own anecdote: For a month, she and her two male friends experimented with a paid premium version of Tinder, Tinder Gold, which in addition to letting you swipe on singles around the world—the free version being location-based—allowed you to see who had *liked* you, a less intentional method of approval than the swiping. (OkCupid had this feature too, I saw, represented by a star and escalating number in the upper right-hand corner of my profile; when I clicked on it, the profiles of men who had liked me were blurred out and covered by a box that said I, a "total catch," could see who'd liked me by joining the A-List.) At the end of the month, my friend said, each of her male friends had a couple dozen likes, from women who mainly seemed like their type. Despite being about as attractive as the guys—one of whom was actually very hot—my friend had over four thousand likes.

The Bergman guy was thirty-two, six foot one, straight, thin, white, Asian, atheist, spoke English native, Korean native, and German fluent, had attended university, smoked occasionally, drank often, sometimes did drugs, Taurus, and 91 percent compatible with me. In his first photo he was smiling, not looking directly at the camera, at a party, in flattering pink light, wearing a normal shirt; there was the sense that people were moving and laughing just beyond the frame. In another he was kissing a terrier. In another he was climbing a rock. He had a long face, a narrow chin, hair like male movie stars in the nineties (the swoop), and very defined calves. He liked cooking and chess and worked as a teacher. One can take in this information much faster when it's presented in bullet points, with selective bolding and a lot of white space.

Ignoring a concerning mention of something called Relationship Anarchy (capitalization his), I replied that my other Bergman favorites might be red flags and I would prefer to get to know him before I revealed so much about myself. Though (or because) it was after midnight he responded immediately—a green dot next to his username indicated he was online— with *haha*s and more questions. (Though admittedly boring his personal favorite was *Wild Strawberries*.) He was cogent and nonrobotic, worldly, getting of it, not at all bad. After about fifteen minutes I noticed that I was sitting in the dark messaging with a guy from a dating website at one in the morning and said I was going to bed but that we should meet for a drink this week, my schedule being open; he said tomorrow at this bar in the Reuterkiez? The bar was highly rated on several platforms. Fine.

I woke up to more messages, not from him. The necessary sifting had the desired effect of pulling me away from social media, and although the waste of time was functionally equivalent it felt productive, almost as if I were meeting new people. When I abandoned my inbox and began scrolling through the men the app suggested for me—sortable by Match %, Distance, Last Online, Special Blend—I was surprised that many piqued my interest, not as potential subjects for my personality experiment but as people I might actually want to date. The Special Blend seemed to know what I wanted and fed it to me endlessly. I envisioned myself hitting it off with an Italian postdoc, an American artist, a German artist, a German engineer, another German artist, a Spanish artist, a Spanish Marxist,

a Moroccan PhD candidate studying ancient languages, a Slovenian journalist, a Russian translator. Even an Australian project manager, working
at a startup, and a British bartender/DJ compelled me with self-effacement
appropriate to their jobs. In our imagined meetings my role was always di-
minished, my only emotions a sense of giggly ease and magnetism, relief at
like-mindedness. Objects online are less sexy than they appear, I reminded
myself, not believing it at all. I began to regret agreeing to go on my first
date with Bergman, who was not as enchanting as some of the others, many
of whom seemed happy, well-adjusted, and self-aware. I'd had no idea I'd be
able to be judicious. How could there be so many people with whom I might
have a believable relationship? I sent a few messages to the matches who
met my height requirement—all copy-and-pasted except for a calculated
reference to something specific in the man's profile, making sure to change
each missive before I sent it off so as not to reveal this was an assembly-line
effort—and got up to make coffee. The ex-boyfriends are thinking of, but
not mentioning, the times when I Gchatted or text-messaged them some
particularly worded opinion or fiery emotional missive, something that
sounded as if it had just then erupted from a core of intense feeling that they
would have believed genuine if I hadn't already sent it to them a day or two
before, in the same incensed tone and often the very same verbiage. Haha
i suck, i'm the worst, bad1!!!, I'd always say, and then try to forget about it.

. . .

RELATIONSHIP ANARCHY (RA) IS A PHILOSOPHY THAT REJECTS
definitions and rules, Bergman told me, drinking a Moscow mule, the ring
on his pinky distracting from an otherwise normal outfit. The ring hadn't
been featured in any of his photos. He had a disarmingly soothing accent, a
combination of springtime allergies and having grown up in Sydney with a
Korean mother and Scottish father, an upper-class Commonwealth fluidity
atop a bed of congestion, garnished with a distant staccato. Everything he

said sounded right, even when it was totally ludicrous. The hair, shiny and thick, long but not too long, likely contained some subtle product, suggesting confidence and control. He had studied German in school and had lived in Berlin for seven years, but when he spoke the language to the bartender the consonants didn't manage to transcend the softness of his voice, though she replied in her own accented German and not in English, which is not how anyone ever responded to my attempts, even when I thought they were competent.

RA was conceived in 2006 by a Swede named Andie Nordgren and its adherents believed that because love is not a limited resource, traditional hierarchical relationships that treat it as such are not just unnecessary but harmful, perpetuating toxic retrograde attitudes that equate love with ownership. One should allow space in one's life for the kind of intimacy that can be cut off when one designates a single person as special and reserved, and therefore owed and owing. Even designating a category of relationship as special and reserved was poison: Romantic relationships are not better than platonic or familial ones. The ingrained belief that romantic love should be life's organizing principle is inextricably linked to patriarchy and the oppression of minorities, the poor, and immigrants, among other populations. The resulting expectations kill love at the root. When caretaking duties are foisted onto individuals and families rather than supplied and paid for by the state as they should be, the state must make it seem like this is the natural and noble situation. Propaganda. Marriage is obviously propaganda, but so are all conventional relationships, because all conventional relationships cannot help but situate themselves in relation to marriage, whether they are like marriage or on track to marriage or on track to being like marriage or not; marriage is all encompassing and cannot but enforce hierarchy. Thus, ritualized domestic exclusion begets systemic exclusion via our admiration and craving for exclusivity. He cleared his throat, failed, tried again, and took a very small sip of his drink, the ginger sting of which did not seem to help. Relationship Anarchy explodes not just exclusivity but the possibility of exclusivity, he said, almost recovered, by, well, like the name says, applying anarchist principles to interpersonal relationships—by flattening *all* hierarchies, among *all* relationships. To an outsider it sounds like polyamory—RA naturally eliminates the expectation of arbitrary sexual and romantic fidelity within an individual relationship, thereby lessening the sense of hierarchy among romantic partners—but it's really sort of the opposite. For years, polyamorists have been trying to convince the public that theirs is a community with rules and boundaries. Ours is decidedly not. By defining our lives by what we don't believe in, we can get closer to freedom from pain and oppression; ideally, we envision our world as a constantly (and beautifully) turning kaleidoscope of not-friendships, not-affairs, and not-marriages. There are no commitments, and no guarantee that a sexual and/or romantic relationship will be more "important" than a friendship, because all relationships are free to grow or shrink or change as suits both parties, provided both engage in enthusiastic consent. Saying "no labels" sounds juvenile, he knew, but there were none, only ideals: respect, trust, communication, autonomy.

This was about twenty minutes into the date, when Bergman felt he should make his customary disclosure, making a ninety-degree turn from a lively description of the classes he taught at the John F. Kennedy School, located in the southwest, to "So: before we get any further I have to talk a little bit about how I live," running a tan hand through the hair. I was surprised; his ideological commitments weren't at all visible in his personal style. On my way to the bar I'd decided to tell him that my father had written a seminal geography textbook in the eighties and that he'd recently died, leaving me three million dollars, but I never got the chance. He outlined the above as I nodded with a look of strained neutrality on my face, and when he reached the "Any questions?" portion of the talk I knew this was my chance to speak, so I didn't want to waste it on half-assed fantasies I'd lifted from the lives of people I was jealous of in New York. I began by agreeing that marriage should be abolished. It was a huge and stupid institution that persisted entirely through the various racket industries that needed it, and through sexism and denialism about the human spirit. I was in general in favor of polyamory also, though in practice had found it incompatible with the sort of people I wanted to date, who stereotyped polyamorists as weird, sweaty devotees of certain uncool music festivals. However, I also suspected there was a catch.

I asked him how it worked.

It's about letting other people flow through you, he said, undulating in his seat to demonstrate. You may or may not flow through them, depending on how porous and willing they are. (His words.) Their porousness and willingness, however, is fundamentally and critically not your problem, he said; your problem is you and your own porousness and willingness. Or at least that's how he interpreted it; the great thing about Relationship Anarchy was that there was no blueprint you had to follow.

This didn't really answer my question, but I didn't know how to respond. How porous and willing was I? It wasn't something I'd ever considered. Until recently I'd always lived as straightforwardly as I could, finding strategy tedious and likely to backfire, terrible at hiding things, more interested in the possibilities of disclosure than worried about the risks. This was why I'd become so frustrated with Felix: I cared less that he was a fake conspiracy theorist than that he was cagey, that he'd given me no way to determine in his sudden absence why he was a fake conspiracy theorist. The slim chance that maybe he'd kept it all a secret because he actually believed the theories were true did, at times, really bother me. He was not a reciprocal person. He accepted what you offered and then put it in his pocket and winked at you. Yet it could not be denied that lately I'd been, like him, very impermeable and unwilling. Did Bergman know that? Could he somehow tell? Should I have been talking more? Was my lack of contribution revealing a character? Was I, despite my newfound unwillingness and impermeability, actually completely transparent?

While I was reviewing the nuances of my body language and the few sentences I'd spoken that evening to determine whether I was, despite my impermeability and unwillingness, actually completely transparent, I saw that I'd been tricked: I'd forgotten all about the potential charlatan sipping from a straw in front of me and started thinking about myself. It seemed possible he wasn't being serious—the talking points were too defined and the vocabulary too vague—but it was also possible that he'd given this spiel to many, many people over the two years he said he'd been doing it and had developed a tone based on the pearl-clutching reactions commonly expressed. If it seemed like he was selling something it was because his enjoyment of that thing depended on a diversity of people participating. The number of available sexual partners for the Relationship Anarchist is probably limited, and assuming one of the draws of Relationship Anarchy is weird sex with a variety of people, that limitation may cripple the point. There are social obstacles to doing things differently: People get mad at you. They worry you're judging them and suspect deep down you might be right; they become stubborn and defensive. You need backup, reassurance, affinity. You'd have to be a real believer to keep going, is what I'm saying, so I thought maybe my rush to characterize him as a charlatan was unfair. Though this is also the rationale of multilevel marketing schemes.

The bar was very smoky. The multiple-partners aspect of it was not so hard for people to get over, he said, especially in Berlin, where people are progressive and understand polyamory. The difficult thing was the refusal of any commitment at all, of any kind of anchor. Though you could have anchors, he corrected himself quickly, that's not what he meant. A commitment could inevitably result. What he meant was that there was no pretending things would last forever, no asserting certainties over another person's life. And no essentializing. No understanding another human being through their relationship to you. He didn't like to say "colleague" at work, though the Germans said it all the time.

I asked what individual porousness and willingness meant in a practical sense, like, OK, say he and I were in . . . not a relationship: What would we do?

We would do whatever we wanted!

I had no idea what that meant.

He said: In RA each not-relationship required the full intention of both parties and could be abandoned or expanded by either at any time. Communication was key, but there was to be no bargaining or convincing or even asking; it was about exchange, not power. You could say you wanted an explanation of another person's actions, but you couldn't request or expect one. You could say you wanted to see another person again, but you couldn't request or expect to. This acknowledged the value of an individual's attention and prevented people from taking advantage of each other. It was reciprocal empathic agency. It was entirely selfish and entirely egalitarian.

I said, So your philosophy is pro-selfishness. I didn't mean to sound wry but I suppose it may have come out that way.

He said: Yes. But it's not really. It's more that—for the first time during this speech he seemed to genuinely be picking his words from the air, not reciting, which made me feel as if I'd come up with something original—RA, the way he saw it at least, recognizes that everyone is selfish, that selfishness is what motivates us all, and it doesn't try to fight against that.

Even altruistic acts contain selfish motivations, he added.

Well, yeah, unless it's, like, you're dying for someone, I said. The ex-boyfriends give me no credit. Could a sensitive person do this?

He said yes that was true but anyway: In life, most people say they want to fall in love. By that they mean a few things, none of which is actually part of the emotion. What people mean (ticking off on fingers):

1) They want to find someone who solves—or makes otherwise irrelevant through the delirious happiness they inspire—the umbrella problem of life: What is the meaning of it?;

2) They want to find someone who makes them want no one else, someone they feel totally confident that they are in love with, with no doubts;

3) They want to find someone who they feel totally confident is in love with them, so that instead of going through the painful process of looking deep inside themselves for worth they can outsource the task of identifying it;

4) Later, when such things become worrisome, pangs in the night, at the grocery store, while cooking countless sad dinners for one, they want someone who will take care of them when they die.

This vision of love is totally unrealistic, it just doesn't happen, but there's always the sense that it *could*, and that imagined possibility drives the whole system of despair and broken dreams that has everyone settling for that guy from high school, or whatever, he concluded.

As someone who was at that point and for the foreseeable future loveless—I don't mean that in a self-pitying way, just realistically speaking, look at me—I have to say a lot of this made sense.

Did he sleep with people who aren't Relationship Anarchists?

Yes. After all, it would be a little hypocritical of a Relationship Anarchist not to accept someone else's prerogative. But he did require that they agree to practice Relationship Anarchy with him.

Did this not put him in a disadvantageous position? They could abandon him at any time and have a stable understudy boyfriend waiting in the wings?

He didn't think in those terms. In fact, if he was being honest, he mainly spent time with non-RA, because it was just easier. He had a job, things to do—he relished intimacy and didn't want to wait for people he liked to come around. It was enough to teach them about the philosophy. Usually it was poly people, who were not really a problem—they had a primary partner and would be just messing around with him, or they had a few partners who ended up taking priority. *They're* so used to people freaking out on them about jealousy or commitment or whatever that they end up feeling reassured by the whole thing. So accustomed are they to being the baseline for romantic weirdness that suddenly seeing someone who is romantically weirder than they are is liberating. If you find yourself on a date with a normie, though, you can get into a bit of a dicey situation with expectations, which are counter to the cause.

I asked if it was difficult to operate with this mindset, purging expectations, rejecting impulse. I heard myself asking, and really feeling something as I asked, though these were not priorities I'd ever had before: Is there not something to be gained from obligation? He said that when he was feeling most possessive—or, on the flip side, unloved, alone—he had a process for getting rid of the feeling: He loved ice cream, stocking a selection of flavors in his freezer at all times, and when his heart and soul were gripped with negative emotion he was allowed to eat the ice cream—but only after he meditated for thirty minutes. He sat on his little cushion in his living room and thought about not thinking, and after half an hour, successful or not, he was free, and ate ice cream. He always felt a little high after he did this. I asked how often did he need to do the process and he said that when he first learned about RA he knew—the way people describe meeting the person they'll marry—it was the right thing to do, but it was awful getting started, like withdrawal. After a series of dark horrible days, he decided he had to figure something out and came upon the process when a fellow RA suggested he "put his own spin" on meditation. Now two years later he's down to once a week. I was about to comment that that seemed a high frequency of turning to extreme measures, but when I began to think about how often I felt desperately sad about whatever situation I was in, once a week seemed on par, if not better. I, too, have a fast metabolism, I said, and he laughed.

I asked how it was different from "no strings attached" relationships. He asked if that was really a thing, and I said I guessed not really, no. He said RA was somewhat similar, though because the philosophy emphasizes the value of the individual, it's different from a no-strings-attached thing, which renders the other individual meaningless. Also, he added, RA was an oppositional politics. It wasn't a motto.

We finished our drinks and left. As we stood on the stoop of the bar ready to begin muttering about which directions we were going, he grabbed my hand, looked at me, and asked if I was game.

I was genuinely confused. Game for what? He couldn't have meant to have sex, which didn't cross my mind.

"For Relationship Anarchy," he said. If I wanted to see him again—let's stop calling this a date—I had to confirm a verbal nonbinding noncontract to agree to agree to nothing.

I wanted to laugh, and if he'd been a true cad, I like to think I would have, though I've only laughed at deserving men on rare occasions; I usually freak out when faced with absurd offensiveness instead of looking it in the eye. But out from between the lines of his practiced definitions, a disconcerted loneliness peeked. Here was a person who was, it seemed, serious, who was attempting to structure his life in a way he could stand. It wasn't as if anyone else had come up with something better. I said I was sorry, but I didn't think I could be a Relationship Anarchist, but it was really nice to meet him and interesting to learn about it. He shook his head, looked at me, said he wasn't surprised, and gazed off into the street as if suffering some unknowable inner pain. In his remarkable voice he said, not looking at me, that I wasn't open enough, and he had known that at the beginning, that he could tell, that he could see, and walked away.

I was a little offended. I had just felt private sympathy for him, and instead of demonstrating the painstaking sensitivity his politics demanded, he insulted my character and moped off into the night. Who's open on a first date? I wondered, and then I considered that maybe that was part of my problem.

. . .

THIS NOT-DATE MADE ME COMPETITIVE, ALMOST VENGEFUL—I wanted to prove to Bergman that willful deceit was a surer route to precarious happiness than willful transparency. That a Goldilocks solution was obviously the correct one didn't matter. Going out with strangers I found on the internet quickly became the only activity I pursued with much regularity or vigor, not only because I lacked the vim for regularity or vigor but also because getting people from the internet to go on dates with you was harder than my initial experience suggested. Because I was dedicated to going on many of them, I ended up using the morning hours I'd previously spent reading social media in bed to message potential dates on OkCupid. People chatted, there was banter, and then when you wrote, "ha that's great. want to get a drink this week?" they stopped replying to you. Even when they agreed, they often canceled. I'd been under the impression that men were in it for commitment-free sex, not commitment-free instant messaging, but the gender was full of surprises, which I suppose is part of my attraction to it. Still, I was discouraged, almost hurt, as if I were not trying to lure them with a false personality but with my actual one. Aren't all personalities false?, one of the ex-boyfriends, the most dreamily theoretical and point-missing of them all, the one who once gently debated a friend of ours when she said her dreams never seemed very symbolic, wonders. When I inevitably became disheartened with the men on offer, I tabbed back to social media, where I clicked on articles to open more tabs that remained there to jilt my attention for weeks, developing an even more peripatetic style of reading than I had before. One morning: Marine Le Pen's niece said France, with its Greco-Roman and Christian roots, was facing a choice between globalism and survival. A man with a koala on his shoulder would love to talk to you about Hannah Arendt. An account with twenty-six followers whose photo was just a bright orange circle liked one of my lazy posts mocking a poorly phrased headline. ("What Is Triple Cleansing?" accompanied by a photo of a woman washing her face: "gosh . . . what could it be?") One new email, spam. Some huge percentage of Americans couldn't find Syria on a map; an unfamiliar account I didn't remember following said, "it's surprising there aren't more climate deniers among the Hillary fans, as they've all been frigid for the last twenty years"; a familiar account I thought I'd unfollowed said, "stop trying to make Brexit happen"; a review of *The Idiot* (the one by Elif Batuman) promised "revivifying pointlessness"; two people liked my post, one I knew who had quit his media job to work on a book "about coolness (the social quality, not the temperature)" and the other a politics guy who had been retweeting every post that contained permutations of the refrain "Bernie would have won." No new emails. "Got any book recs?" a message said. "Would love to talk words over tea or beer :) I'm a huge nerd!" Why "the last twenty years"? Someone I'd met once in New York liked my post; an article from a few weeks before explaining how feelings of social exclusion made people more likely to believe in conspiracy theories. I would have liked to assume serendipity, orchestrated by a force so high and powerful that it had to be magic, but it was merely topicality, a combination of algorithms and forces so unexciting that people could only rampage about their effects rather than their causes: things were discussed because they were blunt and shocking, because they appealed to obvious impulses. Discussion begat more discussion, and that discussion begat imitation. People became exasperated with the same things and produced the same thoughts. People said, "This is the article I've been waiting for someone to write!" Others said, "Why is everyone talking about *this* celebrity's likely premeditated gaffe when people are dying from *that* series of cruel events and labyrinthine policies?" A question both entirely reasonable and sweetly quixotic. (A word I learned when it appeared on the drop-down menu of possible moods to assign yourself on LiveJournal, the blogging platform I used in middle school.) No new emails. A Swiss guy said he enjoyed paragliding and cocktails—not at the same time, though. An email from the expat panlist, someone looking for an English-speaking podiatrist. Donald Trump was the dumbest person on earth and there was nothing I could do about it. The dumbness of any one person, regardless of their influence on the world, had nothing to do with me, except that it could maybe make me look good in certain company, but at the same time this fixation, on news, on other people, on gossip, on distillations and opinions, was nothing if not a reminder of how much one could know without actually knowing anything. I could tell you that people I would never meet had just broken up with their boyfriends, explaining why their recent posts seemed unmoored. I could map out social circles and determine whose bitter ripostes were the result of professional jealousies and whose were the result of stress from hardship. No new emails. I clicked on the article about the essential loneliness of conspiracy theorists and stopped reading in the middle of the first paragraph—people who *believed* in conspiracy theories made sense to me and did not require further investigation. A spam email. Most of what I read or started to read online was aimed not at clawing for some difficult specificity but at reaffirming a widespread but superficial understanding, or highlighting the understanding that could easily be intuited by the highest number of people, if they chose to think about it at all. "overheard a guy explaining that jazz was 'like the subway' to his tinder date at the bar last night ?!" A spam email. I perused more profiles. I was getting a twinge in my lower back, never bothering to find a comfortable position because I always assumed I'd be getting out of bed any minute. I went to my Twitter timeline, paused to remember what I was doing there, and then typed in the unfamiliar account's username, @HelenofTroyWI; her little profile photo, of bathing Maria Schneider in *Last Tango in Paris* with red devil horns drawn on, an image that could have been interpreted but was best left not, appeared in the dropdown menu, and I clicked it. Her profile description provided few clues as to her identity: "no ass-play, no exceptions #RESIST." Her location was listed as "Uranus, not mine." She posted several times an hour and replied to anyone who talked to her. Her use of "as" in her tweet about Hillary Clinton supporters suggested British or international English, but such things could seep into anyone's vocabulary, could mean any number of things—it could be part of a voice she'd devised to throw people off. A few days before, I saw, someone had asked her why someone so good at Twitter would want to be anonymous. "I wasn't always anonymous," she replied, "but my tweets weren't good when I was posting as myself." She had about seven thousand followers, so I could assume that when she used her old avatar and real name, the ones I recognized, she'd had fewer. She was followed by fifty-six people I knew, a mix of well-known media figures and niche literary types. "Time for some game theory" (a memeified catchphrase from some self-styled pundit who'd written a very long thread of tweets about Russian collusion in the presidential election that went viral through who knows what proportion of earnest belief and contemptuous irony): @HelenofTroyWI's awareness of arty small-press publishers and past-life book bloggers meant she must have had roots in the literary world; these were not people or entities known in the wider media. The relationship between her avatar and her bio seemed to understand something about expression through form that a journalist wouldn't bother with. While it was hard to imagine that anyone in the publishing industry would want to express the account's mildly controversial political opinions through reactionary edgy offensiveness, hers was a literary impulse, an attempt to project herself, or her ideas, publicly through a slightly different character. The reactionary edgy offensiveness, and its inaccuracies and perplexities, seemed controlled and considered rather than careening and volatile.

I spent a couple of minutes reading her posts and trying to remember who she might be before I became bored and clicked back to my timeline. Even though I knew I had the tools to divine her identity, I stopped caring quickly—what did it matter? This is the struggle with describing social media: it devours importance. It happened when I inevitably found myself on Felix's inactive Instagram account, too; I would scroll through his old posts, pick one I thought seemed interesting—the photos of the Denver International Airport, which is believed to be situated on top of an underground meeting place for the New World Order, as well as home to a cursed blue horse statue named Blucifer, were striking—and then scan through the hashtags and commenters, trying to see if anything looked familiar. Sometimes I'd search the theory online, as if trying to retrace Felix's steps: Where had he found it? What parts did he choose to highlight? But all I gained was a rounder understanding of Truths Hidden in Plain Sight. It was boring. To my surprise, very few of the theories Felix posted had been inspired by the 2016 election, as had been suggested by the news articles I'd skimmed; Trump had merely made existing conspiracies seem more viable. After becoming disgusted with OkCupid and vowing to stop looking at social media the next day, I usually managed to get out of bed by lunch, to do aimless European wandering of the sort I might later romanticize.

"Will you try to stay in Berlin?" Frieda asked one day as I ate yogurt next to her collection of cookbooks and houseplant literature. I realized I hadn't thought about it; if someone asked how I liked living there I made something up. I looked at her blankly, like an idiot, and said, "I don't know . . ." I made an expression to suggest this was a real dilemma I'd been wrestling with internally. My tourist visa lasted another two months, and I had not yet purchased a return flight or come up with anything I'd like to do back in the United States, but I was also clearly having some kind of psychological problem that Berlin, while not the cause, perhaps could not be said to be helping. (The ex-boyfriends would like to interject here, but they feel that would be overstepping boundaries.) I asked her to let me know if she heard of any apartments I could live in when this sublet was over. "I guess if I stay I should take a German class . . ." I added, totally not meaning it at all, and she replied, "Why? English is better."

I had to admit I agreed with her. I spoke to Germans so rarely that the language barrier didn't register as part of the overall experience of living in Germany. Naturally it was limiting in the usual ways—many people, when hearing someone struggle with their language, assume stupidity. Older Germans had a particularly humiliating tone to their typical response, an exaggerated nasal *Heh?* that matched a squinting snarl. Younger Germans just spoke to me in English, which was possibly worse, being politely accommodated for a deficiency over which I had full control. But it was nice to be in a crowd but separate from it, to feel no pressure to participate, and Frieda seemed to be giving me her blessing to appreciate the naughty pleasure this provided. Already superior to the New York subway system in every way, the U-Bahn was a warm bath of incomprehensibility. If a man approached me in the street or at a bar where I was drinking alone and said, "[German]?" I was able to smile apologetically and continue what I was doing without having to awkwardly turn him down. Most people, as that tourist's cliché goes, spoke English, but the men who approached strange women in public were, on average, much worse at it. One day a man outside my apartment—short, wearing a T-shirt that said WHATEVER, smiling too much—managed to ensnare me for almost ten minutes, eager to practice, asking asking asking, what I did, why I was in Berlin, what is it like to work as an architect, and after he informed me that he had just come from an allergy test and I had to ask him three times what he was saying, I watched him realize it was futile, that having to stack English phrases together for the length of the beer he was about to propose we have together would be just too exhausting, that his English accent probably wasn't as good as he'd been led to believe. I said I had to meet a friend and walked away quickly in the opposite direction of where I actually needed to go. Whenever I overheard a native English speaker—the Weserstrasse was almost entirely Anglophone in the evenings—it was unbearably distracting. It was like everyone was having caricatures of conversation, always explaining their recent breakups or noting the prevalence of good bars in the neighborhood, and soon enough I would remember that all the elegant European accents around me were probably conveying ideas equally vapid and wisdom just as conventional, and I would imagine trite observations filling in the empty space around me until I could not see or hear or breathe. I couldn't tell if Germans actually spoke more quietly or if I just perceived them as quiet because I didn't understand what they were saying. Americans are often considered loud and obnoxious, but that might have been because our language occupied a rare position in being both outlying and recognizable, and therefore invasive.

Six weeks after I arrived, though it felt like a year, or one very long day of moderate but continuous drinking, it was mid-April, and the woman I was subletting from emailed to say she was going to stay in Portugal because she had fallen in love with an oboist. Was I interested in keeping the room for three more months, at least? For some reason, I was. I'd have to get a visa, but I'd heard it wasn't hard to do—after all, Felix had done it—and despite my moping I didn't want to go back to New York because it would feel like I'd wasted my time, so I said sure, I'll waste more, until it can be retrospectively determined not wasted.

As soon as I made this decision, I could think of nothing else. Maybe I would get an apartment with a balcony and stop hating percolated coffee. Maybe I would give up the online dates and fall in love with a German who would teach me his language, allowing me to surprise him with my natural proclivity for grammar. Maybe he would be from Hamburg—stable yet able to party, reachable by train yet sturdily seafaring. I looked up how to stay there legally.

The blogs had thousands of words of advice. The gist of it was: The experience is harrowing but ultimately fine if you are from the United States and especially if you are from the United States and white. I could apply as a freelancer for what was referred to as the "artist visa," the sound of which I liked. To do this I would have to compile many documents proving German society's need for my unique services and confirming I was unlikely to require government assistance, which I'd present to an interviewer at the Ausländerbehörde, a word I couldn't help mistranslating in my head as "hoard of foreigners." I was advised to make an appointment to avoid long and sometimes impossible wait times at the office, which had limited hours despite need.

When I went to the designated website, available in a passive English, the first available appointment was four months away. Having warned of this, the blogs were smug, and they relished taunting me with possible solutions, none of which were ideal. I could book an appointment and wait, though my standard three-month tourist visa would expire in a month and a half. I could stay in the country as long as I had an appointment scheduled at the Ausländerbehörde; all would be fine as long as I did not miss the appointment, or attempt to leave the country before the date. I could also show up very early in the morning and try to get one of a limited number of walk-in spots, distributed by a take-a-number system, though none of the blogs seemed to have been written by someone who had managed this. To be clear: I know this is boring. I decided I would demonstrate my superiority to the blogs, which presented these options as either-or, by showing up one day to try and walk in as *well* as booking the earliest available appointment, in late July. I looked up a recommended freelancer's plan to cover the health insurance requirement, which the blogs did not explain well except to underscore its chief importance, and then clicked over to my email, where I had three new messages from the expat panlist. Buzzing from mild productivity after weeks of desultory web browsing, I replied with interest to a post seeking an English-speaking person to "walk" nine-month-old twins every morning from eight until eleven and got an answer back right away. Both the woman who posted the ad and her husband were artists who worked from home, she American and he German, and now that they could stand to leave the babies to someone else for a couple of hours, ha ha, they guessed they couldn't put off work any longer. Their apartment was about twenty minutes away from mine, and we agreed to meet there the next day.

I had managed to get a bike by this point, from a very tall Dutch woman selling it online—"It's not stolen," she assured me, though I hadn't asked—so I rode it there. While I talked with the parents about my work as a freelance tax preparer in the U.S., I let one of the babies hold my finger and put it in his mouth as the other sitting up uneasily waved a brightly colored giraffe back and forth in front of his face. As I was explaining my job, my skills with spreadsheets and the pleasure I took in being able to soothe panicked scramblers, I knew it was a bad lie—a freelance tax preparer would have little need for a side job walking babies—but the inappropriateness didn't seem to faze them. The two pursuits, accounting and babysitting, could be united by a desire to have a real, nontheoretical effect on people's lives—to help them in confusing and stressful times, to be a small relief. It was only after I had made meaningful eye contact with both of the babies that the father, Holger, told me they'd met with a girl just before me and they were going to hire her, but if it didn't work out they would call me. Though I had no stake in an early-morning babysitting job—indeed it probably would have sucked—I felt deflated, and on a date that night with a guy who did copyright law, I complained about it as if I were really, really disappointed. He told me I seemed like a very passionate person and squeezed my shoulder when we parted.

The next day I was running along the canal in the newly springlike weather thinking about whether I would like to be hit by a car when I missed a call: The girl had not shown up to walk the babies that morning, could I start tomorrow? The pay was seven euros an hour. I called them back and said sure. I added in my knowing-girlfriend voice that it was very strange that the girl had just not shown up, but the mother, Genevieve, replied, "Oh, that's just Berlin."

. . .

DEAD BEHIND THE EYES AND WARM, THE BABIES WORE COORDI-nated but not exactly matching outfits and, I was told, would wake up and cry if I remained stationary for too long. As Genevieve and I strapped them into the oblong pods of the double stroller, maneuvering their chubby arms as we needed and hushing tremors of sadness with our sweetest feminine voices, she asked me if I was happy Tax Day was over. I was tucking what I believed was an unnecessary blanket under a floppy leg and paused, confused; I was certainly not unhappy Tax Day had passed, but I didn't know why my feelings about it were being asked of me by a recent acquaintance at eight in the morning in a foreign country whose tax season I had no idea about. I smiled with my mouth closed and said, "Who isn't? Though of course as a socialist I believe the problem with Tax Day is that it doesn't make enough people unhappy, ha ha," and as she clarified, "I'm sure it's very busy for you this time of the year," I remembered my lie and rued myself. She stood up and looked at me suspiciously—or maybe I just believed it was suspiciously—before handing me the keys to the lock for the stroller. I tried to convey the air of a quiet, kept-to-herself woman who compartmentalized her life and who had taken on a side job as something to do, like a housewife or retiree. People were constantly taking part in strange and unimaginable situations—why not me? I'd told her I liked children. When you stopped to consider that many women like children enough to manufacture their own, it seemed markedly less strange that a gainfully employed tax professional of reproductive age might like them enough to spend fifteen hours a week in their presence for pay that is low but nevertheless would cover rent plus some. (My rent being so low that I am not going to tell you what it was, teetering as I am already on the border between likable and loathsome.) Maybe I wanted to practice caretaking. Maybe I was using it to distract myself from a problem or issue in my life. Genevieve didn't know. It was absurd that people would just hand over their supposedly prized children to young and inexperienced strangers. Maybe I was doing an art project aimed at illustrating this. She'd better hope not.

Outside the babies squirmed and murmured as I paused to put on a podcast, an uninteresting interview with an author who had written a book that sounded uninteresting, and then I began to walk. The neighborhood was empty, the way I always wished New York could be when I had to get up early and go somewhere and entered the subway to find it already full and irritable at 7 a.m. and, knowing it had to do with class and gentrification, felt guilty about my annoyance at this. I regretted all the Berlin mornings I'd spent scrolling through my phone now that I knew such quiet expanses were at my disposal. The grocery store on the corner was closed; the line of mannequins in loud ball gowns posed in the dark window of a Turkish bridal shop; a single businessman strutted toward the U-Bahn as if he knew he shouldn't be there. I crossed the street and the stroller bumped and caught on the cobblestones. As I crossed Kottbusser Damm to assess a bakery's offerings the author laughed about how irritating it was to be asked to what extent her novels derived from her life, without saying to what extent her novels derived from her life. I walked past a group of Turkish women who looked at me and then looked at the babies. I was a normal age to have children so they might as well have been mine, but something about me, maybe my clothes, which were shabby, or my aura, which was ambivalent, told them I shouldn't have them in my possession. After a while I peeked in at them and they were sleeping cutely, round cheeks flushed and pouched against their baby pillows, spittle glistening on their tiny lips, tufty hair tufting upward. The author said she thought having children contributed to the form and style of her books, written in stolen moments, necessarily short sections, simple, aphoristic sentences, more of an essay than a novel at times. Lots of women were writing fragmented books like this now, the interviewer pointed out. Having read several because they were easy to finish, I couldn't help but object: this trendy style was melodramatic, insinuating utmost meaning where there was only hollow prose, and in its attempts to reflect the world as a sequence of distinct and clearly formed ideas, it ran counter to how reality actually worked. Especially, I had to assume, if you had a baby, which is a purposeful experience (don't let it die) but also chaotic (it might die). Since the interviewer and the author agreed there was something distinctly feminine about this style, I felt guilty admitting it, but I saw no other choice: I did not like the style.

I tapped pause on the interview and switched to an episode of a long-running sex-advice podcast that began with a woman who said she had been with her *partner* for five years and although she loved him a lot she had one problem, just one, which was that he really liked anal sex and claimed he could only get off if her anus was very tight and there was not much lube. @HelenofTroyWI may have had a point about ass-play. The babies made light discontented noises when I stopped moving.

About an hour later, having taken random turns while heading in the general direction of where I would need to be at 11 a.m., I found myself outside a coffee shop from which emerged the beaming woman from Los Angeles I'd met at the bookstore dinner. Nell. She remembered me. "Where did you get THOSE?" she shouted down the street. She hugged me and bent down to look at the babies. At that moment I was gripped by the certainty that she would one day force me to come to the bathroom with her, not just into a waiting area but into a single-occupancy restroom itself, for no reason other than, I guess, bonding. She was wearing indeterminate layers, several earrings in both ears, rings on most fingers, and a bright orange lipstick, and she had cut her hair into a bob that hung straightly around her chin. I pushed the stroller slowly back and forth as I explained that I liked her hair and had gotten a job walking babies for two artists in Neukölln. She interrupted me as I was about to broach the subject of visa advice. "Do you want a coffee? I'll get you a coffee." She went inside as I continued pushing the stroller, babyish muttering emitting occasionally, back and forth like I was doing an ineffective exercise, and a couple of minutes later she was handing me a cappuccino. "It's just been awful!" she said, laughing at the dreadfulness of it all. "I have to leave my apartment this week! The landlord's daughter is coming back from Iceland early! She 'finds the people really too weird'!" I told her that at least she could now try to find a place with a shower, thinking that remembering this detail would show I was interested in her life, and she said, "Ja, but finding an apartment in Berlin is impossible." I asked her if she spoke German and she said, "Ja. Danke Mutti!" She was a dual citizen and so would be useless in helping me procure a visa, so I didn't bring it up. She said she had to go to a flat viewing now but still wanted to do the writing group with me and tapped her email address into my phone before daintily getting on her bike and riding away. I always said one of the reasons I didn't want children was that I would be devastated if I had a boy, but sometimes I felt I didn't understand women at all.

MAYBE IF I WROTE LIKE THIS I WOULD BETTER UNDERSTAND them.

*

A GERMAN PROGRAMMER WITH LONG CURLY HAIR MESSAGED ME and we met at an anarchist café with board games and chairs barely clinging to their remaining upholstery. I'd always liked the idea of dating a programmer, despite not knowing if that's what they're called anymore. Coder? No—developer. I found them difficult to communicate with and felt that if I met one who could make me understand what programming was it would be a sign he was my soul mate. "But who makes the back end for the back end!" I cried, nearly knocking over my beer as I showed off my vocabulary. "The back end for the back end?" he replied. I ask every developer I meet this question and I never remember what they tell me. He invited me to a movie screening on the roof of a parking garage the next night, but I told him I was going to Leipzig to see an exchange student from my high school play in a hardcore band. He said, "Ah, do you know the band?" I said I didn't know the band and usually only listened to classical, "and some jazz."

*

A CANADIAN GRAPHIC DESIGNER WHO HAD BEEN IN BERLIN FOR two months, struggling to find work, was intriguingly nihilistic. He was supposed to move here with his girlfriend but at the last minute she decided she wanted to stay in Toronto and, effectively, dump him. I asked him if this was surprising and he said, "In retrospect? Yes." I asked him what he meant and he said he had never imagined a future with her and had even talked with his buddies about what he would do if he got to Berlin and decided he didn't want to be with her anymore, but now that she'd left him and defected from their exciting new plan he couldn't stop thinking about her and feeling they were certain to get back together someday. He didn't seem *very* upset about it, just a little upset, so I had to take him at his word. I said, angrily, that if I had actually been looking for someone to date, I would have been very discouraged by this. I told him he should not be on dating apps, even though I didn't care what he did with his life. I said that my beloved childhood dog had died that morning and I had to go mourn him.

*

I WAS STARTING TO GET ANNOYED. THESE PEOPLE JUST WANTED to talk about themselves. They weren't giving me a chance to talk about my characters.

*

ONE THING THAT SURPRISED ME WAS HOW LITTLE I THOUGHT about having sex. Some of the guys were attractive, if not downright hot.

One had a sexily crooked mouth. Yet to have sex with one of them would have been preposterous.

*

MAYBE I WAS TOO GOOD AT LISTENING. LISTENING, EVERYONE SAYS, is essentially female. Like 46 percent of the nouns in the German language.

*

I DECIDED TO GO ON A SERIES OF DATES ASSUMING PERSONALI-ties based on the twelve signs of the zodiac. This would, I imagined, provide structure.

*

ARIES: I WAS A MASSAGE THERAPIST, YES, BUT MORE IMPOR-tantly I was an acupuncturist, I said to a serious Argentinean translator before I began proselytizing about pressure points and energy flows. Whenever he expressed a doubt or tried to suggest an alternative interpretation of something I said, I snapped that he was being sexist. I *loved* acupuncture. Sticking tiny needles into strangers was my *calling*. I sometimes got tears in my eyes just thinking about the beauty of the human body and spirit intertwined. I took his hand, very soft—he was clearly not someone who performed manual labor or even played an instrument—looked in his eyes, and pressed my thumb and forefinger into the wing between his thumb and forefinger, saying it would help with tension in his head and neck. He said nothing. I was pressing quite hard as I told him I would start my own acupuncture practice someday, hopefully in Berlin. He said he was jealous of my commitment, that he wished he cared about translating from German to Spanish and from English to Spanish as much as I clearly cared about acupuncture. I looked at him with a sympathetic smile and said I felt very lucky, to have known for so long that this was what I was meant to do. "One needs a purpose," he said, wistfully, and I really did feel sorry for him, because we might have gotten along otherwise. "I wish it were enough just to exist."

*

I'M GOING TO STOP THE EX-BOYFRIENDS RIGHT THERE: YES, I know astrology is fake. It's not real. But as I've said to them before, who cares? It's real enough to influence how real people think.

*

SEX SCENE: A COUPLE OF MONTHS AFTER FELIX MOVED BACK TO the U.S., I showed up to his new apartment unannounced and a little drunk. When I was outside his building, I rang his bell, and he buzzed without calling down, probably thinking it was someone who lived on a different floor and had forgotten their key. A minute later he was opening his door to my knock, surprised and then trying to conceal his annoyance. From the entryway I could see his kitchen table, where an aluminum takeout container and bottle of beer sat next to his laptop, open to YouTube; he didn't let me in immediately but instead asked if something was wrong. It was as if we had not spent the last months speaking all day every day, relaying thoughts and feelings. As if I had never told him important, closely held things about my life's recurring themes, about how the way I perceived myself misaligned with certain realities! I hadn't felt like I was *dying* to see him, just that it would be nice, but being obviously unwelcome heightened the stakes of the visit. I doubled down, putting on a beaming smile and saying no, nothing was wrong, I just wanted to see him—not "to say hello," not "to stop by," but specifically to see him, Felix, an apparently simple desire meant to signify something deeper. Because of this phrasing, or so I imagined, he would have to shut down his well-meaning girlfriend, with her unabashed love of him, if he wanted to continue to be alone. A mistimed kiss on the mouth. He stood aside to let me in, and I sat down on the couch with programmed ease; I'd only been there once before, when it didn't look like an apartment that belonged to anyone. (He hadn't asked for my help with the move, and when I offered he acted shocked, as if helping him move would be a horrible burden and not something friends and lovers did so often that it was a trope to provide pizza in exchange, and said he had hired people.) There were still a couple of small boxes in the corner, the miscellaneous stuff you transport every time you move, half-filled notebooks you might read in a nostalgic mood six years from now, notices from past banks, desk figurines, snow pants wrapped around a fragile vase. He had gotten a plant, a waxy Monstera, about three feet tall, and it bobbed like a curious prehistoric pet when either of us stood up or crossed the floor. There was nothing mysterious about Felix's apartment, nothing that suggested it contained somewhere within its three rooms a secret laboratory or hidden trap door or child pornography, but still I felt I was seeing something I wasn't supposed to. A framed poster on the wall advertised an Italian movie I'd never heard of, least of all from him.

He offered me a beer, took his own, sat next to me on the couch, leaving a little space between us, and asked as if it pained him whom I'd been having dinner with. I put my legs on his lap and told him I'd been at the Thai place down the street with Jordan, a friend from college, who wanted to meet him; they were neighbors. He said that would be nice and took out his phone, swiping and tapping at it a couple of times and, when the song he wanted didn't play immediately, pointing the device at a speaker in the corner, though the gesture was useless, a reflex from growing up with remote controls. Following more frustrated fingering of the cell phone Ethiopian jazz began to play, and he set his hands on my shins. It was winter and the radiator hissed. We talked about our days and the primary debates, and though he wasn't coarse or rude or even unwilling, after the initial display of mild reluctance I wanted to push him, if not toward intimacy then at least toward some affection. I sat up from my position lounging against the opposite arm of his sofa and took his face in my hands. When we kissed, I realized he too was drunk, maybe drunker than I. He softened and pulled me fully onto his lap, and we kissed a little while longer before he pulled away and smirked, his eyes lazy, looking so much like a teenager that I recalled being sixteen, in a car on a hill. Unlike his previous facial expressions this one was not forced or concealing; he took my hand and brought it to rub his erection, which was pressing against my inner thigh otherwise. I'd been operating on the adrenaline produced by my attention-seeking but upon his display of agency I suddenly wanted to leave. I mimicked the soft cooing of porn stars and noticed as I did the brightness of his living room, the stark unremarkability of the scene I'd walked into, the rug not quite big enough for the space, the curtains ugly and concealing no secrets at all. This had the effect of making me feel like a fool, and at once I needed to recoup my pride. Willing to risk seeming inept I started to rub his penis on the outside of his pants faster—too fast, I knew, to be pleasurable— and he soon put his hand on top of mine to slow me. In the unnecessarily low tone of sex he told me I looked hot; he must have seen himself as rescuing me from self-knowledge. I kissed him as if in response and as we parted I didn't say anything, just kind of smiled, like I had some kind of plan that was better than taking off at least some of our clothes and having sex but that I was not going to reveal just yet. He said, "Baby," not to direct me or request anything of me, just to declare, and although I hated the falseness of the endearment, the huskiness he brought to the kinds of words he'd never say in a nonsexual context, I felt a little happy that he'd called me something I had to assume he meant nicely.

Still, I didn't want to have sex with him. Why? I don't know. Perhaps laziness. Perhaps a desire to maintain the illusion of an uncontaminated metaphysical state. The brain chemistry is altered during sex, plus penetration does what it does, psychologically. A man I nearly had an affair with once told me, as we lay close but not touching on a blanket in the park, that women having heterosexual P-in-V sex could not fuck, only be fucked; I replied that there was a great body of literature that debated this very question and then despite his pleading never fucked him. But still: he had a point. One wants to be able to fuck a man while actually fucking him.

Felix and I had sex often, and it was good. I had plentiful orgasms, in quantities that made friends ask about vibrators. Because I had come there, at night, having drunk enough to be playful but not enough to be worrisome, having put my legs on his legs, having batted my eyelashes, I didn't feel I could just say, "I don't want it," without offering some physiological excuse. I had wanted it earlier that very day, which had probably contributed to my decision to drop by. Yet not even the most genuine-seeming dirty talk could yank me out of this not-wanting; I wanted to have sex so little that sex was all I could think about. I saw her, the me of five minutes in the future, having to look at the wall as she undulated not too fast or slow atop this uninteresting structure, having to prop herself in some straining way, having to prepare a look of pleasure on her face, having to decide whether saying "I want you to come" would expose her disinterest or sound as if she craved his orgasm. I kept to my sophomoric secondary fondling until finally he unbuttoned his own pants with his left hand as he fingertipped my waist under my shirt with his right, still kissing, and I started to move away, almost imperceptibly, the slightest recalibration, just to prepare my body to disengage from his. As I moved my upper body backward Felix unbuttoned my pants and rotated his hand around unnaturally to slide it between our bodies and onto my crotch. After a minute of this I removed the hand and he used it to pull his dick out of his boxers. What was to be done? I decided to give him a blowjob.

As I moved down his body, shimmying his pants down so that he sat with his bare ass on the couch, he put one of his hands on the back of my head, not intending to actually do the job of downward movement but merely encouraging it, as if he had come up with this idea himself. I became sad. It was my responsibility to go down on him, not necessarily now but sometimes, and if I didn't do it now, I would have to do it some other time. I could not go two weeks without giving a blowjob, or having sex. This was not a policy, simply a reality, and one that I rarely stopped to consider. Imagine if you were in a functional sexual relationship and then one party just started refusing to have sex. It would no longer be a functional sexual relationship. The sex is required. I mean, not *required*, but strongly encouraged. If I were dating a man who would not go down on me, I would not be dating him. I know a guy who really believes that the power differential between (heterosexual) men and women is no clearer than in oral sex, during which only one gender can look up at the squirming other while simultaneously performing her favor/duty. When he first posed this analysis I laughed and laughed, exactly what he was afraid of. He thought I didn't understand what he meant, so he tried to explain. "The guy can, like, perk his head up, but not *while* he's, uh, eating you out, not *at the same time*," the guy said. "He can't communicate with his eyes that he could hurt you." I was in hysterics. I had tears in my eyes. I explained that while I got what he was selling I just didn't buy it and said that just because the power could not, in this one specific instance, be seductively communicated it didn't mean it wasn't there; even men like him, I said, narrowing my eyes, trying not to smile smugly, were very strong, or at least stronger than me. You felt this when you fucked them, or rather were fucked by them. They could kill you more easily than you could kill them; in many cases you could kill them, but it would be harder, require more strategy and planning. You would also have to overcome your ingrained sense that you should not kill this person. What's more, I added, there was the porn, which taught men to desire eye contact while they receive blowjobs, so they often *tell* the woman to look up at them, in order to monitor in real time the effect their dicks are having on her face. I pointed out that many men like it when the woman gags; in fact, some *want her* to gag, and is this not humiliating, to be physically below someone sputtering and coughing and eye-watering in service entirely of their sexual pleasure? Women may want to gag as well, but again, there is a whole body of literature debating what this means; for the purposes of this anecdotal argument the gagging signified humiliation, whether desired or not. He said, "Well, *I* don't make women gag!" reddening with regret as he did. I said it seemed that what he was actually afraid of was humiliation and he was forgetting that sex required either not looking or looking stupid. He held up his hands as if in retreat and changed the subject to the question of whether it was true that teenagers were having a lot of anal sex, as had been reported.

Felix's penis felt inert and unalive, like a small squash. I tried to get all of it in my mouth and gagged; I had never and would never be able to, but I always had to try. My eyes watered and I pressed on, varying my rhythm when I remembered to do so, licking his balls when I remembered they existed, keeping my fingers and thumb in a firm but banana-safe hold. Although I have no way to understand the passing of time during sex it felt like it would never end, like he was withholding his orgasm to demonstrate not only that he had won this battle but that I had been immature to conceive of a casual evening together as a competition in the first place—that if I continued to, I would lose. The music was nice and I wanted to know the artist. When it was over I swallowed, as I always do, and went to the bathroom to wipe away the smudged mascara from under my eyes, and then I spent the night.

*

FUCK! I MESSED UP THE STRUCTURE. THAT ONE WAS TOO LONG.

*

TAURUS: MY FATHER ABANDONED MY MOTHER WHEN I WAS FIVE years old, taking much of her collection of Royal Family memorabilia with him. The British DJ expressed his apologies. My father had wanted to sell it for drug money, she'd said, and I had to believe her, because I never saw him again, though I also couldn't remember the Royal Family memorabilia, which, I later learned, were basically worthless. I only remember that he smelled like cigarette smoke and spent his days in the basement. Once, when I was nineteen, he contacted me on Facebook, and I deleted the message immediately. I never regretted it, no. It was stubborn, yes, but I was a stubborn person when it was justified, when I could pair my bullheadedness with a seething rage unrecognizable to me during the rest of the placid and contented life I had built entirely for myself by working my way up the ladder at a successful company until they did exactly what I wanted them to do, which was transfer me to Europe. The memorabilia he'd left behind featured the lesser royals. What are their names? Beatrice and Eugenie, right. A Beatrice mug. Excuse me, but fuck him. Now all I really wanted to do was settle down with someone sturdy and reliable. I was self-sufficient, of course, with my years of accumulating savings distributed in a variety of funds, but one wants a partner, you know? To talk to. To make dinner with. The question had been if my parents were divorced. The DJ's were, too, but it was amicable, nothing like that. Just recently, yeah. A year ago or so.

*

ALREADY THE PROJECT WAS REQUIRING MORE RESEARCH THAN I'D anticipated. I'd thought I knew a fair amount about astrology, particularly for someone who didn't believe in it, but the only signature traits I could really recite if pressed corresponded to my own sign. It turned out to be incredibly boring to learn about the made-up characteristics of other people.

*

I'VE BEEN WONDERING IF SEX CAN BE IRONIC. I THINK AT THE end of the day probably not, as much as we would like it to be.

*

ALL MY EX-BOYFRIENDS WERE GEMINIS, I TOLD AN INDIAN POST-doc, wasn't that strange? He had no idea. What was I? *Also* a Gemini, I replied. Isn't *that* strange? He, playing along but clearly apprehensive, couldn't determine how strange it was unless he knew the typical Gemini traits, but he assumed the coincidence was to do with some kind of feeling of alliance I cultivated among those with similar birthdays. Why would I cultivate a feeling of alliance among those with similar birthdays? I wanted to know. Why does anyone do anything? he wanted to know. Actually, he wanted to know, what did I do? Like, for a job. I told him I was a Jill of all trades, unable to commit myself to any one field, because I found everything so interesting. There was nothing more thrilling to me than an internet rabbit hole, I beamed. I sometimes felt Wikipedia had been invented just for me.

*

ACCORDING TO THE BLOGS, THE MOST IMPORTANT PART OF THE visa application was proving you had a health insurance plan that complied with German health insurance requirements. It could NOT be traveler's insurance. Traveler's insurance was much cheaper and easier to apply for.

*

CANCER: I WOKE UP ON THE DAY OF MY DATE WITH AN ESTONIAN marathon runner and went swimming at a historic pool near my apartment. The pool was in a grand hall, built in the early twentieth century to look ancient and Roman, decorated with mosaics and enclosed by thick columns, and it was a women-only swim day. There were no lap lanes, just a divider between the shallow end, where women in burkinis waded back and forth, talking, and the rest of the pool, where chaos reigned. I tried to swim laps normally but no one else was, so I felt disruptive. I emerged an hour later feeling like I'd had a cultural experience but not an athletic one, and when I arrived at the appointed bar that night I still felt sensitive to minor annoyances. The marathon runner's lateness did not help. I asked him if he'd ever had any psychic experiences, saying that he seemed like he had, and he said, "Wow, yes, how did you know that?" I said I was very intuitive. All his visible ligaments suggested clairvoyant energy. I asked him what the biggest problem in his life was and he said his finances. I asked him why and he said he didn't have a job. I said that must be hard and he said no, it was actually quite easy, except for not being able to pay for anything. His main activity in life was running and that was free, except for the shoes, which companies would send him for free. I nodded a lot and said that seemed like it would be difficult, even though it did not, and that I was worried for his joint and foot health.

*

THE EX-BOYFRIENDS ARE FINDING IT ODD THAT I WOULD SAY they're all Geminis. What's the point of lying about that?

*

A MAN WHO PLAYED THE BANJO CANCELED OUR PLANS SO, APPRE-ciating the weather, I went to a bar with outdoor seating near the Reuterplatz. I had just ordered a beer when the perky voices of my countrywomen jerked my ear. I was two tables away from them, one blonde California type with a dog in her lap and one with short dark hair cut to swoop across her face and a larger dog lying at her feet. There was no noise from the street except for the occasional rumble of a car over the cobblestones, and I could hear everything they were saying as if it were being broadcast over speakers. Conventional wisdom about eavesdropping—that you should not do it—seems to ignore the important point that it is often unavoidable, especially when the targets of your eavesdropping are not engaging in the usual discretionary gossip tactics—lowering their voices, avoiding identifying proper nouns, looking behind them to make sure no one compromising is in the vicinity—because they believe no one within earshot can understand their language. I entered the conversation in the middle of a party scene: The dark-haired woman, a little drunk, had been introduced or been told to introduce herself to a man because she was really into this one kind of techno and didn't really know anyone else who's into this one kind of techno. She and the man had a really good conversation; he could recommend certain club nights that featured the kind of techno they liked; it was unclear whether they practiced the techno themselves or just enjoyed it. They smoked a huge joint and she thought he was cute, but at some point the girl had to abandon the conversation to use the bathroom, and when she came back the man was gone. Hours later she returned to the room where they'd met and saw that he was lying on the ground, half inside and half outside, with his legs on the floor of the balcony and his upper body on the floor of the bedroom. The woman asked him if he was OK and he said yes, would she like some speed, and she took a little and then went home. Besides that? Work was going well but she really wanted to focus more on her music. She was excited about getting a new tattoo tomorrow, with an artist who was expensive and had a long waiting list but was very good at flowers. The tattoo would be located on her bicep and about the size of a twelve-ounce can, though they don't do ounces here. The blonde woman was planning a trip to Italy.

Suddenly the large dog was no longer at the dark-haired woman's feet but out on the sidewalk next to the restaurant's little outdoor patio, barking. Turning heads collided with a childish shriek; then a pause, followed by a sustained wail. Called by both the blonde and the brunette in anxious unison, the dog trotted back over and lay down in its original spot. For a moment the boy, encircled by his skipping and apparently unbothered brother, stayed there in the middle of the patio with his arms over his face in anguish, crying and screaming. The heads of the restaurant swiveled back to their companions or looked nervously around the corner, wondering if the child had someone to console it or at least remove it from the premises. The girls were soon identified as those culpable, and they looked only at each other, their eyes locked in nervous giggles, the brunette's hand on the dog's collar. Finally a tall man, salt-and-pepper hair, Birkenstocks despite the chill, emerged from behind the building and approached the child, his pace slow and even, and when he reached the boy he did not crouch down to comfort him but merely looked down at him as he thrashed and flailed. Finally, the man put his hand on the boy's head. The girls, still laughing, not maliciously but nevertheless, began to hiss at each other that the man was looking at them, and the tension of the situation stretched smiles across their faces in anticipation of confrontation. The blonde one held her thin hand against the side of her face, shielding herself from his gaze; the brunette had her back to him and seemed to understand her vulnerability. The man, his hand still on his son's curly little head, looked at the women in silence for about thirty seconds, the blonde occasionally updating the brunette on his continued presence, until finally the brunette turned around, offered a meek wave and smile, and said, in English, "Sorry, I'm sorry," gesturing toward the dog's collar, which was still in her hand though she had twisted awkwardly around to face the father. The man, whose flair for drama was clearly honed, waited a beat before nodding silently and turning away. A short woman appeared, a lumpy swaying laundry bag hanging off the handle of her empty stroller; a brief recitation of events occurred, and the group walked away. I wished that I had seen what happened, to know if the child had somehow taunted the dog, if the dog had actually made contact with the child or just barked at and scared him, but I had not been paying attention. "Oh my God—what an asshole," the brunette said. "I'm going to get kicked out of the country because some man can't watch his own kid."

*

WHAT'S AMAZING ABOUT THIS STRUCTURE IS THAT YOU CAN JUST dump any material you have in here and leave it up to the reader to connect it to the rest of the work. I was going to cut that dog story, but why should

I? It evokes a mood. It relates to my themes. When I saw it happen it was somehow incredible; I was watching earned self-consciousness mutate into unearned self-preservation in real time, something I usually only saw online, where it was easier for the unbelievable to remain that way.

*

@HELENOFTROYWI ON ASTROLOGY: "PEOPLE LIKE TO SAY ECO-nomics is astrology for men, and I agree: economics is the more compli-cated, useful, interesting, and rational version of astrology"

*

I ONCE BROKE UP WITH SOMEONE WHO TOLD ME MY REASONS for doing so were "not believable." I replied that I couldn't believe he'd said that. When I told a mutual friend about it, she replied, "Well, you're a hu-man woman, not a book!" I said to her what I said to him, that the advan-tage of switching from fiction to non- was that you no longer had to worry about being believable.

*

AROUND THIS TIME, I WOKE UP ONE MORNING DISTURBED BY A vivid dream. I won't describe the dream, but I will summarize the lesson I believe it hammered home: I felt trapped, almost claustrophobic, by my inability to talk to Felix, and I wanted to ease the tension I felt between us with a jokey text message, like in the morning after a fight, or an admission of insecurity that I hoped would weaken his resistance to self-exposure.

*

THE GERMAN HEALTH INSURANCE I ULTIMATELY CHOSE WAS called TK, which had an English version of their website that advertised "above-average benefits and services." I knew for many days that I would choose TK but I put off doing anything to make the choice. It wasn't until I came home after having three drinks at a bar, where I was stood up by a thirty-seven-year-old experimental trumpet player, that I went to the TK website, downloaded the application form in English for "People In Work," emailed it to myself, and departed for the Späti where you could print stuff. When I entered the Späti my drunken sense of purpose propelled me to attempt German, and the man behind the counter either did not understand or pretended not to. "Drogen?" he asked, laughing. "Drogen? You want Drogen?" *Drogen* means "drugs." *Drucken* means "to print." Sober I would have been floridly embarrassed. I sat down at computer 4 next to a muttering large-headphoned teenager who had chat windows splayed across his screen. The German keyboard inserted *z*'s into my password and I had to type it three times, funneling my fluid concentration into the task. Finally the familiar customized background (leopard print) and list of recent chat contacts appeared. I clicked on the email I'd sent myself. I downloaded the attachment. I wanted TK. I hit Drucken. I logged out of my email. I left the computer and then returned to make sure I had logged out of my email. Having nothing to do with me the teen jolted in surprise and pulled the headphones away from his ears, as if trying to distance himself from a loud sound. At the counter the smug employee examined my paperwork as if making an assessment and winked as he handed over the TK form. I paid him in coins and when I got back to my bedroom I put the form on my desk without looking over it and fell asleep in my clothes.

*

I WONDERED IF MY DESIRE TO TALK TO FELIX WAS NOT REALLY A desire to talk to Felix but a desire to talk to someone I knew well, seriously, in depth. I was avoiding any kind of go-there conversation, it was true, but I couldn't remember the last time I'd had one with anyone, and despite his caginess about himself, Felix was very responsive to others, seemingly authentically so. His voice didn't shift into a faker register when he gave a compliment. He looked you in the eye. He seemed like someone who had certain things he didn't want to talk about, which might have been true for a number of reasons, and so he seemed to have all the facets of his life story under control. He was especially good at concealing the possibility that one of those reasons was insecurity. I suppose it was also comforting to be around someone who seemed to have no doubts, only frustrations.

*

AFTER I PRINTED OUT MY TK FORMS, I FELT I HAD MADE GREAT strides. I permitted myself to not think about them for a week.

*

LEO: I PREPARED FOR A DATE WITH A CHAIN-SMOKING AMERICAN who worked at a call center by listening to "I'm Too Sexy" and making my hair big, thinking, This is a sign that goes all out. After fifteen minutes he admitted he had recognized me on OkCupid because he followed me on Twitter and remembered my old profile picture, from before the one where I have my hair in front of my face, and in advance of the date had read all of my writing available online. I had not even considered trying to look up anyone I'd been on a date with. I said, "What do you mean, everything?" He said, "I mean everything." I said, "OK. But not, like, my college-newspaper columns?" He said, "Yes, even those." I was uncomfortable but also euphoric. I was addictive. He could have, if he'd wanted, come up with a theory about me. He knew more about me than I did. Unable to offer him an alternative personality, I homed in on what his compulsion to "possess me intellectually" (my words) and subsequent admission of that compulsion might have said about his feelings about his family, education, ex-girlfriends, and self-worth. I posed therapeutic questions and messed preeningly with my hair. I let him buy the rest of the drinks. Every time he asked me what I thought about an issue I said something like, "Well, as you know, I said it better in December 2014." Though I felt he was owed at least a kiss at the end of the evening, having spent the majority of it intimately discussing the idea of me, I said that I never kissed on the first date because I was a real germophobe, and I used the pause that followed to bid him quickly goodbye.

*

AT SOME POINT YOU HAVE TO ADMIT THAT DOING THINGS IRON-ically can have very straightforward consequences.

*

THAT EPISODE IS AN EXTREME VERSION OF WHAT HAPPENS WITH dating apps generally: The getting-to-know-you process is fabricated by the exchanging of profiles, and each person gets to foreground what they want you to know, which is usually banal information about preferences that would not necessarily be frontloaded because in spontaneous interactions people respond to the environment and/or build on what has been said before. In meetings arranged on dating apps, both parties possess information from the get-go that would ordinarily trickle in as it was relevant, making the date more like a job interview. Each person feels uncomfortable starting a conversation with, "So: I know you like bad music. Explain why you like it?" because it's weird to admit knowing that sort of thing about someone you've never met. But what else are you going to talk about? The weather? Not when the contraband info is front of mind.

*

A SIMILAR THING HAPPENS WHEN YOU MEET, IN PERSON, SOME-
one with whom you have interacted on social media. On social media, you
publish your opinions, your beliefs, your likes, your dislikes. You do this
in a more *organic* way than you do on a dating profile, but the effect is the
same: you approximate a character. Or a character is approximated; I'm not
so sure it's fair to say intention is a major factor most of the time, though in
the cases of certain reality stars and opinion columnists, the people who are
obviously not approaching social media in *good faith*, who are manipulating
it, there's got to be some amount of intentional sleight of hand. Anyway,
I'm not talking about provocateurs or celebrities; I'm talking about regular
people. We publish these things because we want other people to read them.
If we didn't care about people reading them, we would just keep a journal or
write notes on our phones. Users who are particularly good at getting other
people to read their opinions and beliefs acquire a following, become known
to lots of other users. We can't really blame the followers for doing exactly
what we wanted them to do, which is pay attention to us and, inevitably,
remember some of what we say. In fact, we probably find the fact that they
pay attention to us extremely relatable, since we find ourselves fascinating. If
we didn't find ourselves fascinating, or at least want other people to find us
fascinating, we wouldn't publish these things about ourselves.

*

ON THE U-BAHN I REMEMBERED I HAD WRITTEN AN ARTICLE IN
which I interviewed women about whether they sat on public toilet seats,
and I included my own view that it was fine, unless there was visible evidence suggesting otherwise. I could have been lying in the article, but I
doubt that possibility would occur to the chain-smoking American, whose

kiss I had rejected on grounds of germophobia. As the train approached my stop, I felt bad. What if he concluded that both of my claims were true, and that I thought he threatened more germs than a public toilet seat?

*

THE CONSEQUENCES OF PUBLIC CHARACTER BUILDING ARE NOT as fun or useful as the fantasy of social media fame suggests. It's always odd to encounter one of your followers in the noncomputer world and they say something like, "I loved your tweet about moisturizer!" or "I wanted to ask you what you thought about this subject you think quite a lot about." How do they know? Because you, thinking this was exactly what you wanted, told them. You told everyone.

*

THE SHY READER IS YELLING, "I DON'T FIND MYSELF FASCINAT-ing!" If you don't find yourself fascinating, then what are you so protective of? And why are you yelling? You just can't win.

*

VIRGO: I ARRANGED TO MEET A FRENCH PROJECT MANAGER, thirty-two, at seven fifteen at the desirable window table, which I reserved, at a tapas restaurant on Weserstrasse. Businesslike and wearing a crisp shirt, which I borrowed Frieda's iron to press, I asked about project management as if I did not know it was totally bullshit. He said it was entirely about organizing other people's schedules and streamlining projects, which meant, paradoxically, that his schedule always had to be open, in order to accommodate emergencies or unforeseen complications. I said that this was not an example of paradox but of irony, and regardless, I did not think I would do well in such a job because I would be focused on constantly rearranging the near future until it reached the optimum conditions. I had a problem with optimization generally, I said; I always wondered if there was a better way to do things. *This* was paradoxical, since by wasting so much time wondering if there was a better way to do things, I was guaranteeing myself suboptimal conditions. Anyway, I said, I was a poet and a bartender, and I liked bartending because it gave me time during the day to write my poems, specifically four hours a day. I told him that the poems all followed a certain pattern that was very hard to explain because I had come up with it myself using math and angles. He said that he was sure his job was a paradox, not ironic, and he thought ultimately that poetry should be more spontaneous and expressive than my description of my process suggested. I stuck a toothpick into the precise center of an olive and then waved the waitress over for the check.

*

AN ORGASM CAN BE IRONIC, CERTAINLY, ESPECIALLY IF IT IS DRAMATIC.

*

EARLY ON, DURING A LONG NIGHT OF DRINKING AND MAKING out in the corner of a bar, Felix asked me if I had any sexual fantasies. Usually when men ask this they get a horrible smug look in their eyes and become a different person; Felix managed to ask it naturally, to encourage a natural response, partly because we were drunk, partly because we were at ease with each other then, still wowed by our feelings and not yet bothered by each other's negative qualities, and partly because we'd been talking about some recent viral article concerning a strange sexual fantasy. I turned around—I'd been sort of leaning up against him in a booth—and replied that I wanted to fuck him with a strap-on while he read the novel I was working on.

*

MIRACULOUSLY, AT A BAR AND THANKFULLY NOT WHILE I HAD
two babies in my possession, I ran into a man I'd slept with a few times
in New York just before meeting Felix, a cable news producer who wasn't
looking for commitment because he was too busy being a cable news producer. I had always maintained we both stopped talking to each other at
around the same time. Now, something was different about him, namely
that he had a long, bleached-blond mustache, a long, bleached-blond mustache so weird and disturbing that when he began approaching me, I didn't
recognize him and felt briefly worried. It didn't seem like the sort of mustache that would stab me, but it did seem like it would talk to me for many
minutes about increasingly sexual topics. It wasn't until the mustache asked
if I recognized it that I did: Jon. I said oh and laughed and put my hand
over my heart as if he had startled me. He nodded apologetically. He was
in Berlin on vacation, his first in three years! I didn't want to be obvious
but there was no getting around that the main point of interest between
us was the mustache, so I asked what the deal was. He said his roommate
had bleached her hair the day before he shaved off his beard, and feeling
mischievous he got the idea of bleaching his mustache, because he always
waits to shave the mustache until the end, just to see how it looks, as many
men do. Though the bleaching was time- and effort-intensive—he had to
breathe through a straw while it was on his face—he had intended to keep
the mustache only for a few hours, just so he could take some pictures and
then go back to looking normal. Once he took the pictures and sent them
to friends, however, they became dedicated to the mustache's debut in public, and they dared him to wear it out. Being a little drunk by this point, he
agreed. That had been six days before; it was unclear, to both me and him,
why he still hadn't shaved it. People scooted away from him on the subway.
A woman in the street seriously shielded her young daughter from his view.
The night before, he'd been at a bar where he overheard a group of girls say-

ing, "EW—SHAVE THAT OFF," and he'd gotten so upset that he'd confronted them, saying something like, "I know my mustache looks stupid, but I'm a real person with feelings, OK?" They asked to take photos with him. He knew now that it was self-aggrandizing to think he would be able to play this character in public and not identify at all with the character. "I sometimes do a persona, you know?" I knew. "But I guess I always assumed I could distance myself from it, because the persona wasn't *me*." I said that when the persona was attached to your face it becomes a whole different thing, and he chuckled kind of wearily. Thinking I should change the subject away from something so painful, I didn't tell him that my boyfriend had died recently but I did say I'd just moved here, and he said "finally!" and congratulated me: "You always wanted to do that." I wondered if he was confusing me with someone else because I certainly had not, and also where he found the authority to say I had "always" wanted to do anything. He looked at me in a way I interpreted as pitying. Maybe he thought he had dumped me. Though I had not thought much about him since we parted ways, I suddenly wanted him to grab and kiss me and confess that he had thought of me the whole time, or at least ask me if I had time for a drink. He did neither, and after he went back to his seat, I left.

*

I'M NOT VERY GOOD AT THIS STRUCTURE. I KEEP GOING ON TOO long.

*

A FRIEND ONCE INTERPRETED MY ASTROLOGICAL BIRTH CHART, and she was stunned by the clarity of what she found. Two predictions came out of it that I still think about, one being that I would always "have difficulties with paperwork." I can't remember what birth time I'd given her or if I'd contacted my mother to ensure its accuracy, so on top of astrology not being real, it's possible the conclusions were irrelevant. Nevertheless, the paperwork thing: haunting. But also rewarding, because anytime I do my taxes I feel I have triumphed over my true nature. I suspect my friend resented me for some reason, or was making fun of me for something, because trying to nudge someone toward a lifetime of self-reflexive anxiety about paperwork is mean.

*

LIBRA: I STARTED MESSAGING WITH A GERMAN PHD STUDENT, who talked about social media and translating slang in literature. I asked him some questions about his research. He answered them intelligently and asked if I wanted to meet him the next night. After ten hours went by and I still had not responded, he sent a second message: "If I do not hear back from you, I will remember you as the person with a lot of good questions." I replied as soon as I saw it and we had two drinks at a popular bar called Ä. We talked about the academy; after years of indecision, during which I plagued my friends with endless vacillation, I had dropped out of a PhD program in the States because it had beckoned me to peek into the telescope of my future and what I saw was very depressing. When he asked me what I'd been studying, I had to think of something specific: a subject not too far-fetched but that wouldn't require me to know any German. I almost said early modern English history—an aunt of mine loved the Tudors—but caught myself. You would be doomed if you were studying early modern England and did not even know how to buy cigarettes. My face got hot. I tried to look away as if pained—the decision to leave had been a difficult one. Gender studies. "Oh, this would be very interesting now, no?" he said. I kept looking at my reflection in the window next to where we were sitting, fluffing my hair, as I discussed my fury about injustice.

*

ANOTHER JUSTIFICATION FOR THIS STRUCTURE IS THAT IT MIMics the nature of modern life, which is "fragmented." But fragmentation is one of the worst aspects of modern life. It's extremely stressful. "Fragmented" is a euphemism for "interrupted." Why would I want to make my book like Twitter? If I wanted a book that resembled Twitter, I wouldn't write a book; I would just spend even more time on Twitter. You'd be surprised how much time you can spend on Twitter and still have some left over to write a book. Our experience of time is fragmented, but unfortunately time itself is not.

*

KNOWING THIS I CAN'T HELP BUT FEEL THE BOOKS OF COLLECTED tweets you occasionally see displayed on tables at Urban Outfitters would be better as novels or memoirs that contain no tweets.

*

SEX SCENE: LYING ON MY STOMACH ON MY BED READING A BOOK on a summer afternoon as the air conditioner raged in the window, I felt a tickle on the sole of my right foot. Instead of turning around, or laughing loudly and demanding the person responsible stop, I kept my body still and eyes focused on the book, allowing my foot to twitch if it had to but otherwise staying in position. After several seconds of tickling the finger moved slowly and daintily from the sole to the ankle, the inside of my calf, the pit of my knee, and the inside of my thigh. The finger, obviously, paused. I turned the page. The finger began to trace small circles on the inside of my thigh. It moved to the hem of my skirt and under to trace the bottom of my ass. I knew that if I stopped reading I would upend the delicate unspokenness of the sex we were about to have, so I turned another page. There was a full palm on my hip, and then another mirroring it, firmly. The air conditioner shifted to a lower gear, my skirt now hiked up. I was wearing uncomfortable underwear.

He asked what I was reading. I told him the truth. As he grabbed my ass and began to massage it, he asked if it was good. I said it was very good and that he should read it. He said not to let him interrupt, pulled down the underwear, and began to eat me out from behind.

A few years ago there was a video series, called *Hysterical Literature*, in which porn stars sat at a desk reading aloud from their favorite books while, under the desk and off camera, someone stimulated them with a vibrator. It was shot in black and white. Each of the actresses begins reading carefully, as if they have strategized and practiced, but within a couple of minutes they begin to falter. The pauses, jagged and sudden, increase in frequency and duration; exhales become heavier. They have to stay focused on their books—one of which is *American Psycho*—and you can see them try to remember this as the exercise goes on. Just keep reading. About halfway through the women begin to quiver perceptibly, and giggle. One woman begins to jiggle a leg. Another stumbles over the word *magnanimity*. It wasn't explicitly a competition about who could read for the longest without coming, but I would have treated it as one. Eventually they all give up in one way or another, some theatrical, gasping, moaning, imitating Meg Ryan, others looking down, shuddering *yes*es and *oh*s, smiling knowing they are being watched. After I came once he fucked me, same position, flat on the bed, with his hand under me so I would come again, his breathing forceful and humid on my hair, whispering urgent *fuck*s until he pulled out and came. Instead of rolling off to the side he lay on top of me for a moment, heavy and sticky, a kiss on my shoulder, until I said, in a cutesy squashed-baby voice, that I couldn't breathe.

*

ONE MAN, ADVERTISED AS TWENTY-EIGHT, SHORTER THAN I, AND working in Berlin for a year on an exchange through his company, an adult study-abroad student, brought a little baggie of grapes to the park bench where we met during his lunch break. "These grapes are just so good," he crooned at the baggie. "I don't want to share these grapes with anyone." I became jealous and angry. I plucked a grape and threw it into the grass. Then I winked, crossed my legs, and extended my arm across the back of the bench; according to a Scorpio friend, Scorpio is "the sex one," though intentional sexiness divorced cynically from the act of sex is a quality many women will be familiar with, regardless of their astrological origins. The guy lived in an affluent part of town in an apartment owned by his company, which had even booked his flights for him, and he was taking a mandatory German course for which he never did his homework. I flirtatiously asked if that wasn't annoying to his classmates, who required his participation to learn, and then flirtatiously asked to hear his accent. He refused to even say hello or goodbye. On the weekends he went to an Irish bar in the Europa Center or clubbing with his mates. I took one grape and found it very good, but I qualified that grapes have a much lower potential for goodness than other fruits.

*

WHEN THE THIRTY-SEVEN-YEAR-OLD EXPERIMENTAL TRUMPET player wrote to me again, I deleted his message without replying. About a month later I realized that he hadn't stood me up—I'd gone to the wrong bar.

*

THE WEEK REPRIEVE I'D GIVEN MYSELF TO NOT THINK ABOUT health insurance passed. For my purposes there could really be no better name for a German health insurance company. I didn't make it up.

*

OF COURSE I WAS NEVER GOING TO FIND LOVE OR EVEN BRIEF satisfaction this way, going on fake dates. I knew that. Not everyone is looking to find love or even brief satisfaction all the time. Yet a small part of me mused that once I had become all the zodiac signs, there was a very slim possibility that I might achieve a complete understanding of humanity . . . and, by extension, my*self.*

*

SOMEONE POSTED ON FACEBOOK: DOES ANYONE HAVE RITUALS for moving house? I typed into the comment box, then deleted before I posted it, "Packing and complaining." Not what she meant.

*

THE BABIES BEGAN WAKING UP EARLIER DURING OUR WALKS, and they were increasingly difficult to keep from crying in the public spaces available to me.

*

SAGITTARIUS: TO ANOTHER PROJECT MANAGER, I EXPRESSED A desire to be constantly in motion, cycling through phases of life and the locations in which I experienced them every two to three years. I would never get married or have children or envision my life more than five years in advance. After Berlin I planned to move to Chile, where I would learn Spanish and read Neruda. I offered to pay for the drinks multiple times, even though he kept reassuring me, in faint, bewildered tones, that we should just deal with that at the end. The man, a neutral Swede with geometric wrists and precise gestures who had enjoyed the translations of Neruda he'd read, was wearing a shirt with an elaborate collar made by a popular designer I recognized, and I asked him how much it cost. He said he got it on eBay and if you bought designer clothes anywhere else you were an idiot.

I laughed, and then said I had in my past racked up nearly twenty-five thousand dollars in credit card debt, which began innocently enough with some bill-paying issues but then escalated because I was taking too many taxis and buying too many dinners out, and then I started doing a lot of coke. I had wanted to spend time studying philosophy, so on top of all this I kept the amount of time I spent working for pay to an absolute minimum. I decided as I watched him watch me skeptically that I wanted to have sex with him and made a very straightforward comment about how difficult it must be to take off his unusual shirt, but because I had been so obnoxious the innuendo made my personality seem even worse and he left after the first glass of wine.

*

EVENTUALLY I WENT ON A DATE UNASSISTED BY THE DATING APP. I noticed a guy at a Greek café on a Monday, and then on Wednesday, and then on Friday as I was checking Twitter and looking miserably at the TK form, which despite my drunken initiative I had not yet filled out, he came over and asked me if I would go to a bar with him that evening. So simple! So old-fashioned! I said not that many people hit on you in person anymore, and when he doubted me I said I'd just read an article about women who refuse to date anyone they didn't meet on an app. He said, as if unable to stop himself, "Well, we'll have to get married," but then he seemed to be embarrassed about it.

*

I DECIDED THAT I SHOULD SOON PICK A DAY TO TRY TO GET A walk-in appointment at the Ausländerbehörde. I picked May 29, a Monday. I would show up at 4:30 a.m. and wait, surrounded by more deserving applicants, for the doors to open at seven. When I asked Frieda if she would come with me to interpret she said, "No, it is really too early." I said she wouldn't have to come until just before seven and she looked at me and said, "I knew that when I made my answer."

*

CAPRICORN: I HAD MOVED TO BERLIN TO FOCUS ON MY CAREER AS an entrepreneur, I told an Australian hairdresser. His business was mainly house calls, on his bike; when he asked what sort of business I was starting I said I didn't know, but maybe he and I should collaborate on an app. Maybe many hairdressers would want to advertise their services on our app, where they could also post profiles and before-and-after photos, and where users could schedule appointments for hairdressers to come to their houses. Seamless for hair! Hairless! No. Less hair? No. It would have to be a pun, though, because there are so many opportunities to make puns out of hair. He said he didn't feel like he needed an app; he liked getting business by word of mouth, which had served him well so far, and he would feel stressed by something in his phone constantly telling him he had the opportunity to work more. I said I didn't understand that but after years of alienating those around me with my ambition I had come to accept that some people were just not ambitious and that was OK. More for me, ha ha. When he began to talk about himself, I acted closed off and dismissive, nodding with my mouth closed, inscrutable.

*

AN IMPORTANT THING TO REMEMBER WHEN LYING, TO REMAIN cool and not nervous, is that other people care much more about themselves than they care about you. It never occurred to me that some of these men might be faking it with me.

*

I TOLD MYSELF THAT THIS WAS WHAT SEPARATED ME FROM FE-lix: I never used the average person's presumed self-centeredness to make the men think I was something they might want in order to manipulate them long-term. If anyone had wanted to go out with me again, I reasoned they would have had to have something seriously wrong with them, and it was for their own good that I was unavailable. One wasted night is a fun story, not really wasted. A wasted extended period of time is likely to inspire you to waste even more.

*

THE EX-BOYFRIENDS THINK THIS IS OUTRAGEOUS SELF-EXONERATION and delusion, which surprises them, because I was always so grounded be-fore, ha ha. They feel some obligation to finish, having gotten this far, but they have to admit, they're looking forward to reading other things.

*

AQUARIUS: I REMARKED ON WHAT WAS, TO ME, THE MOST AN-noying difference between Europe and the United States: no one brought you tap water here. Were Europeans walking around dehydrated? Did they need less water? The Turkish ad salesman laughed and said they were just lazy and didn't want to have to get up to pee all the time. He had just been skydiving and when he asked if I had ever been skydiving I said yes, and then I said that it was unfortunate that it was a cliché to say you enjoyed "trying new things," because I just loved trying new things. I was trying to teach myself to DJ, for example, because I also loved new technologies. I watched his facial expression flicker at "DJ" but he dutifully asked what sort of new technologies were arising in techno and I said most people just used their laptops, but there were lots of different programs and that maybe once I got good he could design a brand for me.

*

WHEN I WAS SEVEN YEARS OLD MY MOTHER TOOK ME TO SEE THE film adaptation of Louise Fitzhugh's 1964 classic children's novel *Harriet the Spy*. The movie starred Michelle Trachtenberg as a sixth grader who keeps a notebook of "spy" observations, which include field notes on "missions" (breaking and entering) as well as mean commentary on her friends and family. The notebook is a classic black-and-white marbled composition book with the word *PRIVATE* taped over the front; this mandate is ignored by the rich popular bully, Marion Hawthorne, who finds the notebook while Harriet and her friends, Janie and Sport, are playing in a park. Marion, in a precocious houndstooth blazer, gathers the class around and begins to read aloud, to the tiny Michelle Trachtenberg's freckled distress. "The only thing more pathetic than being Marion Hawthorne," Marion begins, in her taunting nasal singsong, "is wanting to be Marion Hawthorne." Janie and Sport try to stop her, but their entreaties only spur Marion to flip to the pages detailing their own shortcomings. "Janie really creeps me out. I wonder if she'll grow up to be a total nutcase." "Sport is so poor he can't even afford food. Why can't his father just get a real job?" "If I was the boy with the purple socks, I'd hang myself." Etc. Harriet's friends abandon her, joining a collective "Spy Catcher Club" to prevent her from carrying out her missions. Her parents confiscate her notebook after her grades drop; eventually, there's a *Carrie*-esque scene involving blue paint. Harriet begins to enact cruel, specific revenge, made possible by her sleuthing campaigns, on all the kids individually, deepening their animosity toward her. It sounds dark, and it is. The resolution happy ending only arrives after Harriet's former nanny, Rosie O'Donnell, advises her to apologize to everyone and to lie about how she didn't mean the cruel things she wrote.

When I saw this as a child, I didn't take away the lessons intended, which were that lying or omitting the truth is sometimes necessary to maintain friendships, and that if you're going to keep a private notebook you should be careful about where you leave it. Instead, I began to fantasize about undergoing Harriet's dramatic ordeal myself. The idea that everyone I knew might care about my private thoughts was appealing, as was the possibility of people knowing my negative internal monologue without my having to tell them. When the class became obsessed with making Harriet miserable, all I could see was that they were obsessed. I asked my mother to get me a black-and-white composition notebook and began to write down all the mean stuff I could think of. My report focused specifically on one friend, Kayla, who lived down the street; I wrote that she had stringy hair and that I never had fun when my mom made me spend the night at her house. We had recently begun painting our nails ourselves, and I wrote that I found it disturbing that she painted her toenails with horizontal strokes instead of vertical ones.

A day later, I went over to Kayla's house with my notebook ostentatiously guarded at my chest. "This is my private notebook," I told her. "I got it yesterday. You can't look at it." She asked what I wrote in it. "None of your business," I said. After we spent some time on her swing set, I left the notebook in the yard and went home. Soon after, my mother received a call from Kayla's mother, saying that Kayla had read my abandoned private notebook and was crying. I can't remember if I was punished—it's possible I wasn't—but I do remember panicking as soon as I realized that what I'd done would have consequences beyond being sent to my room. I had ceded my thoughts in exchange for becoming the focus of attention, and now I had less control over who I was to other people. Kayla and her mother would forever see me a certain way—as a careless little bitch who didn't know what she was talking about. But a careless little bitch who didn't know what she was talking about is not as bad as what I actually was: someone who would rather other people think of her as a careless little bitch who didn't know what she was talking about than not think of her at all.

*

PISCES: I LOVE SLEEPING, I SAID TO THE MAN WHO HAD JUST bragged that he slept four hours a night. He was German and worked at an art gallery and wrote articles for magazines and wore nice shoes and glasses. What's more, I had vivid dreams that I loved to describe to other people. For example: Last week I dreamed that an ex-boyfriend had called begging me to come to his house, but when I got there it was under construction. There was dust everywhere, except in the bathroom where he could be found sweeping up pine needles, morosely. For example: Two weeks ago, I dreamed another ex-boyfriend was lying on the floor of a large and endless high school gymnasium, rolling around like a modern dancer and yelling that I needed to stop drinking so much because it was giving me breast cancer. Later in the dream I was flying over Albuquerque, which I somehow knew was Albuquerque, in a very small plane. For example: Three weeks ago, I dreamed I was in a field of wheat and a man I'd never met before was speaking to me in Russian, but I somehow knew he was my brother, reincarnated after having died when I was eight. The poor German man said quietly that he was sorry and asked if I kept a dream journal. I said yes, every day. Then he asked if I was liking Berlin and I said that it was OK except that I had been scammed out of a deposit for an apartment, being a very gullible person.

*

DID I EVER CHEAT ON FELIX? YES. OF COURSE. I CHEAT ON EVERYONE.

*

WHEN THE MAN WHO ASKED ME OUT IN PERSON WALKED INTO the bar, I thought that if he was interesting and we got along I would just tell him the facts, that after spending a few years in New York working for a popular but negligible website I had come to Berlin because a boyfriend I was about to break up with died and I had felt so strangely empty that when the idea to go to Berlin appeared I latched onto it, relieved to return to inclination. The boyfriend, I would add, had been operating a fake conspiracy theory account on Instagram; he had always given off an air of deceptive mystery, the evidence of which one could never quite put one's finger on. If it went really well I might even confess to having lied to pretty much everyone I'd met so far in Berlin, a guilty and distraught look on my face as I did so, admitting that it was an obviously psychological coping mechanism that I could nevertheless not overcome . . . until now. It would be whimsical, pitiable, and direct, a strong introduction that would balance vulnerability with originality and self-awareness. With Americans you had to worry about an extended trip to Europe making you seem moneyed. What do you mean, you had no program? No job? No fellowship? But people from other countries—this guy from the café was British, and hot, with that tousled hairstyle British men have—so he knew what plane tickets could cost, how easy it was to not save the money for retirement or the purchase of a home but instead spend it on carefree visions of canals and language-barrier bloopers. Yes—if the guy from the café was interesting and we got along, I would acknowledge that my situation was strange and my response to it selfish but I would assure him that I had undergone significant reflection and now felt "over it," did not think so much about Felix anymore, no longer connected the word *grieving* with myself, and was vowing henceforth to stop lying to innocent men I met on the internet. I could add that I believed I had reacted this way because my sadness about Felix's death was incongruous with my structural view of him as a delusional, perfidious, and generally awful person, and this produced within me anguish and confusion that manifested in mimicking the delusions and perfidy that had made Felix so awful. In addition to probably offering me some catharsis, my confession would serve as a handy test to see if the guy was too sentimental about death. Anyway, it had been almost six months. Four months. It was only when I saw people in the street who resembled Felix, the square head, the smirky walk, the strutty smile, that I remembered why I had come to a country where I didn't speak the language or know anyone in the first place.

The guy from the café and I looked at the menus without reading them, established that we would both be ordering red wine, and cautiously approached the notion of getting an entire bottle—he began the sentence and I finished it nodding. I got out my wallet and he accepted my ten euros before noting he thought we paid at the end. He was being polite; he knew we paid at the end; I felt stupid, remembering all the times I'd been left clutching unwanted currency as the waitress whisked away to fill orders or smoke a cigarette, but at least I was thus far unburdened by obligation. The hazardous candles cast a flattering dark, and this place had a chandelier made out of rusting mattress springs, a replicable ingenuity that was nevertheless impressive. Because he and I had not met online I opened with, "So. What are your interests?" to approximate the experience of meeting online, and I delivered the question matter-of-factly, crossing my right leg over my left and grabbing my wine glass as I did so. He laughed and said, "Continental philosophy," adding "just kidding" a little too soon for the joke to click, though it was good to know he knew the term "continental philosophy"—I was also on this plane, intimidated by things I was aware of but did not fully understand. He asked if a profession counted as an interest, and I said that in New York it would but here no. He was trying to write a novel but it wasn't going well; instead he had procrastinated by writing a cookbook, for which he'd received an advance of thirty-five hundred pounds. When pressed for more details, he explained that the cookbook included meditations on various ingredients, often with references to their occurrences in art and literature, and was based on recipes his parents had made separately. "I guess it's kind of a memoir in herbs," he said, smiling, performing well a sentence he'd almost certainly said dozens of times. "It's a little gratuitous, and a little embarrassing, but." I said there were far too many gratuitous and embarrassing memoirs by women and not enough by men, so I thought it was good for balance. Feminist. I didn't mind this sort of thing as long as the book didn't pretend to be anything but a memoir in herbs if indeed that's all it was. In fact, I liked it. Were his parents divorced? He raised his eyebrows and said no but if they had been, wouldn't that be quite a personal question? I said, "Only if you think parents matter." He asked if mine were and I said yes. He said he was sorry and I docked two points. Among his subsidiary interests, "hobbies," he did not mention coffee or specific types of alcohol or "travel," which was a good sign, though he did say, unapologetically and without irony, that he liked podcasts. I said I listened to podcasts every day and enjoyed the experience about one out of ten times, knowing, as I watched his subtle frown, that I was being mean. He asked how did I find the time to listen to podcasts every day and I explained: I worked nights as a pub crawl tour guide for an exploitative company that required me to wear a dorky polo shirt and never paid when they were supposed to, so during the day I had a lot of time to take walks, which I liked because they revealed a Berlin that did not cater to screaming tourists as well as kept me away from the internet, which did not work on my phone. He laughed. I asked what his novel was about and he said he absolutely would not tell me. He had lived in York, Sydney, Hong Kong, Cape Town, Sydney, Cambridge, Bangkok, Tokyo, and, for three months, Los Angeles, until he finally admitted he should just move to Berlin—his mother was German, a fact somehow omitted from his biography until this point—after a relationship with the friend he was staying with in the U.S. soured. I asked if his novel was about male friendship and he said no. I asked if it was about globalization and he said no. I asked if he liked Tokyo and he said yes, but it was expensive, which didn't really matter because he had rich parents, but he nevertheless preferred Bangkok, which was cheap but was also the only city in Southeast Asia that had a middle class. He knew it was problematic to feel comfortable in that kind of situation but he did not believe individuals were responsible for the systems in which they operated. Besides, he added, the humidity was an equalizer. He rolled his own cigarettes and was smoking them continuously, though he swore he only did that when he drank. I waited for him to ask, "And what are *your* interests?" but he never did. A disappointment bloomed within me, but I refused to start talking about myself without a prompt. I kept asking questions—he had a sister but she was delinquent, he had lived in Berlin for a year, alone in an old GDR apartment block in Mitte that he suspected was going to be renovated soon, such that he might be kicked out. After I exhausted him he asked if it got boring, introducing myself to tourists every night, explaining where I was from and why I had moved to Berlin over and over, giving them the same restaurant recommendations and tips for beating the crowds on Museum Island. I told him no because I made up a different story every time. Last night, for example, I was a burlesque dancer. He looked at my breasts with exaggerated skepticism, which I appreciated. "People will believe anything," I said, "especially if it's a little unbelievable." He said, "Oh, will they?" and asked me why he should think that I was who I said I was if I was such a practiced fabulist. I smiled naughtily and said he shouldn't. Really circuitous, I know. I asked him to roll me a cigarette and he said of course. I went to light it on the candle and he yelled, "No!" It is, apparently, considered bad luck for sailors. We sat silently smoking for a moment, careful to blow away from each other, as the din of the room filled in around us. He asked if I would like a glass of water and I said I would, and through the entryway I could see him at the water station, pouring a glass and gulping it down entirely, like a child who has been running around outside with his friends and who, upon breathily crossing the threshold to his kitchen, is greeted by a motherly arm holding a drink. He poured two more and brought them back.

I suppose it was the longest I'd gone without having sex since I lost my virginity, but a few months is nothing serious. Nevertheless, now, as he looked me in the eye while setting down my glass of water, the stupid little things that people do when communicating desire, I was struck by the prospect before me. I could have sex with a confident, functional, good-looking man. I realized then that I had been worried about it, the question of whether he wanted to sleep with me. Throughout our conversation, little worries dashed in and out of the back of my mind: Was he just humoring me? Were my conversational missteps overpowering? Did I seem boring or crazy or preoccupied with some issue that he did not want to be hustled into helping me resolve? I realized right then, with the dumb locking of eyes across the flickering table, that I no longer needed to worry. When I was younger I had relished my role as a sexual gatekeeper and made a fool of myself, dangling the key in front of boys at lectures, boys at parties, boys in the dining hall, laughing, flirting, teasing, until finally I gave in and went home with everyone. Now it was chastening, to know I was pretty enough and socially aware enough and young enough to more or less get whatever I wanted. Maybe we could have had an interesting discussion about that, about the discomfort of being at the peak of your powers, of being able to manipulate even your disadvantages into tools, but I was not going to bring it up. It was not very relatable, especially to men, though he was charming enough that he would probably relate. I didn't have a strong inclination to sleep with him or not, but I liked, too, the nerves that came with having to decide. He leaned across our wobbling table, avoiding the dangers of candle and wine glasses, and kissed me.

Instead of sex, I'm ashamed to say, I imagined our relationship: He would be initially very sweet and progressively less so. He would always leave our mornings-after at a reasonable hour. Eventually I would have to tell him I'd lied about my biography, and he would be upset, but it would be because he was allowed to be, not because it truly hurt him. We would keep small things from each other because neither of us really understood ourselves and we would not want the other person to uncover such intimate knowledge first. I would constantly ask if I should stay in Berlin or go back to the United States, and if it was worth the trouble to learn German, and he would never offer anything but a sincere effort at logic: If I left, x; if I stayed, y. He, Z, would never be a factor, because a man should not affect a woman's right to choose what she does with her life. Similarly, his tenderness would be calculated, never shifting into vulnerability; I, in turn, would demand from him some sign of emotional seriousness, though not because I really wanted it, not because I had ever felt in love with him, but because I would want to know he had felt in love with me.

Or maybe it would have been completely different and I was succumbing to my emotional turmoil. Maybe he would have broken the spell. He said, "I am going to get up and go to the toilet, and when I come back I am going to ask if you would like to come home with me." He stood up, maneuvering around the crowd of low tables, and turned the corner. The bathroom had a single toilet, no urinal, and was located at the end of a short hallway across from another loud room; he would have to wait. We had shared a carafe of wine, almost certainly more than one liter, we had noted, and combined with the cigarettes and the noise and the low light, I was drunk. The nerves proliferated and I no longer liked them. I picked up my jacket and left.

*

WHAT CAN WE LEARN FROM LITERATURE? SOMETIMES THINGS may feel like they've been going on forever, but really it's only been about forty pages.

*

THE EX-BOYFRIENDS MEAN THIS IN THE MOST LOVING WAY, BUT they're feeling like they really dodged a bullet here.

NELL'S WRITING GROUP CONSISTED OF HER AND ME SITTING IN her salon-like bedroom on Karl-Marx-Strasse and discussing issues of plot and structure, her being "not really into style." When I blinked at this, she added that she appreciated it in other writers, but it just wasn't really for her. Since I was mysterious and unproductive and never brought any work to shop, I didn't feel I had the right to object.

After three sessions I decided I would ask her if she would come with me to the Ausländerbehörde to help me apply for a visa. Since I'd contributed no writing to our writing group, in a way she owed me. In another way I owed her, as I had not given her any material to later mock in her own semiautobiographical novel, but I wanted to hold on to this transactional understanding of our relationship. I gave her feedback (three specific compliments, followed by a constructive piece of criticism that was substantive but never as big as the biggest compliment); she could give me early-morning translation skills. Before our first meeting, she sent me a three thousand–word story about a woman who had a compulsive acupuncture habit, written from the perspective of someone who seemed to have never heard of acupuncture or women, and I told her the moments conveying the appeal of *wellness* trends were apt and she should worry less about depicting the peculiarity of the trends through the unnatural voice. When she herself expressed a hair-twirling guilt about her own penchant for burning certain incenses to effect specific changes in her life, which she said helped her feel less "neurotic" though she knew it seemed "woozy," I said, "If you have an imaginary problem, an imaginary solution usually works," which Felix used to tell me whenever I made fun of myself for doing yoga. (Well, I would point out, arguing against myself more than him, yoga is actually exercise.) I touched her forearm confidentially and said I had a huge jar of turmeric powder, an alleged guard against inflammation, on my counter. "Turmeric!" she exclaimed, gesturing toward her own kitchen. It was only after I left the apartment and was passing the closed discount shoe stores and chain bakeries that I realized telling someone who was basically an acquaintance that her problems were "imaginary" was pretty rude. My problems were certainly imaginary, but I did not know what hers were. If you want to become a nondescript yet consistent presence in people's lives, able to take advantage of their companionship without investing emotionally, offending them is not the best way to go about it. The next time we met, she said she would have loved to help me with my visa interview but couldn't because she was going to Venice for the Biennale that week.

People I had no reason to trust assured me the visa case I had constructed for myself was solid: registration with the police; a bank account with more than ten thousand euros in it (thanks to the previously mentioned rich friend, who smugly agreed to smugly transfer me a huge sum so that I might print out an inflated balance before transferring the money back to him); fictional letters from three fictional freelance employers testifying they would employ me for x hours per week at rates of y for copyediting work, copywriting work, and article-writing work; a falsified letter from my mother, translated into German by Google translate and corrected by Frieda, testifying she would give me one thousand euros per month should

I encounter financial trouble; my résumé; a photo of my university diploma; a printed portfolio of several of my articles; a financial plan (I would have no expenses); and a passport photo I took in a booth in the Hermannplatz U-Bahn station, the greenish light casting a murderous mauve look to my visage. I assembled all these in a large binder, having been told by several blog posts and one acquaintance that Germans *love* binders. A woman I met at a very bad poetry reading told me she had gone in with a letter from an employer whose address was listed as "Mary-Jane-Strasse 69"—they had been joking around in the office that day and forgotten to change it—and she was granted her work permit within a month. A musician from New Zealand told me he received his visa the same day he applied. A man from New Jersey said, "It was always easy for Americans, but it's even more so now," raising his eyebrows and gesturing, I kid you not, at the falafel he was eating. When friends back in New York asked why I wanted to stay in Berlin I took to mimicking the responses of other people, like these: It was just "so different" here, so "chill," the clubs were "amazing," nobody worked, and now that the weather was getting warmer you could drink outside! The socioeconomic benefits of legal outdoor drinking should not be waved aside as mere frivolous recreation! The New Yorkers could not argue—everyone was leaving town these days—but as I said these things I sounded much dumber than I had when I lived there, as if I'd been overtaken by some exploitative self-help program, so I hoped they suspected something was wrong.

The only problem was that the TK form was very confusing and confusingly translated, containing requests for health insurance card numbers and exemptions and cancelation confirmations. One section was titled "Recruit New Members and Win," but it seemed to be more of a hypothetical opportunity, acknowledging that I myself might have been recruited and that someone else might win, but also to remind me that in the future I could put myself in the shoes of a winning recruiter. When I tried to visit the company's office in Friedrichshain to discuss the form with an agent—assuming a phone call, without the aid of body language, would be impossible—I could find no office where an office had been promised, just an eerie car dealership and a discount grocery store. I walked around the block and stood in the grocery store's parking lot with my neck bent over my phone to look at the map I'd loaded in advance, trying to find some hidden alley, a fork in the road, a cul-de-sac that would make clear where I'd gone wrong. I finally gave up and, though I'd spent the entire morning looping the babies around the disused airfield that had been converted into a public park, watching early-morning rollerbladers speed up and down the tarmac, and feeling sympathetic for the remaining twin who had not yet said his first word, I decided to walk around after my failure. I knew I was just east of Felix's old apartment; with the hope that I might run into an ex and confirm he looked worse than when we were together, I started off in that direction and decided to let my navigational intuition guide me. I could have looked at the map on my phone, yes, but I told myself I would not.

I'd spent weeks in this neighborhood but didn't know it well. From east to west, it transitioned from industrial, to quiet and neutral, to aggressively familial, to Felix's Kiez, which was touristy and insufferable at night. Scattered throughout were the dirty and mad holdouts of legendary squats and DIY venues that had once ruled the area, whose heyday we were sad to have missed; their offspring today were either unobtrusive or flying combative banners in response to attempted evictions. I'd been to a show at Rigaer 94, somewhere around here, which had been raided and reoccupied since, its doors cut out at least once; Frieda had told me about a new squat a bit farther north, in an old carpet factory that belonged to the owner of a fast fashion company. On the other side of Warschauer Strasse was the major draw for bright-eyed money-spending tourists and self-righteous expats, Berghain, the former power plant that now housed the best club in the world, bounced by a notoriously scrupulous and face-tattooed doorman whom the tourists inevitably came to resent and the expats pretended not to revere; the club had so far resisted succumbing to badness by seeming to ignore the conversation about it, remaining popular enough that it could continue to reject the sort of people who would make it unpopular. When the subdued apartment blocks gave way to obvious renovations and facades decorated with kid-friendly murals advertising peace and acceptance—"mom graffiti" as Felix had it—I knew I was close. The neighborhood was at maximum capacity in terms of places to buy customized T-shirts. A pirate-themed ice cream shop was just opening, though it was after noon. A Vietnamese place I may have been to. A tram rambling down the middle of the street. The Platz that hosted a popular flea market I'd never been to. It felt a little like I was stealing Berlin from Felix, like I shouldn't be there, even though he never liked living there and had, for all intents and purposes, failed at it, based on any typical metric of life success for an upper-middle-class white man with bohemian inclinations: friendships formed, local language learned, sustainable income procured, artwork made. Yet he was constantly mentioning the two years he spent there—I'm pretty sure it was two years, there was some documentation—and whenever he appended an anecdote with some version of "I lived in Berlin so," or "In Berlin they do it differently," I would respond, "Oh, you lived in Berlin?" as if that were the first I'd heard of it. I would never do it like he did it. The health insurance forms were surmountable and I was going to surmount them, at which point I would act as if it had been no big deal.

When I reached Simon-Dach-Strasse, I knew I should turn left, pass the bar where we'd had our first "date," and then turn right to end up in front of the door to Felix's building. It was ridiculous of me to suggest that I might not be able to find it again; I knew exactly where it was. I could probably get someone to let me in if I wanted, but there would be no point in that. His roommates might still be living there—the apartment was very cheap, rented through an old contract, and it would have been foolish to abandon it—and if I ran into them they might recognize me and ask me questions. I would just walk past the building, have some kind of emotional experience, and then continue on across the Oberbaumbrücke, where I would look at the TV tower and the Spree before walking back into Kreuzberg, cutting a straight line through Görlitzer Park, across the canal, and into Neukölln. When I turned left and saw that the bar we went to wasn't there anymore, I almost cried, which was pathetic. I hate crying, especially about facts of life. Bars closed all the time, for all sorts of reasons, and most of them had been settings for first dates that didn't lead to everlasting love. What was that bar to me? What was any bar to me? I'd been there a handful of times, all of which were now tinged with betrayal. Yet I was desperate to find some great significance in its closure. I think it had been there for years, but not that many years, and regardless, I hadn't been going to it for years. It was so cheap, and the bartenders were rude. Briefly I tried to blame gentrification, the shrieking children all around me and their huffy parents waiting to pick them up from Kita, but I had no claim to that complaint and no basis for the assumption even if I could have made it. I turned right onto Felix's street and no longer cared to see his apartment, but it was there, fine. I was already having my emotional experience.

Waiting at the corner across from the sausage stand I noticed graffiti that read "UGLY BOYS" on the side of an apartment building, but I was too sad to take a picture. On the easy ascent to Oberbaumbrücke a couple waited for their strip of souvenir photos at the Photoautomats there. In New York photo booths were popular at parties and weddings and in bars, but the photos they produced usually appeared new, in color, too detailed. Sometimes the booth came with "props" to help subjects convey kookiness—comically large sunglasses in neon colors, false mustaches attached to little wooden sticks. But in Berlin the booths looked antique, and the photos were a grainy black and white, though the booths had only been installed throughout the city in 2004, as part of a *project*, as if Berlin needed more opportunities for nostalgia. The woman waiting had a spiky ponytail that suggested she straightened her hair with a flat iron; the man wore a zipped-up sweatshirt and boat shoes. I'd never asked Felix to get our photos taken together when I visited, and he never suggested it, and I knew why, because it would have been cheesy, because everyone did it, but still I wished I had one, if not to reject an opportunity to be sentimental about it then to have a set of flattering photos of myself appearing to have a good time. The photos were always flattering—high contrast, dramatic shadows, blurring imperfections—and the people in them always seemed to have stumbled into the booth in a moment of playful joy, never caught uninspired for a pose, probably because they were usually drunk or high. There were a few photos of Felix and me, our faces always mockingly serious, never smiling, always taken by one of us awkwardly holding a cell phone in front of our faces and so to a certain extent provisional. I had some saved on my phone that I'd avoided looking at; when I finally did go through them, the first thing I noticed was how uncomfortable I looked to be photographed. My face was thinner than I imagined it, my hair was not as boring as I was always complaining, but I felt ashamed to be next to Felix, who managed to look both aloof and comic.

. . .

MRS. DALLOWAY SAID SHE WOULD FILL OUT THE HEALTH INSUR-
ance forms herself. Blistered and home I lay on the floor in my bedroom and tried to work up the necessary courage, saying to myself in my head several times that I would get up after ten more seconds. The floor was a cool, ugly laminate, inconsistently installed and hilly, with a few peeling edges here and there, and because dirt just sat on top of it, I could feel little rocks and bits incorporating themselves into the backs of my arms and embellishing my T-shirt. There was a vacuum in the hallway next to the front door that I'd recently tried to use but couldn't figure out how to turn on, and because I'd been living in the apartment for two months I didn't feel I could ask Frieda how it worked without making it clear I had never vacuumed my bedroom, or any other part of the apartment. I could have used a broom, but I did not. She knocked on the door.

"Come in," I said.

"Oh," she said. "You are on the floor?"

I agreed with her. I said I was trying to gather the strength to fill out my health insurance forms, which didn't make any sense. I recited some lines, which I had apparently memorized.

"Do you have them in German?"

Since they were German health insurance forms, they were available online in German. I had not even considered this as something that could be helpful to me. I got off the floor and sat in front of the computer.

In fact, the form I'd been attempting to fill out was not the correct form at all. Frieda stood over me like a parent helping a child with her homework and navigated me to the page I needed. As she scanned the health insurance application for foreign nationals not required to enroll in the German pension scheme, her mouth moving silently over the long German words, she interrupted herself. "By the way, I am here to ask if you can borrow me a tampon?"

This opportunity to be reciprocal cheered me up immediately. Could I ever! My tampons were unusually stylish. The nature of occasionally writing women's interest stories meant I had at some point been signed up as a subscription member for an organic tampon company, which every month for about a year had sent two boxes of tampons—one regular and one super, both in tastefully patterned packaging—to my apartment in New York, as well as a newsletter full of mantras like "We are worthy of the ability to be the sovereigns of our own bodies." It would be a medical emergency if a person needed all the tampons they sent, and I always donated half. I brought the rest to Berlin because they were nice—I had not realized there existed such variability in tampon quality until I used them—and because I'm cheap. It also seemed like a good way to avoid a translation problem at the drugstore. I rolled my chair over to the end of my bed, pulled out my bag of tampons, and handed one to Frieda.

She looked puzzled. "What is this?"

"It's a tampon. I know, it's a little cute. For every box they sell, the company donates a box to a village in Africa." I sounded much less cynical about this project than I knew myself to be.

"But . . . how does it work?"

Knowing Europeans mainly used tampons designed to be inserted manually, as in with one's finger, I opened the tampon and demonstrated the applicator system.

"You throw it away? This seems very wasteful?"

I agreed.

"Do women in Africa use tampons?"

I said definitely, at least some did, but that the donations might also be pads and that I thought that if it wasn't a question of religious/cultural norms it was a question of access, or rather that the questions of religious/cultural norms and access intersected. What's more, menstruation stigma truncated many girls' educations. I gave her a new tampon that had not been part of a demonstration.

"Do you buy these tampons without knowing the point of them?"

I said I had gotten them for free through work.

"Ach so." Her eyes returned to the form. "Do you make more than forty-eight hundred your-ohs pro month?"

"Yes."

"OK—"

"No! I'm joking."

"Ah, OK. I thought it was a little weird. You wouldn't need to live with me." She wrote down every difficult-to-understand question in my notebook, numbering them as she went so I could follow along on my own later. She refused the offer of more tampons than the one she immediately needed and left.

I emailed the application to myself to print and clicked over to Twitter, thinking I'd earned some time mindlessly registering others' impressions of the world. It was, as ever, both placating and stressful, the stakes of any comment or discussion unclear except that they were high. I replied to posts by people I knew but had never met in person and took solace in the idea that to someone else I might seem like part of a clique. I assumed they all assumed I was in New York; I had said nothing online about going to Berlin because there was no reason to say anything online about going to Berlin, and if there were no reason to mention it then it would read as bragging or out of touch. None of the people who followed me were in Berlin, or had followed me because I frequently posted commentary on Berlin, so Berlin was, coming from me, irrelevant. If I wanted to brag, there had to be plausible deniability for the boast. For example: I had posted about leaving my job because I was excited for people to stumble upon a detail of my life and have to think about it, taking a moment to resituate me in their vision of the world. But I had also done it so that people would stop "pitching" me pointless things on the behalf of corporations and cultural producers. I watched someone with sixty-four followers who was studying for an undergraduate degree in literature accuse a prominent television critic of classism and go unacknowledged. I watched someone with two thousand followers accuse someone with seventy-five hundred followers of exhibiting racism at an event that no one repeating the accusation in outrage had attended, though they would all *love* to see a video. @HelenofTroyWI, inspired by Twitter's biannual widespread discussion of bagels, tweeted that having Manichaean opinions about food was a sure sign someone was bad in bed. I watched a female writer, A, say disparaging things about another female writer in generalized passive-aggressive terms; I was able to figure out the latter's identity, B, by messaging someone who I suspected disliked A because of various comments she'd made in the past. That led me to the profile of another female writer, C, who was saying that if she possessed a collection of traits that described B and only B she would kill herself. Having met none of these women but read their writing, I was on Team B. I considered posting something underhanded to express my allegiance to the approximately twelve people who would know what I was talking about but did not, thinking about what might happen if A saw it and then one day I happened to meet her. I asked my source if A had some personal problem with B and the source replied that she had no idea, but they didn't seem like natural allies, did they? Political urgencies dissolved into complaints about the heat wave in New York and the functioning of the subway and Why French Women Embrace Their Dark Circles and Watch a BBC Anchor Stare into Space for Four Minutes on Live TV. My spine curved. My hands were clammy on the keyboard. Into the soft underside of my forearm the cheap desk burrowed a straight groove. I heard Frieda leave the apartment, slamming the door to make it close all the way. I responded earnestly to a funny woman's earnest request for book recommendations. I mocked a conservative commentator's mixed metaphor. I found it hard to believe so many people felt as cynical and blasé about North Korean nuclear missile tests as their jokes about hoping for "the sweet release of death" suggested. I read more portions of articles, collected silent approvals. Occasionally I would notice my shoulders tense and hunched up close to my ears, so I would sit back, straighten my spine, grab them with my hands, and hold them down as a reminder of where they were supposed to be.

When it had gotten so dark that I couldn't read the notes Frieda had made for me I shut my computer decisively and the room brightened around me. I was going to get a falafel. I put on my shoes and jacket and checked for my keys three times, feeling unfocused yet paranoid, like I was forgetting something important, or like I was going to look down and find myself naked in front of a crowd. Experiencing so much of the world two-dimensionally, staring at an object without being in the same scene, made walking into the twilight feel like moving through a painting or a film. Leaves were impressionistic patterns daubed on pastel apartment buildings, people on the sidewalk blurs of motion veering startlingly close to me. Casinos with papered-over windows in racecar colors and ads for cell phone companies stood out for their garishness and guided me forward. I'd recently seen a headline that claimed staring at screens too much wouldn't cause permanent blindness, so that was good, but there was also a sense in which such reassuring articles disappointed. It was easier to think of technology as something that was happening to me rather than acknowledge I was doing something with it.

. . .

"THE NEIGHBORHOOD DIDN'T USED TO BE LIKE THIS," GENE-vieve was saying as she loaded sippy cups into the basket beneath the stroller. "It's a cliché, but it's true. When we moved here, it was just Turkish families. Quiet. If you wanted to go to a bar with other, you know, young people you had to go to Kreuzberg"—Kreuzberg being a five-minute walk away, almost literally across the street—"or you had to go to the German bars where they hated you and pretended not to understand your accent. My husband's"—she always called Holger "my husband" even though I'd met him at least four times—"parents lived in West Berlin in the eighties and when we told them we were moving to this neighborhood they were scandalized. It was dangerous. There used to be dog shit everywhere." I was about to say there was still dog shit everywhere, imagining vividly the large pile of orange-flecked excrement I'd seen a woman bike through while trying to maneuver around construction on Weserstrasse, but she cut me off. "No. You have no idea. It was *everywhere.*" Finally, she got to her point, to recount the distressing events of the night before: "Last night the bar downstairs—which is run by this just awful woman—was hosting some kind of trivia night or something and it was so crowded that, like, twenty people were just hanging out on the sidewalk at midnight. On a Tuesday! We've had to call the police three times already, and last night we didn't because it always falls on me and I just didn't want to, I couldn't stand the idea of having to talk to her little wobbly head with her giant earrings. Once she saw my husband in the street and stopped him and said, 'Your wife is a little high-strung, hm?'" I expressed surprise at the audacity. "Yes! I'm serious! The fucking nerve! They always open the side door to air out the smoke because they have that stupid fucking ledge thing, or whatever, so the entire place is just entirely smoke, and the smell just wafts all the way up the stairs. Even Uwe, a really nice old man, who's lived on the fifth floor for three decades, smells it, and you can also hear just basically everything people say down there, like clear, full sentences. And always in English. So, anyway, the boys were up all night, so sorry if they're a little grumpy. Isn't that right, boys?" She touched each of their noses.

The cocktail bar she was referring to, directly under her balcony, was owned by an American couple, and it was always crowded, loud, and full of smoke, which caused them to open their side door onto the apartment building's ground floor and make the entire stairway stink, loudly. The drinks cost more than at similar bars around the corner, but that didn't matter, because this bar had a little lofted space in the back, accessible by ladder and about ten feet long by four feet wide by four feet tall, where it was even hotter and darker and smokier than the rest of the place. You could fit about six hunched-over people up there, seated in a single-file row, which as everyone knows makes for optimum conversation. I'd been on a date there, and because I was seated next to the ladder I heard the childlike wonder expressed by each new person who climbed it when they reached the top. There had been neighborhood meetings and building meetings, and the residents had tried to be understanding, but the bar owners were stubborn and vindictive, rolling their eyes in stained jeans and looking at each other meaningfully to convey the absurd tedium of what they were being put through. "If you want quiet nights, don't live in Neukölln!" the woman had said, angering the tenants who had, in buying cheap apartments in the area when it was quiet, perhaps not realized they had made this happen. Poor Uwe. A few months before, the bar had had a fire, and the renovation period was the most peaceful time of Genevieve's life, except for the dread she'd felt about the idea of the bar one day reopening. Hoping to distance myself from the patrons of the bar, to whom I was demographically identical, I said its popularity was ridiculous anyway because the cocktail bar around the corner was cheaper, bigger, and decorated like a jungle. "A jungle!" I said again, to the babies, who laughed at my wide eyes and jazz hands.

A few days before, panicked and trapped in bed, I'd been toying with the idea of paying someone to accompany me to apply for my visa when I admitted to myself that I interacted every day and on shaky power-relationship terms with the perfect person to help. Genevieve spoke fluent German, had no professional obligations at any specific time, was used to waking up and functioning at early hours of the morning, and owed me a cosmic and practical debt for underpaying me to care for her children, the two things most precious to her in the entire world. She had also surely been to the immigration office and probably resented German bureaucracy for one reason or another; she would commiserate as well as consider this an opportunity to avenge whatever wrongs the country had in her nearly twenty years of residence committed against her. I decided to ask her when I brought the babies back. I set off with surprising optimism toward the bourgeois market hall near Görlitzer Bahnhof, which was empty in the mornings and so a good place to wait out the weather; that day it was grotesquely humid. Unfamiliar bugs had begun to appear in my room, long, skinny ant-like things with wings that looked like tiny translucent ball gowns, but they didn't seem to fly. The babies slept immediately and anytime they began to murmur I would do a lap or two around the market, past the dormant stalls offering veggie burgers, tapas, Southern barbecue, Peruvian empanadas, Korean fusion bowls, expensive bread. Janitors or maintenance men occasionally looked at me curiously, but they never seemed to mind me being there.

When I returned to the apartment I took a moment outside to compile my story, each detail a twig in my nest of harmless lies: While we were out walking, I'd gotten a call from the friend who was supposed to go with me to translate for my visa application interview early next week. She was sorry but she just couldn't go—some "presentation" at work. I considered saying the friend had had a "family emergency" but I didn't want to accidentally curse anyone. No, presentation at work, simple, straightforward, a nuisance for me, a minor injustice for me, not too many details. It was possibly slightly New York–seeming—I was under the impression that most young people in Berlin would never have to wake up at 7 a.m. to prepare for a presentation—but it was also my impression that young people in Berlin tended to prioritize their own interests over those of others, which means the imaginary friend could have been making up an excuse to get out of taking me to the visa office. Or it could be that the presentation was moved to 9 a.m. and she wanted to make sure she wasn't late. I could pretend I had no idea what the presentation was and that the excuse seemed suspect to me as well but suggest that she wasn't a good enough friend to ask about it. I rang the doorbell, which was my custom, since I didn't have a set of keys. The door buzzed.

"What's wrong?" Genevieve asked as I rolled the stroller into its parking spot in the entryway wearing a look of mild distress. "Were they really awful?" I told her no, they slept pretty much the whole time—they must have been tired!—but that etc. I knew I should have worked harder on my German so that I could do it myself, but it was too late now. Woe, me, tormented not only by my situation but by the guilt that comes from its being of my own making. I wasn't on top of everything, I had procrastinated on certain requirements, but deep down I was good, and shouldn't I be allowed to choose to live for a year or two in a foreign country if I wanted, for the hell of it?

"Oh my gosh," she said. We each unbuckled a baby and started up the stairs. "What time is it? What day?"

I was careful not to answer too quickly. "It's so early. The thing is that . . ." I explained and looked around nervously.

When I finished she looked relieved. "Oh, 7 a.m. is great," she said. "It'll go much faster. I'll go with you." We had reached the apartment and she was getting her keys out of her pocket. "I'll be up anyway! Holger can stay and watch the babies till we're done! Girls' morning out!"

While she was unlocking the door she turned back to me with an expression of light bemusement on her face. "Can you get a visa to be an accountant here? Don't you have to get a certification or something? Germans love certifications."

Coruscating worries about what would happen when someone figured me out had come and gone, come and gone, but I'd always assumed that that someone would be one of the dates I didn't care about. I imagined one guy might tell a friend about his recent bizarre date with an American who wore x kind of glasses and was y tall and had z dental quirk, to which the friend would reply something like, "That sounds like an American I went on a date with! Was her name Cassandra?" to which the first date would reply, "Oh, no—her name was Audrey, she recently composed a concerto," to which the second date would reply, "Ach so," and they would begin to talk about something else, assuming they had been on dates with different women, until I happened to walk into the same bar about ten minutes later to simultaneous shouts of "That's her, Cassandra!" and "That's her, Audrey!" and I would have to spin on my heel and flee, never getting the chance to introduce myself as Sophie to the third date who was there waiting for me. Imagine if you were on a date with a woman, younger than you but not too much younger, pretty but not the most beautiful woman you had ever seen, interesting but a little reserved, funny but not as funny as people who are funny professionally, and fifteen minutes after she told you her name was Jane and that she was a librarian, a man, taller than you, better-looking than you, more confident than you, came up to her and said, "Hey, Melissa. How's it going?" You would be very confused, and probably affronted for reasons you could sort of understand but wouldn't want to. Of course, instead of a slapstick moment involving actors of little consequence, I had set myself up for an awkward confrontation and loss of income by telling the worst, most unbelievable lie to the person I saw every business day. You're not going to believe me when I say this but I'm actually not very good at lying. If I'd been better at it I could have easily come up with an explanation—there was a visa for people learning German, which could have worked for me—though it would have been harder to justify later when I had my big binder of contradictory visa application materials clutched to my chest outside the immigration office. I was trapped in an ill-conceived narrative.

I stammered as the baby on my hip tangled its fingers in my hair. I flushed with discomfort. Genevieve went inside and while she began to unwrap the other baby to assess his diaper I imagined her looking at me the way a mother on a television show looks at her daughter's rascally boyfriend, the one she likes and really believes in despite his being from the wrong side of the tracks. She was going to take me in and reform me, encourage me to get a haircut, buy me some suitable clothes for job interviews. That would be a terrible approach to take toward a compulsive liar who cares for your children. I said, "Oh, I'm applying as a writer. I make most of my money doing accounting, but that's not what I'm applying for—I'm sure there are like five certification tests you have to take, ha ha, plus it would help to speak German. I'll keep doing taxes for a couple friends from here, remotely, but yeah, I'm applying as a writer." She looked up from the poop. "Oh," she said, a pleasant epiphany on her face, maybe a tiny bit of betrayal. "I didn't know you were a writer. What do you write? Can I read any of it online?"

The baby squirmed, angling its body toward the ground. I put it on the floor and sat next to it, shaking a rattle in front of its face and attempting to look casually mesmerized by the miracle of developing life. I told her that yes, I'd published kind of a lot of stuff online but nothing I was particularly proud of, just stuff, you know, quote-unquote articles, really I was here to work on a novel, but I could send her something if she'd like. She said that would be great. "Or on Monday you can read the several examples I have printed out in my VISA BINDER," I added, to which she replied, oh, good, Germans *love* binders. I said I'd heard, spun the baby in her direction, said, "Go see mama!" and left. I planned to forget to send her the links until after Monday, and in the meantime to assume that as a newish mother of twins she would be too busy or forgetful to look up her competent and reliable babywalker's suspiciously extensive online publication history.

That night I canceled a date with a Greek musician and went to see a boring movie at an art house cinema on Potsdamer Platz. Though the city has several movie theaters offering original-language films or those with English subtitles, there had always been something preventing me from going, like I didn't belong there and so shouldn't partake of civic enjoyments. The weather had improved since that morning, and I was in bed scrolling through the dating app, finding problems with everyone, when suddenly I felt like seeing a movie and it was as if I had woken up. I biked down Oranienstrasse through Kreuzberg much faster than necessary, maneuvering around flashing double-parked cars and running a couple of yellow lights behind an older man on a technological-looking bike in a high-visibility vest, though the sun would not set for another two hours.

I was biking past the still-crowded Checkpoint Charlie when I heard a loud clattering behind me, a rev, and a bright green Trabant shifted to overtake me, smelling of gasoline. A sign on its side advertised trabi-safari.de; it was being driven by a man in what looked like an era-appropriate hat. Within half a block I was in front of an apparent competitor called Trabi World, housed in a bright-yellow building with two Trabis on the roof, one stretch and bright orange, the other painted like a giraffe. An "I <3 Berlin" Trabi out front was flanked by other paint jobs on either side. T-shirts in faded East Berlin sorts of colors hung in the windows. In front of me I approached two girls on bikes taking up the right side of the road, their knees splayed as they pedaled leisurely side by side. I rang my bell. As they veered out of my way I heard one of them, Australian accent, say, "They're made of plastic! Yes, I'm serious!" A long stretch of Berlin Wall was to my left, dividing the street, which was renamed after the communist resistance fighter Käthe Niederkirchner, from the former Nazi headquarters that is now a history museum. The concrete was crumbling, the remaining graffiti was blurry and old but often ebullient and occasionally funny—"Rob—call me!"—and pieces of rusted metal frame were visible in places, warped, and there were holes wide enough for people to fit through. Across the street were tacky signs attempting to explain, in paragraphs and paragraphs recounting when it was built, how many people died trying to cross it, how it went up overnight, Brezhnev, Reagan, but they didn't really make any sense.

When I reached the end of the physical Wall, I continued to follow the double row of memorial cobblestones that charted its past course down the street. I turned right and approached the tall shining buildings looming in geometric harmony. The glass and windows gridded to the sky were a disappointing familiarity, the realization that Europe wasn't all my idea of Europe but also sometimes an idea of America, or of the future. At Potsdamer Platz I heard David Bowie warbling in my head "Had to get the train / From Potsdamer Platz," as I always did when I came upon some mention of Potsdamer Platz. More groups of the pleasantly confused and foreign teetered on the edge of the sidewalks as they waited for the signal to cross. People bobbed in and out of my lane, shocked when my bell warned them they were about to be hit by a bicyclist on their vacation. A couple of multicolored hunks of Wall remained on the square, disintegrating historically next to their informative panels. The S-Bahn sign announced the area in sans serif and I remembered the first time I came here, alone, in the rain, the day after the day after I met Felix, intending to visit the Neue Nationalgalerie, which had a collection of degenerate art. Though I would eventually find the museum closed for a years-long renovation project, before I made it there I got turned around and ended up in the gift shop for the Museum of Film and Television, looking at postcards of Marilyn Monroe and Charlie Chaplin until I could muster the nerve to ask an employee where I could find Wi-Fi to see if Felix had continued our email flirtation. The cinema was next door and the movie was boring, but a few days before, the city had entered the mild and euphoric two-month period when it is never technically night, so when I came out of the theater it was still light out.

. . .

I WAS ON THE PLATFORM TO CATCH THE FIRST S-BAHN AT 4 A.M. on Monday, accompanied by a quiet man drinking and a couple making out. Once Felix and I came home from a bar at 7 a.m. on a Wednesday and the scene was the same. These memories had begun to appear to me neutrally, as mere factual associations, something about which to say, "Huh," without pausing for a swell of emotion. The little hut selling pastries and bad coffee at the station was closed and I knew I would regret my snacklessness.

The part of Moabit where the Ausländerbehörde is located is stubbornly bleak, with a smokestack visible in the distance as you disembark from the train station and see the signs for the immigration office. You turn right at the gas station and follow the river. Across the water a block of perverse apartment buildings painted in lime green, carnation pink, popsicle purple, and terrible yellow is visible above the trees, the website for the rental agency responsible emblazoned in bright red across the facade. You'll know you've arrived when a mural depicting parents and children of several races standing in front of the silhouetted landmarks of Berlin welcomes you in French, German, Turkish, English, and Spanish.

I had expected there to be more of a line, but after checking the long list of nationalities posted on the information building I took my place outside the entrance for Egypt, Ethiopia, Algeria, Angola, Antigua and Barbuda, Equatorial Guinea, Argentina, the Bahamas, Barbados, Belize, Benin, Bolivia, Botswana, Brazil, Burkina Faso, Burundi, Chile, Costa Rica, Cote d'Ivoire, Dominica, the Dominican Republic, Djibouti, Ecuador, El Salvador, Eritrea, Gabon, Gambia, Ghana, Grenada, Guatemala, Guinea, Guinea-Bissau, Guyana, Haiti, Honduras, Jamaica, Cameroon—this is in alphabetical order in German—Canada, Cape Verde, Kenya, Columbia, the Comoros, the Republic of the Congo, the Democratic Republic of the Congo, Cuba, Lesotho, Liberia, Libya, Madagascar, Malawi, Mali, Morocco, Mauritania, Mauritius, Mexico, Mozambique, Namibia, Nicara-

gua, Niger, Nigeria, Panama, Paraguay, Peru, Rwanda, Zambia, São Tomé
and Príncipe, Senegal, the Seychelles, Sierra Leone, Zimbabwe, Somalia,
St. Kitts and Nevis, St. Lucia, St. Vincent and the Grenadines, South Africa, Sudan, South Sudan, Suriname, Swaziland, the United Republic of
Tanzania, Togo, Trinidad and Tobago, Chad, Tunisia, Uganda, Uruguay,
Venezuela, the United States, and the Central African Republic behind
about ten other people. Other buildings had longer lines, but nothing as
bad as the photos I'd seen online had led me to believe; maybe the blogs
were out of date, or their authors had arrived later. It was 4:40. A woman in
front of me holding a Nigerian passport yawned and said to the man with
her that it was so much better since the students were moved to that new
building in Charlottenburg. He said yeah, well, students are disorganized
and don't think to make appointments ahead of time. She said accusingly
that he'd said he wasn't mad and he didn't have to be like that. He said he
wanted coffee. She said nothing would be open, especially here, gesturing
wearily around. After about five minutes a man holding a stack of maroon
passports got in line behind me and began shuffling them like playing cards.

I'd gone over my application the night before and decided I didn't need to
worry about smoothing over the details for Genevieve. I wouldn't have been
able to disclose to the German government that I worked as an accountant even
if I did work as an accountant, because it would suggest that I either wanted
authorization to work as an accountant in Germany, which I surely would not
get, or planned to bill clients under the table in Germany. The picture that my
binder painted, of a young writer looking to strike out as a freelancer in a new
land (with support from her stable upper-middle-class background), was not
inconsistent with what I'd suggested to Genevieve I'd suggest about myself.
My résumé was vague enough about the nature of my writing work for the
website, and if she asked me about it I could say I'd left it vague in order to
seem more legitimate as a freelancer to the German government, though I'd
done it to seem less legitimate as a writer to her. Besides that I hadn't lied to
her about anything else. My inflated bank statements would resemble those

of an unambitious freelance accountant, I thought. Rationalization is a sign of weakness, Felix had said once, but I'd thought it was just a sarcastic joke about Donald Trump.

The line was quiet. My anxiety at being found out was overlaid with sleepy apathy. At around 6 a.m. employees began to arrive, walking briskly and uncaringly past us to their various posts, and we all watched them like dogs under the dinner table. I thought it would be funny to cheer or ask for an autograph. I tried to read but mostly just stood there. Genevieve showed up at six forty-five with two coffees and croissants. "The boys have been up probably about as long as you have!" she said, surveying the now somewhat daunting line behind me. "We'll definitely get a spot today, good for you."

When the doors opened everyone engaged in futile crowding and Genevieve and I looked at each other in mock exasperation. A woman yelled, "No, you do not! I am here first!" and a few people laughed. After about fifteen minutes we reached a booth where a rigid man asked to look through my binder, nodded at it, gave me a number, 013, and told us to wait on the second floor. Genevieve asked in German how long he thought it would be and he said, she translated for me, "No idea. Maybe one hour, maybe two hours." The entire complex was hospital-esque, each floor consisting of an alternating pattern of waiting rooms and hallways lined with offices. Many signs printed from Microsoft Word warned of common mistakes and misunderstandings. In our waiting room a digital television screen displayed two columns of numbers, the assigned case numbers on the left and the room they were to report to on the right. As in all number-based line systems these did not appear in chronological order, or any other sort of order. Also on the digital television screen was an image of an analog clock that was about thirty seconds ahead of the identical, actual analog clock hung next to the screen, above a closed door bearing another print-out sign that read, in English, "Do not cross the barrier until you are permitted." When a number on the screen changed, a two-tone electronic jingle sounded; because we were in one of a series of waiting rooms in a long hallway in a building full of long hallways, the ding-donging was almost symphonic as it issued randomly up and down the floor, causing me to look up in precious hopefulness very often. The only people who looked nervous were a young couple a few seats down from me. An hour passed. Employees would periodically emerge from their offices seeming dubiously friendly to welcome their next appointment. Realizing that, in addition to lying to her, I had conscripted a new mother of twins to spend an uncertain amount of time sitting in a waiting room miles away from her children and their needs, I apologized and thanked Genevieve a few times. She said it was fine, she didn't care about her children. More time passed. Genevieve asked if she could look through my binder and I had no credible way to object. I could see she'd gotten to my bank statements when she asked, "Why did you want to work for me?"

By this time I'd abandoned my fantasies of tearful confession met with confused but sensitive acceptance, so I told her that I'd just wanted something to do—I'd moved to Berlin without much of a plan, I said, and it was a little depressing to know so few people and have so little to do. I added that I liked children and thought they would be soothing in a time of political upheaval. It occurred to me that I might seem like I was taking a job from someone who needed the money more than I did, or indeed that I might have actually been taking a job from someone who needed the money more than I did, though it wasn't as if I didn't actually need money. I found myself explaining further: I learned basic tax code after college because I wanted to work on writing without having to worry about getting a full-time job, and my grandpa was a real accountant, a CPA, and I had all these fond childhood memories of watching him with his spreadsheets and his pencils behind his ears. Sometimes, I was told, he would look over at me and make a comment about itemized deductions or the earned income credit that I couldn't possibly understand, and I would respond very cutely in my baby voice. I wasn't a CPA now, no—for most people's needs you don't need to be certified. There are lots of freelancers

in New York, and most of them never think to ask if you're certified, especially when you're cheaper than H&R Block. I couldn't do audits, but why
would I want to? Seriously though, I wanted to stop doing taxes, which
was part of the reason I came to Berlin. I hated math, I was just good at
it, and though I'd initially been sympathetic about the panic inspired by
government bureaucracy, now it took every ounce of patience I had not to
lecture all the people who put off doing their taxes until the last minute and
expected me to comb through their receipts in forty-eight hours. I could
charge extra for that, yeah, but it was still infuriating, and what was more
infuriating was that it was part of my job to remain calm and reassuring
even as my clients treated me like a computer. Most of these people had
no excuse—they were totally capable of paying, just lazy. No, yeah, the
plan is to switch to writing, which I'd studied in college—I nodded at the
binder she was still holding to indicate there was proof of my degree within
it—and then maybe start doing free or, like, sliding-scale tax services for
low-income people once I had things figured out. To do karmic penance for
this lie, I was going to have to actually learn the tax code and start offering
sliding-scale tax services for low-income people, if that was even something
anyone could just wake up one day at 3:15 a.m. and decide to do. People
major in accounting in college. Genevieve nodded and said she was glad
she'd found someone who was so good with the boys, so she hoped I didn't
start hating them, too! Ha ha. No, they're too cute.

When the demonic jingle announced 013 it was dreamlike, surreal, ten
forty-five. I jumped up and said, "It's me!" and elicited chuckles from the
elderly couple who had just sat down nearby. Genevieve and I walked purposefully to the smiling woman standing outside room 155. She had maroon hair styled like a porcupine and said, "Ute. English?" I said yes but uh
and looked at Genevieve. Before she could reply for me, Ute shook her head
and waved her hand and said Genevieve couldn't come. "I speak English,
fine, OK." OK. The blogs had not prepared me for this at all. I passed an
apology to Genevieve as I was whisked into the office and the door was shut

behind me. There was, as a blog said there might be, a small cat calendar on Ute's desk.

"Zo," she said. "My English is not . . . great, but this doesn't matter." I said all Germans said that, even though their English was great. She said, "What?" I said never mind. She asked what I was applying for; I had printed out a cover page for my binder with the German name of the visa on it, which I pointed to. She took the binder and asked what my job was. I said I was a writer. She said ah, a writer. She said, "Do you have health insurance?" I said yes and stood up from my chair unnecessarily to flip to the printed-out evidence of my health insurance, which I had finally managed to procure with Frieda's guidance; it was ultimately very straightforward. She looked at it and then flipped through the rest. She said, "Do you have your passport?" I said yes and gave her my passport. She said, "OK. You go outside. I will call you back when I'm finished." I did this and apologized to Genevieve again.

Five minutes later Ute came out of 155 and beckoned me to return to her office. She said my application looked good, but it would have to be approved by some sort of official body, the name of which I didn't catch, which could take up to three months. I said, "Three months?" and she said yes but it wouldn't be a problem, probably. When it was ready I would receive an email with a date, time, case number, and waiting room number to return. She put a sticker in my passport that said, according to her, I could stay in the country but was not authorized to leave and come back. I didn't have to pay until the visa was ready. I said, "That's it?" That I might just decide one day to move to a foreign country for no real reason and be able to do it with relative ease felt like a con. She said, "Yes, welcome to Germany," and she picked up a little flag on her desk and waved it without changing the expression on her face at all.

CLIMAX

ACROSS THE COUNTRY GERMAN PARENTS STILL IN POSSESSION OF television sets watched the weather reports with concern and quickly relayed the forecast via text message or email to their progeny in the capital. Do you have to go to work on Thursday? Remember to close the windows. The progeny frowned—it was only Monday, and their parents were annoying—but they nevertheless tapped over to the appropriate app, not feeling confident in TV news reports or their parents' ability to relay them. Three days in advance the weather app was mostly useless, but next to Donnerstag and Freitag it did display a cloud icon with a little lightning bolt under it. Further investigation suggested a storm was coming. The Germans began to discuss the impending weather with their friends and roommates and colleagues, who confirmed the projections, adding to the exciting and portentous atmosphere. Among the friends and roommates and colleagues were expats, who warned their friends, mainly other expats, understanding the helplessness of weather to be compounded by the helplessness of never reading local news. I heard about it from Frieda, who was in the kitchen cheerfully grating an apple over muesli while I removed my clothes from the washing machine. Wet pieces of flesh were flying across the countertop; one soared dangerously close to my clean sheets. "What time do you see the babies on Thursday?" she asked, juice glistening on her fingers. I told her I got there at eight and finished at eleven. "Good. It is going to rain really hard," she said. "My mother said, on the news? They are saying one of the worst rains in one hundred years." Since we lived on neither the ground nor the top floor and as renters did not take responsibility for water damage to our home anyway, the gravity of the situation was lost on us. I could buy some groceries to avoid having to eat whatever I had in my cabinet on Thursday, lentils, old garlic, toast, oatmeal. If I didn't it would be totally fine. "Luckily it is not supposed to start until later in the day, I think."

The day before was hazy and hot. I woke up sweaty, biked sweatily to pick up the babies, and after an hour and a half of walking sweatily took them to a park where shade had nothing to offer us. They crawled in resolutely opposite directions as Dan Savage advised a twenty-three-year-old man to let his girlfriend of five years dump him because she had been giving him clear signs that she was trying to do so. They were young! They should fuck other people! I ate bland crackers, designed to be consumed by sucking, from a resealable container Genevieve kept in the pocket at the bottom of the stroller. Since I had teeth I didn't have to wait for them to disintegrate in my mouth, so I failed to take advantage of one of their only benefits. I'd taken a short video of the babies on one of the first days I walked them, and I took my phone out to watch it, comparing. One of them grabbed a stick and began to swing it near his face, so I put down my phone and pried it from his sticky fingers. The other one picked up my phone, to the best of his ability. I moved back, the first one whining now, to pull the phone away, much easier to accomplish than extracting the stick because of the phone's slick design and particular weightiness not accommodating to babies. Both started to cry. I picked them up, laid them on the ground next to each other, and hung my head over them so that my hair would brush against their faces, temporarily mesmerizing them. Then I began to swoop my face toward each of their faces in turn, touching my nose to their noses, making an inane whooshing sound and letting my breath provide a little breeze as I got close to them. Getting them to laugh was an achievement of patience: first they had to stop crying, then they had to look cutely curious, then they had to smile, maybe letting out a preliminary giggle, and then they had to laugh. It wouldn't be long before they were better at German than I was—it was possible, who knows, that they were already better, that they had little bilingual thoughts rolling around their tiny brains, smacking into each other, grasping at intelligible speech with little marmalade hands as something large and difficult to move held them back. I changed their diapers, as perfunctorily disgusting as it always was, and strapped them whining back into their stroller, which was new because their legs had recently become too long for their old horizontal model. Genevieve had apparently forgotten about the discontinuities of my visa binder, or else she had never cared about them in the first place.

After I helped Genevieve carry the babies upstairs and said I would see her tomorrow—"doomsday!" she acknowledged cheerfully—I met Nell for coffee. She was wearing a thrift-store dress printed with giant lilies layered over a white T-shirt that had the word *sex* written all over it in different languages. (It's pretty much the same in most.) The dress was short and she wore it with grubby tennis shoes, one of which had rainbow laces. Since I'd last seen her she'd had a series of feminist epiphanies. "The American government is dedicated to policing women's bodies!" she cried. "We are under attack! I am just no longer interested in straight white men!"

I found this a little bit rich, and I responded that, well, she was a straight white man. Because of the snowball logic of such epiphanies she surely knew she couldn't object, so she leaned back in her chair, shook her head, and chuckled like someone who had it all figured out. "You really have a unique mind," she said. "I never thought of it that way, but I guess you're right. You're right." Despite her bravado I could see I'd hurt her, so I tried to reassure her that I was not mad, or mean. Oh, I'm a straight white man, too, I said, all

I meant was that it seemed inappropriate to claim equivalent hardship with people—I would not indulge the sentimentality of the dualism—who were actually policed and attacked when we were sitting here in Berlin drinking coffee in the middle of the day and had, maybe despite past experiences of mild oppression because of our gender, now emerged more or less capable of handling everything because of our various advantages—financial, educational, alliance with traditional beauty standards, etc.—and that it seemed counterintuitive to say straight white men were no longer interesting when 1) they were who we often slept with, and 2) that was like saying we ourselves were no longer interesting, which was just not true, ha ha. More importantly the declaration suggested that the only interesting experiences out there were related to demographic, which was limiting to people of all demographics. She asked if I'd ever been sexually assaulted.

I was shocked by the abruptness of the question—she was usually hemming and equivocal—and said yes. She said she was so sorry. I said it wasn't her fault. She seemed to want me to continue, to describe the experience, but I just sat there, looking expectant. Felix had offered his followers false empowerment just as the most vocal of his peers were marching confidently into false disempowerment. Had this been part of his thought process? Had he been overpowered by annoyance but still smart enough to know he couldn't express it as himself, an uninteresting straight white man? Nell said she was sorry again, but did I not want to prevent future young women from going through what I did, from being sexually assaulted? I said of course I wanted to prevent future young women from being sexually assaulted, and also women of all ages, and then I stopped again. I was not going to melt into profuse elaboration. She asked how could I say I was a straight white man when a straight white man would never be able to understand what I had experienced? Did I not feel oppressed by the perpetrator's disregard for my *personhood*? I said well . . . I didn't know how to say this without being offensive, and I just wanted to be clear that I wouldn't say this in the context of a policy conversation when I was trying to convince a conservative audience of something, but I didn't really think about it much. She looked like she didn't believe me. I said, What? Am I supposed to lie? How does sacrificing my personality help me prove my *personhood*? I had to believe it was possible for straight white men to approximately understand what I had experienced. A man having sex with me when I have told him not to is not that hard to understand. The problem was not a matter of understanding but of willful denial, which was better disarmed by willful acknowledgment than by willful denial. Had she ever met a male feminist? The kind of guy who just nods and apologizes at you, who begins at the end and stays there, whose obvious belief that there's some trauma at the center of your being makes him so preemptively sensitive to your theoretical difference that he assumes you are unfathomable? Maybe you are unfathomable, but he doesn't even try. *That*, I said, the pseudo-righteous box-ticking kind of giving up, the sense that because I'm a woman I must be approached differently, makes me feel like I'm not being treated like a real person. And I didn't think it was appropriate to equate that experience with the experiences of, for example, women who are raped while trying to seek asylum in the United States, or women who are raped and then cannot access or pay for abortions. I said all women were linked by various or potential experiences but I wasn't going to pretend that we were the same when we weren't. I was aware I was ranting. This was the most I'd ever said to her. She nodded. I said maybe I wasn't making sense but it seemed that what we had was a disagreement about strategy. She said yes. I asked if she'd ever been sexually assaulted and she said no; one time she woke up in someone's bed but she was pretty sure they hadn't had sex. I said yeah, well, drinking, right, and she said yes, exactly. I added that I also didn't like all these op-eds arguing that drinking is bad for women. It was like the fucking Woman's Christian Temperance Union.

After a moment of silence she said in the bright tones of someone who has just started a gluten-free diet that she had stopped reading the news.

Did my eyes widen? Did I look around to see if anyone had heard her? I don't know. I thought of the babies, blinking on the phone, and had the strange experience of wanting to hold one right then, which I took to be an indication not of my innate yearning for children but of my innate yearning for an interaction that made immediate sense. Felix liked babies, actually; they were the easiest people in the world to treat with kindness and generosity. I asked what the final straw in Nell's decision was. She said Grenfell. "I just didn't want to see that anymore," she said. "I know it's bad. I can imagine all the bad things happening every day. I don't need to see them." Though I understood why she would think these things I didn't know what to say. There seemed to be two options for engaging with the world: desperate close reading or planned obsolescence. They were both so clearly rooted in natural impulses and so clearly wrong. I remembered a trick from a journalism class: Don't say anything and they'll keep talking. "I want to get back to *my center*, to really understand myself and my priorities," Nell said. "I used to listen to NPR every morning, the BBC, read *The New York Times*. It's so much better without it. It's the ocean! It's waves! It's always there coming and going! I realized that if something really important happens, I'll know. You can't really escape it, but you can rise above it." I nodded, conveying, I hoped, that I pitied her for having these sorts of futile fantasies. I was not being fair, it's true; I never told her anything about myself or my work, so I forced her to fill our meetings with content. But she was constantly failing the tests I set for her. A man to my left shut his laptop with a sigh. If he was eavesdropping, I didn't want him to associate me with these ideas. "But isn't this the same attitude that got us into this?" I asked, in my nicest, most simply curious voice, appealing to false collectivity. "Conservatives refusing to acknowledge the world as it is . . . only watching horrible cable news that tells them what they want to hear . . . fear—"

Nell smiled. "Exactly. I just don't find that fear is serving me. I have all the right opinions. I know what's bad and what's good. I just didn't feel like it was making me better. Like my ex-boyfriend. Ha ha. I've been doing a lot of baking."

I said I'd heard vanilla extract was hard to find here.

She said she was really focusing more on breads—banana, zucchini, even rhubarb. She said she was going to get fat.

Of course part of my resentment of Nell was jealousy. She seemed to wrestle with nothing, coming to conclusions easily and stating them directly, even if she later contradicted her stated views; shame was something external she merely had to ward off. She believed she had defined personal qualities and preferences and she used them as a foundation to think whatever she wanted, especially if what she wanted to think was whatever she was told. She had multiple passports and enjoyed baking. I did not bake, or cook, and although I knew this didn't matter I couldn't help but consider it a failing. Every time I saw a cake I felt bad. Why couldn't I enjoy this simple pleasure? Why did I compulsively read Twitter instead of learning to eyeball dry ingredients? It was certainly possible that knowing what was happening produced no good—I never did anything about it—and in fact caused harm by making me feel like I was helpless and manipulated, which made me continue to do nothing because I felt, rightly or wrongly but mainly conveniently, that there was nothing I could do. Holding on tightly to the sense that at any moment the governments on whose economies I was dependent could collapse meant that the rest of my days would be lived out in cycles of paranoia and despair followed by shaky you-only-live-once justifications and self-harm. Why keep doing this? Surely someone would tell you before the draft, or the shelter-in-place, or whatever, was about to happen, especially if you were constantly bragging about the richness of a life spent not reading the news.

I said, "Doesn't that make you a little dependent? Not baking, I mean not reading the news."

She said, "Huh. I don't really think about it that way, but I guess I could see that."

I said, "I hate being dependent on people. It's so stressful. It also feels a little selfish?"

She said, nodding with her eyes closed, "I could see that. What's going on with your visa now?"

Although I was almost positive I hated her, relief that someone cared enough to ask drove my needlessly detailed explanation: I described the early-morning trip to the immigration office, a place Nell had never been: its ominous surroundings, the brusque friendliness of the bureaucrat, the fact that I'd brought Genevieve with me and she hadn't been allowed in the interview, the present limbo. I said I kind of enjoyed the purgatorial certainty of my situation now, of having to wait. She asked, "Are you going to learn German?" and I said I didn't know—if I wasn't going to live there for a long time, it felt kind of pointless. She said, "Surely a year is a long time?" I said, "Oh really? I don't think so." She said, "Huh. Wait. I don't think you ever told me why you came here."

I looked away and laughed like a weary woman scorned. Maybe it wasn't sympathy but contempt that would bring out the truth? I could see that. It was kind of funny, actually, I said. Absurd, but funny. Well, sad, also, sorry, I don't want to sound like an asshole, because I was really sad about it. I was only just now getting over it. I took a deep breath.

I'd been dating this guy, Frank, for, like, five years, I said, since the end of college basically, or, like, just after, and all of a sudden he proposed. It was really out of nowhere, which I know sounds wrong. I mean, if you've been together for five years, it can't be out of nowhere, but it felt out of nowhere. Usually you talk about it, right? That's what people usually do, unless you live in, like, the Midwest or something. Anyway, I told him no, I said, and he said then he didn't want to be together anymore, and I said OK, I respected that decision, and he said OK, and we cried and then I felt like I needed to leave the country, so here I was. I'd been to Berlin a couple of years before and really loved it—it was summer, so you know—so I just decided to move.

Nell liked this story. "Oh my God, wow," she said. "I can't believe I didn't know that. It's pretty brave of you. How did he propose?"

I thought she was going to ask why I said no. I chuckled knowingly, as if to myself, for a pause. "Well, that's the funny part," I said. "He came over to my apartment one night when we were supposed to be watching TV and was like, 'I got you a present.' And I was like, 'Oh my God, what?' I love presents. But then he pulled a bright pink Furby out of his tote bag." Nell looked delightfully confused. "I know. I was like, 'Ooooh, wow, my mom waited in line for one of those in 1998!' Pretend-impressed voice, you know. It was funny. I thought he was trying to be thoughtful. I couldn't remember ever talking to him about Furbies, but I was like, you know, it's not beyond the realm of possibility that I had. Anyway, then he was like, 'Here's the batteries for it.' And I was laughing, saying, awesome, let's fire it up! Then I opened the battery thing in the bottom—" pause for drama "—and a ring fell out."

Nell's speechlessness manifested in a hand over her mouth and theatrically wide eyes. Then she cackled. "You're kidding. No. You can't be kidding. No one could make that up. Wow. What a story. Don't you feel *lucky* to have that *story*?"

"I don't know," I said. "I think it would be too embarrassing for him if I ever wrote it. I thought it was really funny, so I laughed, but then it was so awkward, because I didn't know what to say and I had to make something up, but if you're not saying yes immediately in that situation everyone knows you're going to say no. He was a really funny guy. I just didn't want to marry him. Or anybody. I'm too young, besides. I've been going on a lot of OkCupid dates, and I know it's, like, gauche, but I really like it?"

Nell fluffed her bangs with her fingers while making noises of assent. "I'm thinking of trying to date women," she said.

Riding my bicycle, on the way home, I went through the park and while trying to pass a pair of elderly women walking in the middle of the path I brushed up against a bush of stinging nettles and my right calf erupted. I'd never heard of stinging nettles, so I thought I was going to die. I stopped my bike in the middle of the path between two men selling weed and looked at my leg, a thing I wanted to disown and abandon in the park. A splotchy red was already blooming atop the cluster of purple spider veins I occasionally, under nonrash circumstances, looked down at for a jolt of panic. I'd been a fool; I should have appreciated the spider veins when I had the chance. I touched the rash with two fingers and then, worried I was going to spread it to my hand, instinctively tried to wipe them off on my shirt. Now the rash was, I imagined, on my shirt, making its way through cheap cotton to my abdomen. The weed dealers were laughing, probably not at me but I imagined at me, and I wanted to sit on the pavement and cry, to scream at the old ladies who had still not made it to this spot, who were still escorting each other on their carefree European waddle, so far away they couldn't even see the distress they'd caused. Why did no one in this town have a sense of urgency? Why was there a fucking poisonous leaf in a public park? A public park *with a petting zoo in it*? What if an animal ate this leaf? It was so easy to think of others when one needed to. One of the weed dealers muttered promotionally in my direction and I glared. As if I would want to buy marijuana at a time like this! When I was back on my bike I started to cry, and the tears streamed sideways across my face as I sped toward home, my calf still burning.

I saw now that my previous experience with rashes had been quaintly disconnected, the cause always a mystery to be solved. Had I rubbed my elbow on something? Was I allergic to latex after all this time? I'd been so innocent to have thought I knew what a rash was. Only this, now, was a rash. When I got home I tripped getting off my bike and almost fell over; the pedal scraped the other side of the same calf and it started to bleed. I looked at the rash and saw pimply white bumps had risen from the red. A man in a hip outfit—short jeans cinched near the waist with a braided belt, funny hat, geriatric shoes—was smoking a cigarette outside the café next door, ignoring me completely. I sniffed and wiped my face. Everything was terrible, life a series of vindictive matryoshka dolls revealing smaller and more personal horrors until finally you got to the last one, which was you, a tiny pathetic wooden toy that a baby could choke on and die. A clumsy metaphor, maybe, but I was distressed. I imagined the existential matryoshkas had evil slanting eyebrows and black witchy outfits. I locked my bike, went to my front door, paused, went back to make sure I'd correctly locked my bike, went back to the front door, heaved myself against its weight to open it, and ran up the stairs and into the bathroom. I turned on the water in the tub, the cold tap, rolled up my pants, and awkwardly stuck my leg under it. Around the faucet were a few thin hairs, in German blond and American brown, plus a layer of wet dust. I watched for a change in the rash, willing the universe to alter its course so I would not have to go to a German doctor. Nothing happened, but putting water on it was soothing. Eventually I turned off the tap and, finding myself unprepared for the situation, dripped across the floor into the hallway and to my room, where I got the towel I'd used that morning and patted myself dry like I was a pile of delicate berries. Frieda knocked, I said come in, she said there is water all over the floor? I said yes I'm about to clean it. She said, Oh, you have a rash, and I said yes, I brushed up against a plant and it happened. She said, Oh, that's . . . how do you call it in English? She slid her phone out of her back pocket and tapped around. Stinging nettles. Nasty stuff. I said what and she said stinging nettles? You don't have them in the U.S.? I said, No, we have poison ivy. She said, Oh, I don't think we have that one. Anyway it will be fine.

. . .

A LITTLE AFTER NOON THE NEXT DAY THE RASH WAS GONE AND the sky had turned bright and quartery. My room, always in shadow around this hour, got darker, and from my hunched position at my desk I looked to the ominous window. At first it was hard to tell whether the sound came from the rain or the rustling of the leaves that anticipated it. The slim birches swayed as the first few drops warned the roof. From an open bathroom window across the courtyard I heard gargling. There was thunder, and then the downpour began.

OkCupid was frenzied with activity, and I spent much of the day copy-

and-pasting the same bad joke to various men: "I'm sure your inbox has been FLOODED with dates!" Videos from the day were linked and shared. The aisle of a city bus became a riverbed, and travelers lifted up their feet as they continued to text or film the scene. Laughing figures in bright hoods toted yoga mats across a washed intersection. The videos were astounding in a wholesome way; they didn't seek pity for the drivers of submerged sedans or soaked teens watching in awe as waterfalls formed on the steps descending into U-Bahn stations. There was the sense that it would all be OK, eventually taken care of. A shirtless man swam a competent freestyle against what would have been the flow of traffic under a bridge. Upon completion, he stood up and cheered.

While I was eating dinner Genevieve texted, "Wow! Of course don't try to come up tomorrow! Have a nice weekend and stay dry :)" and more hours of nothing in particular stretched out before me. I got into bed with my computer and maneuvered among my reading material—a short story that I'd been trying to finish for a week, a long piece on refugees in a small German village written by a man I'd seen read at a bookstore, a pair of op-eds about how mainstream Democrats could adopt the more progressive agenda favored by millennials, @HelenofTroyWI rejecting both op-eds on the grounds that mainstream Democrats saw their relationship to reckless millennials as fundamentally parental and they only liked children as status symbols of their self-victimization—until a little parenthetical 1 appeared on a tab to indicate I had an email. It was from my friend Orin:

> Hey—sorry to take so long to get back to you . . . Work sucks, as you
> know, but really the problem was that . . . my mom is getting remarried??
> She met some guy at a sensory deprivation tank?? (Her 'float studio') He's
> in his 40s, anti-vax, and when I tell her I think it's a bad idea she just says
> it's not like they're going to be having any children, so she doesn't know
> what I'm so worked up about. It's maddening! I feel so cornered by the
> inadequacies of others lately . . .

Speaking of . . . hope you're OK. I mean, as much as you could be . . . I don't really have anything to say except . . . wow? I'm sorry if it's weird for me to be bringing it up, but I worried people would feel too weird to write you, and I didn't want you to feel like people were avoiding you. I have no idea what you must be feeling, but it shouldn't be that . . . though I don't really have anything to say, I'm on chat for a while if you want to talk.

Like the rash, this email felt immediately disorienting and possibly life-changing. Orin was acting like someone had died. I opened a chat window and typed, "hey. what are you talking about?" Orin replied, "what do you mean what am I talking about?" I said, "i mean: what?" He said, "what do you mean what?" I said "i mean: what? what? what? what? what?" I sent each of these as an individual message, to convey the drama of the confusion I felt, so it looked like this:

i mean:
what?
what?
what?
what?
what?

Many people wouldn't take the extra half-seconds to include the question mark in a casual conversation like this, particularly under such urgent circumstances, but I found the rhythm of holding the shift key with my pinky while my ring finger hit the *?* meditative. As I waited for Orin's reply, possibilities for the category of news quickly eliminated themselves: no one would feel uncomfortable talking to me about politics, no one would associate me in particular with happenings at the website, Orin didn't know anyone in my family or their names. Felix? Felix. Felix had actually saved tons of money and left it to someone nefarious? Someone had figured out his identity and exposed him as the promoter of conspiracy theories? He'd written a hateful manifesto that was discovered and published? Was I associated with any other questionable figures? I couldn't think of any; Felix overshadowed them all. As I waited for Orin's reply, I searched Felix's name, but the results appeared as Orin's message flashed in the unopen tab. "can I call you," he'd written, without the *?* I said yes, and my computer started to ring.

Orin was a sweet, tentative person, though not boring or unfunny. We'd met at a reading shortly after college while he was getting a PhD at Columbia; he was friends with someone I knew from work, and he'd been at the reading in order to think seriously about the aesthetics of alienation. After he finished his dissertation he took a job doing research for a poorly organized nonprofit, which I always told him he should quit. He would nod painfully before saying the incompetence there was so encompassing that he couldn't quit; no one would buy toilet paper or refill the pods for the environmentally unfriendly coffee machine, and it was for such a good cause. I would say that he had a PhD and that if he valued the life of the mind he should not be buying toilet paper and replacing coffee pods because by doing so he was depriving the world of his knowledge of literature. He would nod and then we would talk about our love lives, his always involving some kind of near miss of a date on which I would offer too-late advice. He'd had a long relationship with a woman who left him for a domineering Swedish lesbian; she (the ex, not the Swede) calls or emails him each year on his birthday in order to taunt him with news of her volatile but nevertheless enduring love. Detrimentally trustworthy, he categorically rejected the films of Woody Allen and Roman Polanski, albeit I suspect regretfully, and was a designated driver in college; a woman who would go on to catalyze significant plotlines on a reality TV show once puked in his car. His eyebrows had a pitying look about them, a naturally furrowed upward curvature, and in the winter he wore the same high school swim team sweatshirt every day. I'd never known him to date anyone seriously besides the one woman and had only cursorily imagined what our relationship might be like. (The ex-boyfriends say this is because I don't like nice guys, but they would say that. They should really just sit back and enjoy their coming vindication.)

I answered his call and heard in return, "Hi, how's it going?" I said it was fine; shouldn't he be at work? He said he was taking a sick day. I said, "Ah . . ." He said, "Yeah . . . so you just kind of disappeared! People were worried, but then it was like, she can take care of herself, maybe she needs space . . . Yeah. So, uh, yeah . . . yeah. Yeah. Are you serious?"

I said what did he mean, was I serious?

He said, "You don't . . . you don't know."

I said I didn't even know what I didn't know. Orin hadn't turned on his video camera, so instead of initiating the big reveal I put off what I dreaded would become humiliation by asking if we should turn on our video cameras. I thought if I could see his face it would help me believe I was not being cruelly pranked, though I guess either way this story involves me being cruelly pranked. I just wanted to see his face. Without waiting for his reply I turned on my camera, to pressure him to reciprocate; it translated the dreary lighting in my room into fuzzy shadows that made me look alluringly consumptive. Yet no Orin appeared. He said, "Um . . . I don't want to turn my camera on, if that's OK. I'm doing a face mask right now."

I didn't mean to be insensitive, but I laughed. I asked him what kind of face mask he was doing and he replied, "Please don't mock me, this Felix thing is really crazy." I said, Oh, so it was Felix?

Orin paused. "Yeah . . ." he said, finally. "What's that sound? Is it raining?"

I said yes, it was the storm of a century. He didn't say anything. I said he wasn't saying anything. I tabbed back over to the search results for Felix's name. I'd searched his name many times before, but this time what had come up looked completely different: a series of boxes labeled "Top stories" with variations on one indeed unbelievable headline. "Did you google it?" Orin asked, needlessly; I imagine I wore the light frown of a person who is both aghast and uncertainly impressed. "Which article are you reading?"

Orin waited patiently until I got to the end of the post and finally told him, *"New York Observer."* He'd made himself known the day before, at a party. "I'll just wait till you're ready," Orin said, and I hummed in appreciation, my face clearly working through another report. According to an article on an art website that had been aggregated by several other websites, including the one I'd worked for—Why had none of them told me? Because they thought I already knew? Because they wanted to believe I, supposedly their friend, still read the website, even though they knew I thought the website wasn't very good? Because they were embarrassed on my behalf? There was, I knew, a German word for that—he'd shown up to a happy hour hosted by his old company and integrated himself into a conversation with some former colleagues, who were so stunned they couldn't explain to those who didn't recognize him that the crasher was a ghost, at which point Felix himself explained, saying, according to one attendee, "I faked my death." Whether he'd said this smugly or sanguinely or flatly or remorsefully or in a tone that made him sound as surprised as anyone, the blogs didn't say; they were just news posts, a couple hundred words, though they did link to his website, which I don't believe he'd had before. I opened it in a new tab but kept reading the articles. Did he apologize, if not for the hoax then at least for the fright? The articles didn't say that, either. He didn't respond to requests for comment, but the art blog included quotes from a colleague, whose name I recognized; here was the ladder-climbing sycophant Felix had always complained about, expressing anger and dumbstruck admiration for Felix's project. At a time when millions of people documented their every move on social media and monitored everyone else's, the colleague said, when unearthing obscure gaps and inconsistencies was a popular self-aggrandizing pastime, how had he managed it? "It's kind of a brilliant critique," was the kicker.

I briefly thought of the logistics—the thousand dollars was easy; it surely came from him, from a PayPal account attached to a new, fake email address impersonating that of his mother—but what I wanted to know first was how I'd missed the news. These articles had been posted seven, eight hours ago, in the East Coast morning when they'd get good traffic, and I'd been on Twitter all day during the storm. I tried to remember if I'd seen "A Man Died Five Months Ago. But He Missed His Favorite Bar" headlines and scrolled past them, or if I'd seen the photo illustrating the articles—the same dark, grainy shot of Felix holding a draft beer with his arms in a sort of shrugging position, taken by a phone held at a low, surreptitious angle—pop up in my timeline, something I may have ignored as a digital version of the many Felix look-alikes I'd seen walking around Berlin, no longer worth the double take. Maybe I could blame an algorithm—I'd never been served the story. Being in a different country altered the algorithm, as did the posts I *engaged* with, and I rarely *engaged* with tabloid anomalies, finding the headlines the most delightful part. I checked and found, to my surprise, that I didn't even follow the *Observer*. I followed them. Then I looked at his website: it had a white background with his name in black sans serif font in the upper-left corner. The only thing on it was an "About" page that said he was an artist who lived in Berlin, and when I read it I felt both hurt, like he should have called me, and undeservedly affronted, like this was my city and I couldn't believe he would dare enter it. How long had he been here? Had I seen him somewhere, at a bar or in the street, and assumed he was his own doppelgänger? Returning to the search results, I saw the story had been picked up pretty widely, though just as a brief general-interest item, a quirky fluke. Searching related terms on Twitter, I saw a few people I followed had posted about it, but they weren't the kind of people I paid attention to; it hadn't become a topic of the day, the sort of story everyone could comment on to reliably generate attention for themselves; politics had been too dramatic for another story to take off, and Felix's lack of preexisting notoriety meant he didn't catch on. I guessed my actual friends had stayed silent about it out of respect for me. Someone I didn't know had tried to make a meme out of it, to no success. Felix hadn't said anything absurd or stupid enough to make that work. He took himself too seriously.

Orin asked if I was OK. I said, still frowning and looking at articles, "Uh . . . yeah? I mean . . . he must have really hated dating me! Ha ha. No, ha, uh, I feel like I have nothing in my head," though it wasn't exactly true, and I wasn't trying to hide my true feelings from Orin. Orin said he was sorry in a really meaningful voice and asked if I wanted to hear more details. I said of course. Felix had activated a new Instagram account under his own name. I got my phone and searched it, and it came up immediately: three photos, all of himself, the first posted three days before, the second posted two days before, etc. The first one was a passport photo, white and direct, a fashionable oily shine on his cheekbones, as if death were good for the skin. In the second he was smiling, and it was location-tagged "Berlin – the place to be." In the third he was making an uncanny pouting face, imitating women. It was captioned, "i'm a pretty girl and i'm always late!!" None of this made sense to me as an artistic or personal statement, but his hair was longer and sexier. He had 4,056 followers and followed two accounts, a popular street photographer and @bodegacatsofinstagram. The comments on his three photos so far were moronic, either entirely supportive of "what he did" or scolding. I felt high. Only after we hung up did I worry about having done something unattractive on camera that Orin had seen, though I usually spent video-chat conversations constantly checking on my own image.

Orin had heard about it pretty much as soon as the news broke—someone from grad school had sent him a link immediately, because of his interest in the aesthetics of alienation. Orin was indeed interested, until he was horrified; he said he didn't tell his grad-school friend that he knew the alienated party, though I don't know if I believe that. I didn't care, regardless. I looked up @THIS_ACCOUNT_IS_BUGGED_: it hadn't been updated since January, but it was still there. "Are people talking about me?" I asked Orin, though he didn't know many people who worked in media, who would be most likely to gossip about my role in this. "Not that I know of," he said earnestly, and dutifully added, "but why would they? You're the victim here!"

I thanked Orin for calling me and asked if it wasn't past time for him to rinse off the face mask. He said shit, but was I OK? I said, "Honestly? I'd been planning to dump him anyway, so I feel ... vindicated. But it is weird!" He laughed. I felt guilty for portraying myself as aloof and uncaring—I was OK, but I wasn't going to simply get over it—so I added that I wished it weren't raining so hard because I felt like running down the street or something. Again the tone was wrong, too chipper and wholesome, but I was suddenly exhausted. Orin laughed again and said bye, I should chat him tomorrow if I needed to talk.

I shut my computer, laughed in the dark, and opened my computer again, though when I went back to Twitter I felt like I'd walked into a room and forgotten what I'd gone in there for. How had I missed it? Not just today—the entire time. When I found out Felix had died, I couldn't believe it, but I'd thought that was what it was supposed to feel like. Death is inevitable, something you have to come to terms with, resistant to skepticism even as it produces shock. Should I have suspected something wasn't right? Returning to thoughts of logistics, I saw a flash of my gullibility. Why hadn't I thought more about the strangeness of his mother's phone call, the thousand dollars, the ease with which I'd avoided his funeral unquestioned? Wouldn't there have been a police report or accident report or something from the alleged bike accident that I could have searched for? An obituary? A funeral-home announcement? Why hadn't I tried to do that? Hadn't anyone else tried to do that? No—no one cared, and he was free enough of optimism to be able to count on that. How many people had been duped? Felix had always been one of those people who didn't have many friends—he rarely introduced me to anyone—but he accompanied me to my friends' parties, and was not antisocial at them, so I'd just assumed his somewhat itinerant past and picky disposition meant he didn't want many friends. There was a guy named Matt. People from Berlin, people from work. Was that convenient, or by design? Since he didn't have social media accounts under his own name, it was easier to contain the truth. The person most likely to have encouraged a collective mourning online would have been his girlfriend, and he knew that wasn't my style; he must have created the memorial Facebook account himself, and who would think to question that? Had he created all the accounts that posted on it? I went back to it. A colleague's name jumped out, but otherwise it was all strangers. I clicked on one, but his profile was private, like the one I'd tried to look at before. I clicked on another. Also private. I saw now that there was something similar about their names, which all had the off-kilter spellings beloved by creative but entitled parents. I'd thought that was a product of his being from wealthy Los Angeles. He must have hired a woman to play his mother and call the people closest to him—that had been why the call was so strange. Or maybe his mother was herself just strange, the strange phone call genuine, and he'd had someone play a police officer and call her and say he'd died? Knowing whether he'd tricked her, too, would determine whether he himself had organized his celebration of life across the country, to draw fewer people who (thought they) knew him well, or if his real mother had done it. Had there been a celebration of his life? I went back to my email: a "small, intimate celebration, with family only." So that was for my benefit, and perhaps my unwillingness to attend had meant the hoax would go on longer: there was no opportunity for a coffin-popping surprise. Maybe his parents had died a long time ago, and everything he'd told me about them was a lie.

These questions were so powerless that I suddenly felt like I didn't care, like my capacity to care had been colonized by fortifying thoughts of myself. Again I began to think, or perversely hope, that this was somehow about me. Maybe my joke to Orin was right: Felix had so hated dating me that he couldn't bear having another conversation with me, even if that conversation promised the sweet relief of the end of our time together, so he decided to fake his own death to get out of having it. For a moment I wondered, horrified and nauseatingly flattered, if maybe I'd been the only one fooled, if it was a test of my love I'd clearly failed, but then I remembered the angry and awestruck colleagues, the Facebook page, the blog posts, Orin—you couldn't just fake your death for one person. No—it was crucial that I look this mortifyingly contorted disappointment in the eye. If he'd done it for the usual reasons, financial or legal, he wouldn't have come back so soon, and I couldn't imagine what financial trouble he would be in, with his parents being so wealthy, though I reminded myself that I actually knew nothing about his finances or his parents. Where had he hidden when he was playing dead? Where did his money come from? Who had helped him? How long did it take to plan? Who were his influences? How much did he plot out in advance? Answers to any of these questions might have provided clarity, but even if they were resolved, they would do little to really fill out his character, to show why he'd done it. I knew the most obvious explanation was probably the correct one, that this was intended as some kind of performance art or commentary, but that wasn't gratifying at all. In framing his fake death as a work, he'd built a hermeneutic barrier between himself and the world. One was obligated to think critically through the gesture without psychologizing, even if the gesture was ill-conceived, inelegant, and ugly; otherwise, one would look unserious, personally motivated, biased, obsessed. Fuck, I said aloud. Shit! The intent of his project was obvious, but still I had to spell it out. He had rejected the techno-utopian vision of paranoid collectivity, for which we'd sold our souls and privacy, through the ultimate act of opting out: suicide, but one that managed to evade the usual accusations of selfishness by disguising itself as an accidental death. Would he now out himself as the guy behind @THIS_ACCOUNT_IS_BUGGED_? The statement he was trying to make would have been better publicized by a famous or at least esoterically notorious figure. If he'd had more patience, he could have developed an online presence before killing himself off, though maybe his anonymity was the point. A couple of people who had tweeted about the story wondered: Who is this random guy? By being no one in particular, he'd effectively exposed the tenuousness of the supposedly unprecedented connections linking us now. Who cared about him? No one. Yet were we not all supposed to be at least a little important online? The memorial Facebook page used the certainty social media encouraged to make the lie more believable; though people were more suspicious than ever of *fake news*, bias, spin, scams, and self-promotion, the thing that allowed them to proliferate was the same thing that was seen as a very capable guard against them. Lots of people had posted to the Facebook page; anyone who glanced at it would assume it was legit. A faked death seemed like it would be difficult to pull off, a feat of planning, but it may well have been straightforward precisely because of that appearance. "Let Me Google That For You"—a good joke because increased access to information hasn't really increased our willingness to access it. No one would think to fact-check this random guy; the person most likely to do so was probably me, but he knew I wanted to break up, and he also knew my weaknesses: that I wasn't curious, that I was prone to lazy nihilism, that his death would only exacerbate those qualities rather than send me on some kind of quest for truth. The cynical way he'd revealed his project was entirely self-promotional, a sure means to inflate the follower count on his new Instagram and drive people to his website, but the strategy could easily be folded into the entire statement as a criticism of the inescapable narcissism of social media. Or as a criticism of the appetite for passive destruction the internet promoted in place of engaged inquiry. Regardless, the more popular he got after the stunt, the more right his project would be.

No: What I found interesting about this was not the artist statement, but the artist, even if I hesitate to call him that. You had to be a certain kind of person to fake your death, and I had no idea what kind of person that was. I was overcome with a pathetic urge to understand him. My face was hot, my chest was tight; it recalled the feeling of arguing online with someone you know is never going to get it, someone whose name you might not even know but who is suddenly able to wield power over you. I'd been lured into an intellectual trap and could only blame myself for getting stuck there. There had to be some internal pain or lifelong struggle that had led him to do this! "Why add more suffering to the world," he'd once asked me during an argument about his guardedness, "by handing mine to others?" I saw now that what he'd presented as realistic generosity was actually a hard bargain: if he expected nothing from anyone, he wouldn't have to give them anything in return.

Sitting there, the rain unceasing but easing, I wanted to express all this in an email.

Nothing would come of emailing him. He himself would have advised me, I was sure, to preserve my dignity and resist, and I couldn't deny that he knew a thing or two about winning power struggles. Say something and reveal my hand; say nothing and I could make him wonder as much as I was: Was I mad at him? Had he seriously hurt me? Or had I long ago figured him out and written him off as a selfish hack? Maybe I hadn't even cried when I heard the news. Not contacting him was the best of both worlds— preserving doubt meant I could remain in his mind both dramatic and mature, petty and the bigger person, righteously incensed and at peace with how things turned out. Contacting him meant limiting myself to who I was in the email. I would have to lie down and go to sleep.

Five minutes later I was clicking on Compose, though I had no idea where to start. "Hello Felix, if that is your real name" was what first came to mind. I would have meant it to be ironic but I couldn't trust Felix to interpret it the way I meant it, and if he did get the joke he would assume I wasn't angry, which I was, I think. I typed and deleted, typed and deleted. Eventually I'd written a version of the above analysis, but in a reckless tone that vacillated between dumbfoundedness and contempt. I used the subject line "absolutely totally completely unbelievable" and sent it without checking for typos.

I was laughing again when Frieda knocked on the door. My face must have been red and teary. She asked what was going on, if I was crying or laughing. I said I was laughing but that it was a tragicomedy. She asked what was funny. I said, laughing more, "My boyfriend faked his death!" She made a face unlike any I'd ever seen a human make before—a faked death is often floated as a possibility, but even on TV and in movies it's almost always proven ludicrous—and replied, "What? I didn't even know he died!"

His reply arrived when Frieda and I were on our second bottle of wine in her room; I learned a lot about her that evening, including that she had a large reserve under her bed. I'd been going back to my room to check my email frequently, at her insistence, and it was hallucinogenic when I finally saw the preview in my inbox: "**absolutely totally completely unbelievable** - Hey. It's good to hear from you. I'm not going to apologize, but I will say this: I assumed yo"

Being drunk surely helped, but it was not as strange as it should have been, receiving an email from him. More strange was the tone. Was "It's good to hear from you" a common greeting from people who'd come back from the dead? There was that French/Polish movie—I couldn't remember how the guy in that did it. I was nervous to open it and waited, just looking at the screen, which is not something I'd expect me to do. Finally, Frieda came in and, finding I hadn't yet seen the message, yelled that I had to read what that arsehole had to say for himself.

There's no real point in drawing out the reading of an email. It's not there and then suddenly it's there; that's all there is to it. The dread of opening it is not that interesting. It wasn't much, but the message was impressively calculated, so much that I was almost jealous. All he said was that he'd assumed I knew.

END

A COUPLE OF WEEKS LATER, MY VISA STATUS STILL UNCERTAIN, I was sitting outside a café on Friedelstrasse looking at my German homework, swatting at the wasps edging my cappuccino, wanting to look at my phone but telling myself I was not allowed to do so until I got to the end of my vocabulary column. The day after I found out about Felix, I decided, in a fit of pique, to enroll in an intensive German course that met every day, three hours a day, for a month. Having to communicate in basic sentences was appealing; it was challenging enough to distract me from life's big questions, or any questions besides "Where are you from?" and "What are your hobbies?" After searching various course offerings within walking distance of the apartment, which because of the romantic conditions in Portugal I was now welcome to live in for the foreseeable future, I picked the second-cheapest, a strategy supposedly bad for choosing wine at a restaurant but fine, I hoped, for German instructors. It had a bright green but otherwise professional website that was translated into English well. So far it was extremely tedious. Doing conversation exercises with my classmates was like trying to play tennis against someone without a racket, and who was also a toddler. I pretended to have an overactive bladder so I could get up to use the bathroom frequently.

I was studying vacation words when I looked up and saw, approaching me from the direction of the canal, Felix. He was wearing a pair of jeans and sneakers. Why tell you that? I don't know. He saw me, too. I felt there was nothing I could do to retain my dignity but exaggeratedly put my chin in my hand, like with my elbow resting on the picnic table, and watch him get closer, his expression increasingly inscrutable but possibly pleasant. I had nothing to be nervous about, I thought. Though I didn't believe it I told myself I had the upper hand. I was the victim here. Anything stupid I said or did could be excused on account of betrayal. Not being mad meant not caring, which was fine revenge. If I'd been thinking I would have realized I'd already ceded that advantage with my furious email, but he'd appeared so suddenly that I wasn't thinking.

He stopped when he got to me, there being no hard feelings on his end, and instead of saying hi, or anything else he might have said, he pointed at the last bit of cake on a filigreed plate to my left and asked, "Are you going to eat that?" I said no, and right after he put it in his mouth I said it wasn't mine. Ha ha, ha ha. He said it tasted vegan. I said I often wanted to eat food that was left over at cafés or whatever, but I never did. He said well, it could be poisoned, and I agreed. A pause. He was like any other ex-boyfriend I'd run into after six months apart and the rupture had settled and I'd accepted it was for the best. Looking up at him from my place at the table was a position I liked; it made me feel like a trick victim, able at any moment to stand up and assert my true power. It was also a flattering angle. You should always take pictures of yourself with your phone held above you, looking down at you, so that your eyes look big and your nose small. He was just standing there expectantly and I realized I was the one who'd brought him here, by looking at him intently, by reacting to his presence in a way that defied expectation, so I was going to have to start the conversation, but I had nothing to say. The sun was in my eyes looking up like that, and instead of talking I started squinting dramatically, using my hand to shade my face, and maneuvering my head so his body would block the light. He realized what I was trying to do and began voguing around until I approved his station and said, "OK, just don't move." He was still. I continued looking up at him, now backlit, his stance a little wide to create my shade, until he began to laugh. He said I looked like I'd lost weight. Seeing him in New York, I realized later, was always strange, because he seemed out of context there, almost superimposed onto the streetscapes and apartment settings, but here, on the cobblestones, a half-drunk beer in hand in the middle of the day, he belonged. The sun was beautiful and not too hot. An elderly man walked a dachshund. The wasps continued to hover and land, hover and land. I smiled mischievously though after what felt like a minute of this I began to get nervous and think I was wasting my chance to get some resolution. I couldn't ask a general question or repeat any of what I'd said in my email. But I also couldn't let him go without mentioning it at all, because if I did I would continue to walk around Berlin wondering if I was going to run into him, which I'd been doing since I found out he was there and not dead.

I knew I wasn't going to get anything real out of him, that it would be pointless to try and get him to sit down and explain. But there's something I didn't mention before. I wasn't going to mention it at all, because it's embarrassing, the way it reveals my trifling concerns, what I keep track of, what upsets me. But it's critical to the story, and to leave it out would be self-serving. As a writer you have to think of the reader.

"It's more of a comment than a question," I said, my voice low and flirtatious. I was surprised to hear I sounded not shaky or desperate but cool, really cool, like I hadn't been dwelling on this minuscule detail for the last two weeks, thinking of it and almost nothing else. No, it had just occurred to me then, and since I didn't really care I didn't think anything of bringing up this one minor thing that was just curious, not something that would bother me if I didn't receive an adequate response to it. He smiled and said OK and crossed his arms in front of his chest, still blocking the sun for me.

"That's one of my tweets."

"What?" he asked.

That's one of my tweets. That's one of my tweets. I had been humiliated so much already by this person—I try to hide it, but no amount of positive thinking can erase all the humiliation from this situation—and now somehow without even saying anything he had managed to humiliate me more, compelling me to utter this dumb sentence not once but twice and then later to write it three times. In my own novel! Trying to maintain the knowing tone to my voice that had so pleasantly surprised me just moments before I repeated that that—I'll tell you what it is in a second—was one of my tweets. I didn't care, appropriation was nothing new, and anyway if I'd wanted to preserve that sentence as my own I should have published it in a legitimate form, not on social media. I had no claim. It wasn't that the content of the tweet mattered. I was just saying.

"'I'm a pretty girl and I'm always late!' is something I tweeted," I said, remaining still because of the sun. "I mean, I don't memorize my tweets, obviously, but it is something I tweeted. I remember because I was late at the time." I'd tweeted it from the subway, waiting for the doors to close, late on the way to meet him for a movie, something from the seventies, at Film Forum. I'd felt bad about myself for doing this again, for always doing this, and I was worried we'd end up with bad seats. I hoped he would just go in and get seats as I'd urged him to do in a text message, not to be a martyr by waiting for me in the lobby. At the time I knew or thought I knew that he didn't have social media, so I posted as if he wouldn't read what I wrote. He might have thought the tweet was funny, but he also might have found it deeply annoying, particularly if he was already deeply annoyed about my making him late for this movie. By the time I got there the only seats available were at the very front, on the far right, and I could tell he was irritated but holding it back. After the movie he said he'd never gotten my text message and even showed me that he had not; I said, "Whatever," and that common sense would dictate to get seats. Etc. This is boring. I know that. And I knew reciting it to him would, in addition to being boring, also make it seem like I cared, which would be disadvantageous for extracting any tidbit of information I might be able to get from him. So I just sat there looking up at him and pretending "That's one of my tweets" was a perfectly withering remark. It occurred to me that I might do a lengthy, searching interview with him and pitch it as an article to the website. "A Chat with My Ex-Boyfriend, the Anonymous Online Conspiracy Theorist Who Faked His Death." It would get good traffic. Inevitably an angry response would follow: "That guy didn't really fake his death—I would know, because I did it."

Without breaking eye contact, or what would have been eye contact if he hadn't been in shadow from the sun, he reached into his back pocket and pulled out his wallet. It was the same wallet he'd had when we were together, an expensive zippered thing, now worn at the corners but holding up well. I got it for him for his birthday. He opened it and took out a twenty-euro note. The shades of blue, the gothic windows, the hologram. Holding the bill in his left hand he closed the wallet with his right and put it back in his pocket unzipped, broke his awkward charitable posture, and stood up straight. The sun was in my eyes again and I brought my hand up to shade them. "Yes," he said, maybe pityingly, maybe exasperatedly, maybe patronizingly, maybe guiltily, maybe shamefully, maybe ruefully, maybe matter-of-factly, maybe absolutely, totally, completely devoid of any feeling at all. He lifted my saucer and coffee cup, ignoring the wasps, which dispersed into chaos, and slipped the note under it. "That's part of the point."

Acknowledgments

THE UNATTRIBUTED, PARAPHRASED QUOTE ON PAGE 50 COMES from Norman Rush's novel *Mating*: "Underneath everything in America he sometimes imagined there was a subliminal sound like an orange crate cracking when you stand on it, except that this sound never stopped."

Thanks to my agent, Alia Hanna Habib, as well as Rebecca Gardner and the rest of the Gernert Company. Thanks to my editor, Kendall Storey, and everyone at Catapult, and to Anna Kelly and everyone at 4th Estate. Thanks to Eva-Marie von Hippel for giving this book a home in Berlin.

Many people read and commented on early drafts and sections, including Erika Allen, Callie Beusman, Jeremy Gordon, Monica Heisey, Martin Jackson, Ryan Nees, Hanson O'Haver, Damion Searls, James Yeh, and Matt Zeitlin. Ben Mauk gifted me the perfect title. Special thanks to Dave Wingrave for being an essential reader and patient friend, even though I am very annoying. Thanks to Alyssa Mastromonaco for getting it, and for the support, wisdom, and friendship. Thanks to my family.

Finally, thanks to Jeffrey Kirkwood, whose likeness doesn't appear in these pages at all, though without him they wouldn't be nearly as good. The rest will be for, and never about, you.